Praise for

MURDER UNDER THE M̶̶̶̶

"There is nothing like coastal M̶̶̶̶
Lynn's *Murder Under the Mistleto̶̶̶̶*
to make time during your holiday ̶̶̶̶ ̶̶̶̶ ̶̶̶̶̶̶̶ ̶̶̶̶ Kinsley
Clark and her friends solve the Grinchiest murder in town."

— Barbara Ross, author of the Maine Clambake Mysteries

"Sherry Lynn's latest mystery featuring protagonist Kinsley Clark makes me want to pack up and move to Maine despite the murder. Kinsley is someone that I would love to be friends with."

— Catherine Bruns, *USA Today* bestselling author of the
Maple Syrup Mysteries

Praise for

DIGGING UP DAISY

"In her debut novel, *Digging Up Daisy*, Sherry Lynn does a terrific job at introducing us to the feisty Kinsley Clark and the delightful Salty Breeze Inn located in the small town of Harborside, Maine. Cozy fans will find this to be a fun and fresh mystery with a twist at the end that will give them that most-satisfying aha moment."

— Lauren Elliott, *USA Today* bestselling author of the
Beyond the Page Bookstore Mysteries

"Rife with fragrant blooms, the tang of salty sea air, and delectable lobster rolls, Lynn's atmospheric seaside page-turner will have you yearning for another visit to Harborside, Maine."

— Darci Hannah, author of the
Beacon Bakeshop Mysteries

THE MISTLETOE

Books by Sherry Lynn

DIGGING UP DAISY
MURDER UNDER THE MISTLETOE

MURDER UNDER THE MISTLETOE

SHERRY LYNN

BERKLEY PRIME CRIME

NEW YORK

BERKLEY PRIME CRIME
Published by Berkley
An imprint of Penguin Random House LLC
penguinrandomhouse.com

Library of Congress Cataloging-in-Publication Data

Names: Lynn, Sherry (Mystery writer), author.
Title: Murder under the mistletoe / Sherry Lynn.
Description: First edition. | New York : Berkley Prime Crime, 2023. |
Series: A Mainely murder mystery
Identifiers: LCCN 2023013965 (print) | LCCN 2023013966 (ebook) |
ISBN 9780593546673 (trade paperback) | ISBN 9780593546680 (ebook)
Subjects: LCGFT: Cozy mysteries. | Novels.
Classification: LCC PS3617.U5643 M89 2023 (print) |
LCC PS3617.U5643 (ebook) | DDC 813/.6—dc23/eng/20230327
LC record available at https://lccn.loc.gov/2023013965
LC ebook record available at https://lccn.loc.gov/2023013966

First Edition: November 2023

Printed in the United States of America
1st Printing

Book design by George Towne

The recipes contained in this book are to be followed exactly as written.
The publisher is not responsible for your specific health or allergy needs that may
require medical supervision. The publisher is not responsible for any adverse reactions
to the recipes contained in this book.

This book is dedicated to those who may be struggling during the holiday season.

You're not alone.
My prayer is that you find escape and joy within these pages and have faith that better times are coming.

Chapter 1

The scent of pine boughs permeated the dining room of the Salty Breeze Inn, and the cheery sound of Andy Williams singing "Happy Holiday" filled the air. Meanwhile, a crackling wood fire, built in the original stone-stacked fireplace, kept everyone toasty warm, despite the room's tall timber ceiling.

Kinsley Clark looked away from the festive group of volunteer elves and smiled when she noticed her best friend, Becca, enter the room, plucking snowflakes from her long dark hair. Becca brushed the hint of snow off her wool coat.

"You made it!" Kinsley said. Becca's grin grew wide as Kinsley moved to welcome her. "And just in time, too, we could use you at the ribbon station."

"Ribbon station? I hope you have someone who can teach me how to tie bows, otherwise you might be in trouble." Becca's golden eyes, which mimicked the center of a sunflower, twinkled. She slipped out of her coat and hung it on the back of a nearby chair before greeting Kinsley with a half hug.

"I'm just glad you're here and safe with us now. It looks like the snow started already, huh?" Kinsley asked before the two took a step closer to the table.

"Yeah, and it's really sticking out there—faster than the weather forecaster predicted." Becca's salon-groomed brows fell into a frown. "Not sure I'm ready for winter to rear its ugly head just yet. We haven't even finished our leftover turkey from Thanksgiving!"

"Hey, now, 'tis the season." Kinsley elbowed her friend playfully. "Life in Harborside, Maine, can't be all warm sunny beach days," she added. "Besides, don't you just love the first snow? It puts everyone in the holiday spirit. Which is exactly what we need right about now to prepare for the upcoming boat parade. Next weekend will be here before you know it. I promised the town council I'd have Harborside fully decorated by then, as it's the town's official holiday kickoff party, and I *will* deliver on that promise!" Kinsley pumped an excited fist into the air.

Becca gestured to the group gathered around the table. "Yeah, looks like you rounded up a good group of volunteers to help this year. I'm sure you'll get it all done."

"I did! I actually had to turn volunteers away. Everyone loves the process of helping create these kissing balls that I use to decorate the town. Fa-la-la-la, 'tis the season for help and cheer! I just love this time of year," Kinsley crooned.

"I wish I could share in your enthusiasm and holiday spirit. I just had my third cancellation this week; I'm feeling a little bummed," Becca admitted. "Unfortunately, things tend to hit a lull for the real estate biz during the holidays, as snowy winter weather doesn't exactly make clients all that excited to pack up and move." Becca lowered her voice again and leaned into Kinsley. "Which isn't exactly helping my purse strings and my upcoming Christmas shopping list, if you know what I mean. I might just need a second job to get me through this winter." She sighed.

"Look no further if it's work you're wanting, because I could use some extra hands at SeaScapes. That is, if you're up for it? Besides Harborside needing Christmas decorations, I have several clients lined up who've requested that I prep for their holiday gatherings, too. Seems people are just too busy to handle it this year. They're asking for their trees to be put up and their homes to look festive. Honestly, I was wondering how I would get it all done. You might even find a few new real estate clients out of the deal. The job's yours if you want it." Kinsley shrugged.

"Really? I mean, you're already paying Adam, aren't you?" Becca said, nodding in his direction. "You can't afford to add me to the payroll, too, can you?"

Kinsley lowered her voice to match Becca's. "Well, technically, yeah, Adam's getting paid for today, but that's mainly to help Alice. I can't bear to think of his mother as a single mom handling everything on her own this time of year. Harborside's an expensive place to live and it can't be easy for her. I know Adam gives his mom a portion of his salary, but don't tell him I told you how endearing he is."

"He does? Aw, what a sweetheart." Becca nodded. "I knew you had a keeper with him."

Kinsley ushered them farther out of earshot. "Anyway, I love bringing the community together to craft the kissing balls and I really do appreciate the help. But they're not doing the heavy lifting—I still need to hang them and decorate the entire town.

Between the profits that the town puts aside to pay SeaScapes and the extra clients . . . there's more than enough work to go around. So not to worry, my friend. I've got ya covered." She nudged her friend playfully again with her elbow.

Becca still didn't look overly convinced, so Kinsley continued, "None of that frowny face. I don't want you to stress—especially over the holidays. It's the best time of the year!"

"Kins, you're sweeter than your aunt's Christmas cookies, there's no doubt about it." Becca threw her arm around her and gave a light squeeze. "I'll gladly take the job. Decorating sure does put me in the spirit, and it'll be fun. Plus, the best part? I get to hang out with you!"

Kinsley was glad that her good business fortune could help out her friend and put a glowing smile on her face. Kinsley's landscape and garden business, based out of the caretaker's cottage behind her aunt Tilly's Salty Breeze Inn, kicked into high gear during the winter months. She was solely responsible for all of the town's seasonal decor using mostly natural elements found locally in Maine and it was quite a production. Therefore, Kinsley had convinced her aunt Tilly to let her use the inn the weekend after Thanksgiving to coordinate all her decorating efforts. In turn, she would transform the Salty Breeze Inn into a magical holiday destination that would make guests want to linger. It was a win-win for both of them and the only weekend of the entire year the inn was closed to the public.

"I'm so glad you're here to help this year," Kinsley repeated, taking Becca by the arm and leading her back to the rest of the group. "We need you here—right, guys?" Kinsley looked around the long dining room table and added, "You all remember my friend Becca?"

A bunch of greetings ensued as folks stopped what they were

doing to welcome Becca with a wave, nod, or hello. The group of volunteers were already busy creating the Christmas kissing balls that would be used all over Harborside. The kissing balls, which were made up of round clusters of greenery, were making a comeback. Traditionally, they originated from the seventeenth century and hung from entryways and doorways within a home, so that everyone who passed beneath one would be gifted with blessings and good tidings. Over the centuries they eventually became a replacement for mistletoe. They were crafted from rosemary, thyme, and mistletoe, symbolizing love and devotion. Kinsley chose to use more traditional pine branches native to Maine, though, such as, cedar, fir, white pine, and boxwood. This made it a more symbolic tradition for the town. These beautiful orbs would soon be hung from the light posts on Main Street and sprinkled around the town of Harborside, including at the wharf and marina.

"Oh, Becca, did I overhear you say Kinsley is sweeter than my holiday cookies? She *is* pretty special." Aunt Tilly beamed as she crossed the room with a freshly baked plate of Christmas cookies. "I can't say I disagree with you, but you'll have to taste one and see for yourself. These just happen to be topped with a kiss."

"You heard that?" Becca said, astonished, as a French-manicured hand flew to her chest.

"Her ears are like a bat's; don't let her age fool you," Kinsley said with a giggle. "The woman's amazing! Someone's got a birthday coming up real soon, too. Aunt Tilly's turning sixty-three in a few weeks. We'll have to plan a party!"

Tilly clucked her tongue. "Oh, none of that. When you get to be my age, you don't need a party to remind you that the clock is tickin'." She set the cookies on the table in front of the group of volunteers. "Here, Becca, have one," she further encouraged, gesturing with her outstretched hand. "Hopefully, this should make your effort of driving in the snow worth it," she added, shining as brightly as a Christmas star atop a tree. Kinsley's aunt clearly loved the holiday season, too.

"Ooh, those do look amazing," Becca said, leaning in to examine the plate. "Oh yes, they're the peanut butter kiss cookies!" Becca exclaimed. "Now it's really starting to feel like Christmas around here." She looked to Kinsley with a grin.

"I know, right? Lucky for us, she'll be baking all season long; this is only the beginning. Right, Aunt Tilly?"

"You know I can't help myself, darlin'. I've been told holiday treats are my inn's specialty, and I wouldn't want to disappoint any of my guests," she answered with a devilish grin. Kinsley wondered by the look on her aunt's face if she had a new recipe up her sleeve. Either way, sugar-smacking desserts wouldn't be lacking at the inn the entire month of December. Which made all the visitors who crossed the threshold *and* Kinsley and her friends quite happy, too.

"I'll take one of those!" Adam, Kinsley's summer employee, piped up, stealing one from the plate and immediately stuffing the entire cookie into his mouth. He groaned with pleasure as melted chocolate leaked out the sides of his mouth and he attempted to catch it with his tongue.

"Adam!" his mother, Alice, scolded. "I raised you with better manners than that. You're going to choke to death. Take smaller bites! Plus, the way you're huffing it, that cookie is going to get all stuck in your braces," she added with a tsk. Alice, too, had been swindled into helping as a volunteer. Adam's mom had been recently hired as a housekeeper at Edna's house next door. Which was a full-time job, as Edna Williamsburg owned an oceanside mansion. Alice was also known for making the best bows in town, and she was currently hard at work, twisting and pulling on loops. Meanwhile, Adam's young sister, Melody, played with the rolls of wired ribbon at her mother's feet.

Each of the volunteers bustled around the table, managing their specific tasks. Cari Day, who worked at the humane society, was responsible for attaching chicken wire to the floral Oasis. She then handed them over to Jackie Horn, a busy stay-at-home mom of three, who soaked the Oasis pieces in a bucket of water to prepare them for branches.

Adam was responsible for cutting each variety of pine branch to an even six inches long and then stripping the ends off. Kinsley took the different evergreens that he'd cut and arranged them into piles, so that each kissing ball would have a well-rounded selection of branches.

Mallory Chesterfield, the owner of the local florist shop, Precious Petals, located in downtown Harborside, had donated the winterberry, holly, and dogwood, and was cutting them to size to add a pop of festive color. She had donated these sprigs in hopes of showcasing items from her shop that she used in her floral arrangements. Kinsley thought it a marketing win-win for both businesses. She even suggested Mallory put a sign in her shop window stating that the kissing balls were provided by SeaScapes and Precious Petals.

Pete O'Rourke, the owner of the local tavern, the Blue Lobstah, which was located alongside the marina, had stopped by to lend a hand, too. The New England name to the eatery had everyone in town using his Boston slang. Which is why he'd chosen to name his restaurant after his roots. Pete was busy sticking the limbs into the soaked Oasis and poking his fingers with prickly branches along the way. Occasionally, the group would hear an "Ouch!" utter from the bar owner's lips, and a wounded finger would pop into his mouth.

Tilly provided the group with endless mugs of hot cocoa topped with homemade marshmallow and a dollop of cream. And by the recent looks of things, a large supply of cookies. Candy canes were set in mason jars all down the center of the table in case anyone wanted to stir their cocoa or enjoy the peppermint treat as they labored. These numerous delights enticed the volunteers to happily make a reappearance year after year.

"*Peter*, would you mind adding a few logs to the fire while I run back to the kitchen to check the oven? I don't want to burn my next batch of cookies," Tilly asked.

Kinsley looked over to Pete and lifted her hands in a shrug. Her aunt was the only one in town who called him Peter and seemed to refuse to call him Pete, despite multiple corrections on Kinsley's part. He smiled back at her with his winning smile. A smile that lit his face and made you think he'd just won the lottery. He rose from the dining chair and went straight to the task.

"Becca, would you mind joining Alice at the bow-making station? I'll head over to help Pete load the fire," Kinsley asked. "I'm pretty up to task at my station."

"Uh-huh," Becca teased with a playful swat to Kinsley's backside. "Like he needs the help. But you go on ahead, my friend." She waggled her eyebrows. "It sounds to me like you're just looking for a moment alone with our Boston friend over there."

No doubt, Kinsley and Becca hung out quite a bit at Pete's establishment. And to Becca's credit, Kinsley was the one encouraging it. Something about that Pete O'Rourke had her coming back for more. But it was complicated. They were both remarkably busy with their respective businesses, and time off was hard to come by so any time spent together meant her hanging on the end of his bar. Something she didn't really want to make a habit of.

"He's my friend. Can't women and men *just* be friends?" Kinsley protested.

Becca simply batted her eyelashes and made a kissy face. Kinsley responded with an eye roll before nudging Becca back in the direction of the bows and turning toward the fireplace. Thankfully, Pete had his back turned, oblivious to the goings-on. He was down on one knee and loading logs into the fire but turned when she laid a soft hand on his shoulder.

"Thanks for keeping this going." Kinsley then extended her arms out to feel the heat of the roaring fire. "It feels so nice, doesn't it?"

"Hey, no problem."

"And thanks for helping today, I really appreciate it." She looked at the clock above the mantel and added, "What time do you have to be back at the Blue Lobstah?"

Pete's eyes, the color of blue asters, followed hers, and he, too, snuck a peek at the time. "I hate to leave you hanging, but it's two fifteen, so I probably should head out soon. I haven't hired anyone to plow yet this winter, so I guess it'll be me cleaning the parking lot before the night crowd." He grimaced. "I guess I better get busy on that," he added as he turned to load another log into the fire. He stood and jabbed at the new log with the fire poker, setting it aflame.

Kinsley loved when hints of Pete's Boston accent came out. It usually happened when he was excited or under stress. Right now it sounded like stress, though, so she said, "No worries. I'm finished with separating the branches so I can take over your job and put them in. Again, thanks for sticking with it as long as you have," she teased as she pointed out his wounded fingers. "I do appreciate it."

Pete laughed. "No problem, part of the job." He winked before he set the fire poker back in its holder. "You mind if I take off now, then?"

"Not at all! But you're still planning on helping me with the lobster-trap tree tomorrow, out by the cliff walk, right? I could really use you for that." She gave his hand a quick squeeze before releasing it, and then followed him toward the exit.

"Yeah, I'd be happy to. Just let me know when you need the lift delivered, and I'll make a few calls. I think we'll need a lift to stack 'em, since you were talking about making it thirty-eight feet. I'm tall, but not that tall," he said, chuckling.

"Will do!" Kinsley replied.

The background music suddenly shifted to Mariah Carey singing "All I Want for Christmas Is You." When Pete turned to tell everyone good-bye, Kinsley couldn't help but notice the silly grin splashed across Becca's face. Yes, it was true. Maybe Kinsley's only wish for Christmas *was* for Pete to take special notice of her. But she'd tuck that away for now, like an unwrapped present.

After everyone shared their good-byes with the bar owner, and the volunteers got back to business, Kinsley glanced around the table for a moment to watch them work their Christmas magic. The kissing balls were now hanging from wide red bows and filling up drying racks scattered around the room. She couldn't help but wonder if a chance meeting beneath a kissing ball with Pete might happen this season. Little did she know that less than a week later, kissing would be the last thing on her mind and several of those gathered around this very table would be questioned about a murder.

Chapter 2

The next day, with the SeaScapes work truck fully loaded with the kissing balls, Kinsley and Becca made their way into town. Kinsley hoped none of their hard-earned creations would bounce out of the back of the truck bed, as she did another check in the rearview mirror.

"It's fine." Becca waved a hand airily. "You keep looking in that mirror, but we haven't lost one yet. Besides, if one does happen to pop out, a nice citizen of Harborside will pick it up and deliver it to us. It doesn't take a rocket scientist to know where we're headed with this load." She chuckled.

"I don't want to cause an accident or have someone run one over," Kinsley defended as she snuck another peek in the rearview mirror. "You're right, though. We live in the best town, don't we?"

"We sure do! And soon we'll be swamped with tourists for the holiday season. Expect your aunt's inn to have no vacancies because it's gonna look like Christmas Town, USA, after we finish our magic here!"

"Sounds like someone is liking her new job?" Kinsley teased.

"Hey, between you and me, I would've done this for nothing. But don't tell my new boss." She grinned and then lifted her finger to her lips in secrecy, and then the two broke out in laughter.

"Trust me, your new boss is super glad she hired you." Kinsley leaned over and patted her friend's leg. "Seriously, I couldn't do this without help. Thanks for coming today."

"My pleasure."

"Adam's meeting us, too, so between the three of us, we should have this part of the job accomplished in no time. I'm really hoping to get the lobster tree up by the end of the day."

"Don't worry, if it takes us until midnight, we'll get it done."

Kinsley knew her friend was accustomed to working odd hours, but she really hoped they wouldn't be working that late. She pulled the truck in front of Toby's Taffy, and then put the gear in park. The snowbanks, left over from the previous day's snowstorm, forced them to park a little farther away than usual. "Do you think you have enough room to get out?"

"Sure. Don't worry about my side, I wore my wool socks and high boots in case we had to dodge a few deep spots." Becca tapped the sides of her snow boots and smiled. "I came prepared."

"Excellent. I think we'll park here so we can grab a hot cocoa at Toby's after we finish in town. Despite the sun breaking through the clouds today, it's still cold. Plus, I promised Aunt Tilly I'd pick up the peppermint taffy for her guests. She likes to add a dish of those to each room, along with other treats from town, so visitors get a feel for all Harborside has to offer."

"Sounds like a plan," Becca said as she slipped on a pair of expensive-looking leather gloves.

Kinsley stopped her by digging beneath her seat and tossing over an extra pair of work gloves. "Wear these instead. I don't want to ruin your nice gloves. These should keep your hands warm and keep you from getting pricked from the branches, too. Some of them can be sharp, just ask Pete," she said, giggling. Her mind quickly returned to the bar owner putting the kissing balls together. Kinsley was acutely aware that Pete was never far from her mind. She was glad Becca was preoccupied and didn't seem to catch on to it. Otherwise, the endless banter about their *nonrelationship* would ensue.

"Good idea," Becca said, abandoning her leather gloves to the dashboard and slipping into the work gloves before hopping out of the truck.

Kinsley joined her outside, the sharp wind hitting her cheeks hard. It would be a cold workday indeed.

"Can you move some of those kissing balls so I can get the stepladder out?" Kinsley asked as she leaned deeper into the truck bed to remove the ladder.

"Yup, and I just noticed Adam is across the street waiting. Should I just bring a few over to him, so he can get started?"

"That would be great," Kinsley said with a nod. After removing the ladder, she lifted a heavy-duty Rubbermaid container, filled to the brim, out of the back of the truck and handed it to Becca. "This should give him enough to get started. Tell him to start on this end and we'll bring him more as he goes."

"I'm on it!" Becca replied before she navigated around a snowbank and disappeared across Main Street.

Meanwhile, Kinsley proceeded to set up on her end of the street. While she was adjusting the ladder beneath a lamppost, she looked up to see Chris Chesterfield, a local alderman for Harborside, standing rather close and eyeing her every move.

"Something I can help you with, Chris?"

"Ah, no. Not really."

Kinsley reached into the Rubbermaid bin, plucked out a kissing ball, and began the climb. All the while, she could feel Chris's eyes boring into her. She tried to ignore it and go about her work, but his gaze was unnerving. After hanging the first one in place and descending the ladder she finally said, "Okay, I can see something's bothering you. What's wrong?"

"Oh, it's not that anything is wrong, per se."

"Chris, I really don't mean to be rude, but I have an entire town to decorate before the boat parade next weekend. And it's all hands on deck to accomplish it. Is there something you need?"

"Oh. I don't know. I'm just trying to understand why you think it's fair that you get paid by the town to decorate for the holidays, meanwhile, you're taking donations from my wife. I'm thinking it would be in Harborside's best interest to find someone else for this job. Someone who has a little better business sense and who doesn't steal from other business owners in order to get what they want."

The last comment cut Kinsley deeply, and she fought to maintain composure.

"You know, unlike yourself, Mallory donates a lot to our town," he continued. "And has no problem giving to Harborside for free. But you seem to think SeaScapes should be paid for the work here. It *is* the season of giving, you know."

"Chris, SeaScapes is my job . . ." Kinsley defended, but he cut her off with a wave of his hand.

"Why should my wife be responsible for those spriggy things

and not you?" Chris pointed to the winterberry sticking out from the kissing ball, and then put his hands on his hips and waited expectantly.

"Yes, that's true, Mallory is very kind. And I really appreciate her generosity. The holly and berries from her shop really add a festive pop of color this year. And she was certainly instrumental in putting these together yesterday, too. Your wife's been a lifesaver. But, Chris, she didn't have to do this. It was her choice to donate supplies."

Chris's face turned red, and Kinsley hoped it was from the cold wind whipping around them and not his growing annoyance. But all hopes were dashed when he said, "*Exactly*. Which is why I think she should be *paid* for this job just like you are . . . but it looks like you are just interested in stuffing your own pockets!"

His words hung in the air between them like melting icicles dripping annoyingly on the top of Kinsley's head. She didn't have time for yet another argument with him. Because if it wasn't this, he was picking at her about something else. It wasn't the first time Chris had approached her with an accusation of some kind. And she didn't want to constantly defend her reasoning regarding how she handled her business, but here she was doing just that, yet again. "Look, Chris"—Kinsley breathed deep and evened her tone before continuing—"Mallory wanted to donate supplies so she could showcase some of the products that she uses in her floral arrangements. This is a way to market *both* our businesses. I even proposed she put a sign in her window stating that the kissing balls were provided by both of us, and the additions came from her shop." Kinsley closed her mouth, hoping she didn't set him off further with her directness. By the look on the alderman's face, she had. "Look," she added, softening her tone and laying a gentle hand on his arm. "I think this might be a conversation between you and Mallory. Don't you?"

The alderman's expression pinched.

"Hey, I'm sorry if I offended you. Let me make it up to you. Have you tried the cocoa bombs yet? They are beautiful and delicious! Maybe we can work through this over a hot beverage."

The alderman frowned. "I don't think we need to discuss this further, but I will go in and get a coffee now that you mention it."

"Please?" Kinsley thought maybe if she sweetened him up, he wouldn't leave with a sour taste in his mouth.

"No, we're done here," he said in a huff, turning and swinging the door to the taffy shop open wide. Kinsley didn't relax until the door closed tightly behind him. She took a deep breath of cold fresh Maine air and felt a moment of reprieve before returning to the task at hand.

After hanging another kissing ball and just before she descended the ladder, she noticed a group of boys across the street with Adam, helping him with his work. By the time she reached the bottom, Becca had met her at the foot of the ladder.

"What's going on over there?" Kinsley asked.

"Oh. Members of Adam's hockey team came out to help so he can make it to practice this afternoon. When he told the team he had to work, more than half of them showed up to help him—great group of kids."

"Wow, that's so nice." Kinsley smiled. "At least someone is feeling rallied around and encouraged around here."

"What's with the frowny face?" Becca asked. "I thought you were in your element doing this." She threw her gloved fingers up in air quotes. "What happened to the whole 'best time of the year' speech yesterday?"

The bell on the door of Toby's Taffy jingled as Chris navigated his way back through the doorway, balancing a coffee in each hand. Becca rushed to hold the door for him. "Let me help you with that," she said to the alderman.

Kinsley overheard Chris say, "Thank you. At least someone has good manners in this town," before he turned away from them in the direction of Precious Petals.

"What was that all about?" Becca asked with a roll of her eyes. "I can't imagine something happened inside of Toby's. Jenna and Toby are anything but rude . . . in fact they're the poster children of hospitality."

"No. I think he was referring to me," Kinsley said with a sigh.

"You?"

Kinsley proceeded to share what had happened in Becca's absence.

"Oh wow, I'm sorry. You were having so much fun out here before he arrived. Please don't let Chris get to you."

"Poor Mallory, huh? Can you imagine being married to a guy like him? He's one of these people who must have his finger in everything. It's simply how he is. He should just let his wife handle her business as she sees fit. I mean, what's it to him if she donates a few sprigs from her shop!"

"Some guys can be difficult," Becca agreed with a slow nod as they continued to watch the alderman make his way down the sidewalk, dodging the occasional patch of snow.

"Yes. Which is why I'm still single." Kinsley grinned.

"Is it?" Becca mocked. "Is it really why?"

"Don't tease me, you're still single, too," Kinsley defended.

"Actually . . ." Becca replied before leaving her hanging and walking over to the far side of the truck, out of earshot.

Out of curiosity, Kinsley had no choice but to follow.

They met at the truck bed, where Becca was removing another Rubbermaid container filled with kissing balls. Kinsley stopped her with one hand. "Actually what?"

"That guy at the gym. He asked me out again."

"*Zach?* I thought you said he was too into himself with the bodybuilding thing?"

"Maybe I judged a little too quickly. True, he's all muscles . . . but he's also kinda sweet," Becca admitted in a swooning voice. "He texted me after the date to share how much he enjoyed our time together and how he couldn't stop thinking about me."

"Oh boy."

"I think you'll like him. But I'm giving it the four-week rule before introductions," Becca informed her before lugging the Rubbermaid bin from the back of the truck and then setting it on the ground.

The two shared an informal rule that they didn't introduce new love interests before they had a chance to make their own decision of where the relationship was going. Otherwise, they tended to sway to the friend's perspective, which sometimes led to early unfair breakups. Just like the case of Ted Flaherty, who Becca claimed constantly corrected Kinsley when they had gone on a double date. And Becca had mentioned he left his fingernails too long. Kinsley had never noticed it before. But then subsequently, every time they talked, Kinsley became so defensive when Ted would correct her that she had to break up with him. And still she wondered about him from time to time—despite his lengthy nails. But that was years ago . . . before Pete entered the picture. Was that why she didn't confide in Becca about her feelings for Pete? Was she afraid her friend's perspective might sway her own?

Becca interrupted her reverie. "I'm going to deliver this over to Adam but then encourage his hockey friends to come and get more themselves if they need it. Are you okay with that?"

"Sure." Kinsley was still in her head, thinking about Becca's new love interest. She was happy for Becca, but at the same time knew that if this was someone Becca really liked, she'd see less and less of her friend. It was just how it worked. For that reason, she was glad that she had made the decision to hire Becca, because that would ensure time together—even if it was just for work purposes.

And to heck with Chris. It was her business how she handled SeaScapes. She would regret that decision, though, because it would be the last time they'd see the alderman alive.

Chapter 3

Kinsley and Becca were in search of a warm drink, and the red-and-white-striped awning of Toby's Taffy shop beckoned them to enter. The two were greeted by the sound of cheerful customers and the heady scent of chocolate as soon as they stepped across the threshold. Jenna was taking orders from behind the counter, while Toby immediately moved toward them and scooped up Kinsley in a bear hug.

"Good to see you, Bumpkins!" Toby said as he released her. His thick eyebrows danced animatedly on his face, like Santa Claus. Bumpkins was the nickname the taffy shop owner had given her after the tragic death of her parents. Toby and his wife, Jenna, had become pseudo relatives when her aunt Tilly had taken her and her brother, Kyle, in as their legal guardian. She loved the couple fiercely and would give them the shirt off her back, if asked.

Toby then moved to greet Becca with a half hug as well.

"It smells soooo good in here!" Becca swooned. She traveled to the glass case loaded with cocoa bombs, and Kinsley and Toby followed. The round spheres, decorated like priceless jewels, were loaded with hot chocolate mix and marshmallows on the inside. A myriad of drizzles and sugar-coated sprinkles made each of them look like a classy holiday decoration instead of a treat you'd want to explode into chocolate ruins.

"Which one would you like to try?" Jenna met them at the counter. Her eyes, the color of deep lilacs, danced in amusement as they all waited while Becca scanned the treats inside the glass case.

"They're all so gorgeous, I don't know what to pick! How do they work?" Becca asked, leaning in closer for a better view.

Before adjusting her apron, Jenna smoothed her gray hair, which was tied neatly in a knot at the nape of her neck. "You just go ahead and pick one, we'll drop it into warm milk and stand by to watch the surprised look on your face as it cracks open." She chuckled.

"Yeah, it's kinda fascinating to watch the cocoa ooze out!" Kinsley piped in. "But then you're a little bit sad because it was so beautiful, you hated to be the one to destroy it." She turned her attention back to the shopkeepers. "I bet you're selling loads of these."

"Honestly, we can't keep up with demand!" Toby admitted. "Usually, our taffy sales drop off in the winter, and we expect that to happen. But these cocoa bombs are selling out just as soon as we restock the counter. They've quite literally taken over our saltwater taffy business. Right, Jenna?"

His wife agreed with a nod. "Yes, it's true. And we provide gift boxes as well, so they make a wonderful gift. A seasonal mug with a cocoa bomb? Who wouldn't want that? Tourists seem to love them, too, because our inventory of Harborside mugs is completely out."

"I believe it. They're stunning! Almost too pretty to drink!" Becca exclaimed. "Which one are you getting, Kins?"

Kinsley leaned in and pointed. "I think I'll try the white chocolate one. I haven't had that one yet." The glassy-looking sphere was pure white in color and flawlessly drizzled with milk chocolate. "How about you, Becca? We can't linger too long. I have one hundred and fifty lobster traps donated by the local fishermen, sitting in a heap down at the wharf. I need to get over there and stack them before Chris sends the town council after me for leaving a trip hazard. That would be just my luck."

Toby leaned in and lowered his voice so only Kinsley could hear. "He's still a thorn in your gardening side, eh?"

"Kinda," Kinsley admitted. "But I'm not going to let him get under my skin. I have too much going on this week to worry about it. And it's the best time of the year. I'm not going to lose my holiday spirit over it; I refuse that."

"That's my girl," Toby said, throwing his arm around her and pulling her in again momentarily before fully releasing her.

"How about this? Why don't we drop your bombs in travel mugs? So, you can take it to go," Jenna suggested. "It'll help keep you warm down at the wharf while you're working."

Kinsley looked to her friend for approval.

"Just as long as I can watch it break apart before you put a lid on it," Becca said.

"Absolutely! That's part of the fun!" Kinsley agreed with a nod.

After watching the purely magical demonstration of the cocoa bombs exploding, and buying the peppermint taffy for her aunt Tilly, the two headed back out into the freezing cold. A whip of brisk wind caught hold of them, and they moved quickly to the safety of the truck.

"Brrr." Kinsley shivered as she closed the door tight behind her. Her friend's cell phone sang out in the truck, alerting her to a host of messages, and Becca immediately responded.

Kinsley tried to allow for privacy but couldn't help but surmise by the chatter that her friend was asked to show a house. She took a sip of the delicious cocoa and waited while the engine warmed up.

Her theory was confirmed when Becca asked, "Are you gonna hate me if I ask you to drop me off back at my car? I have a showing appointment." Her vehicle had been abandoned back at the Salty Breeze Inn when the two had started their workday. "I can run over, show the house, and then meet you over at the Blue Lobstah or . . . ?" She trailed off.

"No worries, you go ahead and do whatever you need to do. I can handle it." Kinsley smiled.

"I promise I'll come down to the wharf and help with the lobster tree just as soon as I can. I'm so sorry about this, but these buyers are chomping at the bit. I need to strike while the iron is hot."

"Seriously, it's no problem." Kinsley patted her friend on the arm reassuringly. "Pete said he would help. I'm gonna have him run the lift anyway. You'd probably just be standing around doing nothing. And freezing to death in the cold."

"Ahh yes. I see." Becca giggled. "Probably best I don't interrupt, then. You two might like a little alone time."

"You promised you were gonna drop that," Kinsley warned.

"Yes, boss," Becca countered with a salute.

Kinsley couldn't help but let out a chuckle.

After dropping Becca back at her car and then stopping inside the inn to hand over the peppermint treats from Toby's Taffy to her aunt, Kinsley was finally on her way. Her heart skipped an extra beat at the thought of seeing Pete. Lately, that was a new thing she'd noticed. The uptick of her blood pressure when a chance to see him would occur. She evened her breath and thought herself ridiculous as she tugged at her long blond hair and adjusted it beneath her winter hat.

By the time she'd pulled into the parking lot of the Blue Lobstah, her blood pressure had evened because she had reminded herself once again that neither of them had time in their lives for a serious relationship, so she needed to just squash the idea once and for all. Since losing her parents when she was so young, Kinsley had been resolutely independent. She secretly wondered if that, too, had something to do with it. Was she afraid of loss if she loved too fiercely? Sometimes she felt she could talk herself out of anything—even the good things.

Kinsley reapplied a layer of cherry lip balm to her cracked lips before exiting the truck and dashing inside the restaurant. Pete and Raven stood behind the expansive smooth wood bar chatting, as Monday usually was the slowest day of the week for the eatery. Kinsley was relieved, though, as she didn't want to pull Pete away from his work if it turned out to be unusually busy. She waved a hand in greeting when the two looked in her direction.

Pete threw a thumb behind him. "Did you see the lift out there? They literally just dropped it off."

Kinsley hadn't noticed that the lift had been delivered. She was more preoccupied with settling her jitters and applying lip balm than paying attention to the world around her. "Oh, that's great news!" she said.

"Lemme go grab my coat." Pete turned in the direction of the back room before Kinsley's comment caught him midstride.

"You may wanna grab a winter hat and a scarf, too, it's pretty cold."

"Nah, I'm good. Scarves are for wimps."

Kinsley laughed. "All right, whatever, you goof. I'll meet you out there."

"Be out in a jiffy."

"Sounds good." Kinsley turned on her heel and headed out the same way she had entered. The brisk wind off the water caused her to wrap her arms protectively around herself and then adjust the scarf tighter around her own neck. She walked in the direction of where the heap of lobster traps and over a hundred colorful lobster buoys needed to be arranged. At the sound of a whistle, she turned to watch Pete jogging across the parking lot to join her, and secretly hoped he'd slow down so he wouldn't slip on a patch of ice. His face lit with pure animation when he reached her side.

"Were you whistling at me? Or the enormous mess you got yourself into?" Kinsley chuckled.

"Honestly, it was neither. I was trying to get Stan's attention as he was walking across the parking lot. He just delivered fresh tuna for this week's menu, and I wanted the chance to wave good-bye to him."

"Ahh. Are you sure you don't want to dress warmer for this project? It's freezing out here." Kinsley shivered and then blew on her gloved hands to warm them.

"I'm tough." He grinned.

"That you are." Pete must be, Kinsley thought, to consider heading outdoors without proper attire in these elements, because it was darn right dangerous. But she kept her mouth shut for fear of mothering him.

"Anyhoo . . ." Pete said, landing his hands firmly on his hips. "Looks like we have quite a job ahead of us!"

"Yeah, no kidding. And this isn't the half of it. I also have five hundred feet of garland in the back of my truck and over five thousand lights to add." Kinsley looked in the direction of her truck and suddenly felt overwhelmed. Pete must've noticed, as he put an encouraging arm around her and gave a light squeeze.

"It'll be okay. Becca mentioned you had a rough morning. I promise I won't bite. We'll have fun with this. Maybe it'll even get this ole dog into the Christmas spirit," he added over his shoulder as he moved closer to inspect the lift.

"When did you talk to Becca?"

"She called right before you came."

"She did? Why?" Kinsley heard the slight agitation in her voice and hoped Pete hadn't caught on to it.

"She felt bad leaving us hanging and said if it got late and she didn't make it back, to buy you dinner and put it on her tab. But I insisted she didn't need to pay for your dinner. You can order anything on the house tonight. Consider it my treat."

Kinsley must've had a puzzled look splash across her face because he added, "*What?*"

"You need to make a livin', too, ya know. I have no problem paying my own tab."

"Listen here, girlie. Let someone do something nice for *you* for a change."

Kinsley frowned and apparently Pete caught on to that, too,

because he continued in a more serious tone. "You do a lot for this town, Kinsley. I know you feel some of the elected officials tend to give you a hard time down at the town council, but we all see through that. Chris just needs to have his nose involved in everything." He shrugged. "I wouldn't worry about it. He's been down my throat a few times, too. That's just how he is. I wouldn't take it personally if I were you."

Kinsley was glad that Pete had her back but didn't exactly feel comfortable that other people knew about her issues with Chris.

"I know, but I can't help but feel like Chris has a personal vendetta against me sometimes. I've done absolutely nothing to the guy, Pete. It bothers me that he talks poorly about me and my business behind my back. How would you feel if he were talking about the Blue Lobstah that way?"

"And you know this for sure? That he's talking behind your back, I mean?"

"I mean, he basically acted as if I'm stealing from Mallory by taking her supplies today. It wasn't even my idea! I can only imagine he's blabbing his thoughts to the other members of the town council about me stealing from her, too. It's not the first time he's threatened to remove SeaScapes from working for Harborside. Remember?"

"I know it's upsetting, but the town hasn't tried to push you out, right?"

"Right."

"So don't let one jerk suck you in. It's not even worth arguing with Chris about anything; don't stoop to his level." He shook his head. "If it were me? I'd just try to brush it off and move on."

"I hate it when you're right." She grinned. "Thanks for letting me vent."

"Anytime."

The bar owner stepped into the cage of the construction lift and began playing with the controls. He lifted himself so high in the air that Kinsley had to tent her eyes to watch. She was glad he was the one rising overhead, and not her. The cold wind must've felt awful up there, and she couldn't help but cringe as she looked up at the man not wearing a hat to cover his red ears. He'd likely end up with frostbite due to his stubbornness.

"I forgot to mention the good news!" he yelled.

Pete's comment made her shake off her annoyance about the town gossip. "What's that?"

He lowered himself to the ground before responding. "The artist that made the blue lobstah that hangs inside my bar is making a five-foot fiberglass red one to top this tree! He's donating it to the town for free, too. We can store it in my shed and use it year after year, if you want to."

"You don't think Chris will get after me for accepting more donations?"

"Ah, don't worry about that guy! I'll take the heat on this one!"

"How'd you convince the artist to donate?"

"With my good looks and charming disposition, of course," he teased, and stuck out his tongue.

"No, seriously! How'd you convince him?"

"I said it would be good marketing on his part. I assured him that the local paper would probably do a write-up about it, along with the Harborside Facebook page. I told him, more than likely, it would lead to more sales. I mean, this lobstah tree will no doubt be the main attraction down here."

"That's great, Pete. Thanks! I hadn't decided what we were

going to use for a tree topper. And that sounds like the perfect addition for Harborside."

"Yeah, get it?" His eyebrows danced merrily when he added, "A *Maine* attraction."

Kinsley laughed. She wasn't sure if he was flirting or merely playing with words.

"Anyhoo, I told ya, I gotcha covered." Pete winked before releasing himself from the lift cage and moving in her direction.

"You sure did. Who knew you were this into planning Christmas decorations? Learn something new about you every day!"

"I don't think it's that," he admitted.

"What is it, then?"

"The smile I get when pleasing you," he answered. And then his own face lit in pure Christmas-morning magic.

Kinsley could feel herself blush and turned away. "All right, you flirt. Let's get to work."

"Yes, ma'am!" he replied with a salute.

Kinsley couldn't help but wonder if he'd been in cahoots with Becca, who was saluting her today as well. She secretly hoped she didn't come off like a drill sergeant who made everyone around her jump to attention. That was her brother Kyle's job. He was the one to follow in their parents' footsteps and pursue the military lifestyle. Currently stationed in Germany, Kyle was due to come home on leave from the Air Force for the holidays. And Kinsley could hardly wait for their reunion to celebrate a Harborside family Christmas.

Chapter 4

Kinsley handed Becca the last of the hand-painted seashells to hang on the Christmas tree at the Salty Breeze Inn, when Tilly entered the stately living room. The welcoming space, with comfy off-white furniture and bookcases stuffed with books, was now fully ready for seasonal guests to linger over a glass of eggnog or one of Toby's cocoa bombs.

"Ladies! You've outdone yourselves. The tree is going to be the talk of the inn this year." Tilly beamed as she clasped her hands approvingly and then walked around the ten-foot tree to further investigate.

"It smells good, too," Becca said as she took a step backward to greet her. "I'm so glad we went with the balsam fir and not the Colorado blue spruce. I do like the tint of blue, since we're by the ocean, but I think we were smart to pick scent over color this time around."

"Well, look at you. My new employee learning about trees and all things nature. I'm impressed," Kinsley said, and meant it. Evidently her friend was paying attention when they had visited the tree farm to select the tree for the inn.

"Hey, excuse the gardening pun, but I'm really diggin' the new job," Becca teased with a wide grin.

"Oh dear." Kinsley chuckled. "I have to agree with you, though, we did pick the perfect tree for this room." She nodded approvingly as she studied the height of it within the space.

"I agree, too, my sweets." Tilly wrapped her arms lovingly around the two of them and brought them in for a group hug. "My guests are going to be so pleased when they enter the Salty Breeze and all they can smell is the scent of a down-home Maine Christmas. They'll make it an annual tradition for sure!"

"Oh, I don't know about that, Aunt Tilly. There're some heavenly scents that seep out of the kitchen, too. In fact, what's on the menu tonight?" Kinsley asked, licking her lips.

"Yeah, whatcha serving?" Becca piped in with a gleam in her eye. "I might have to stay for dinner."

"I'm making New England clam chowder, with a side salad. A chocolate ganache cake with white chocolate curls, topped with a raspberry glaze, for dessert. You're more than welcome to stay if you're interested."

"How could anyone not be interested in that? It sounds amazing," Becca cooed, and then linked her arm through Kinsley's. "How do you live this close to her and not gain any weight?"

Kinsley laughed. "If I had a desk job and wasn't hustling all the time with my landscape business, I'd be sunk in the soil for sure. Her menus are hard to resist. And it seems her guests agree, as they keep comin' back for more." After taking a step back from the tree, Kinsley noticed the wire ribbon that cascaded down the side needed adjusting and moved to fix it.

The three were interrupted by the sound of boots clicking on the hardwood floor, and a woman's voice. "What a simply fabulous tree. The Salty Breeze Inn is beginning to look like a place I'd like to stay for Christmas! I hope you're hosting a holiday open house this year?"

Kinsley looked up to find Chris Chesterfield's wife standing at the threshold. She took a deep breath as Mallory entered the room and hoped the alderman hadn't sent her over for further pestering.

Thankfully, Tilly quickly moved to greet her, which felt like a nice buffer for Kinsley.

"Oh, hi, Mallory, how are you this fine day?" Tilly asked kindly.

"Couldn't be better, thank you." Mallory beamed.

"In answer to the question, I'm not sure if I'm hosting an open house this year. Reason being because I'm not sure I can squeeze in a date. It sounds like my nephew might be coming home on military leave, which would take precedence. Thanks for the reminder, though." Tilly's expression pinched. "I'll need to get on it and decide, once and for all. Traditionally, I host a caroling event on Christmas Eve, though. You and your husband are more than welcome to join us; we have a ton of fun. After all, the more the merrier!" Her expression morphed to glee as a new light shone in her eyes.

"Yes, please keep us posted on that. Chris and I are planning to stay local this year and just hosting his brother, Cole, over Christmas. It's always fun to walk through and see your place all decked out for the holidays. We'd be delighted to come caroling, too, if you wouldn't mind a plus-three. Anyhow, speaking of plus-three, I just stopped by to see if my brother-in-law has checked in yet. Have you seen him?"

Kinsley gave a sigh of relief, as it seemed she wasn't the reason for Mallory's visit after all. But the thought of spending her Christmas Eve with the alderman wasn't exactly sitting well. She'd need to get over it for her aunt's sake, though, as Tilly oozed hospitality and would never turn a person away.

Mallory continued, "Cole mentioned he might stay here, instead of at our place. He's allergic to my cat, sooo . . . Anyhow, I was hoping to speak with him before the boat parade." She looked to Kinsley momentarily before returning to Tilly, who confirmed with a nod.

"Ah yes, Cole Chesterfield checked in about an hour ago. I'm not sure if he's still up in his room, or if he stepped out for a bit," Tilly replied. "He mentioned he might head into town to do a little early Christmas shopping. Maybe he was planning to stop in and catch you at Precious Petals?"

"Oh, okay. Well, at least I know he arrived. If you see him, would you please not mention I was here? I'd like to surprise him. And besides, I'd rather Chris not know I was checking in on his brother." Mallory's face flushed pink before she turned her attention back to the Christmas tree. "You ladies do amazing work. I just might have to hire you to decorate the tree for my shop window."

"I'm not sure your husband would be too keen on that idea," Kinsley retorted, and then bit her lip. She wasn't sure if what she had just uttered aloud was appropriate and wished she could hit a rewind button.

"Really? Why do you say that? I think Chris would be fine with me hiring you. Just look at the work you all do!" She gestured with her hand, and they all looked again at the beautifully decorated Christmas tree. "It's simply gorgeous!"

"Honestly, I think he's a little bit disappointed that I didn't pay you for the supplies you so generously donated to craft the kissing balls. You are okay with the donation, right? Did I misunderstand something? Were you expecting to be paid? Or . . ." Kinsley's voice trailed off as she was hoping for an understanding lifeline, and she got one.

"Oh, I see. Well, don't worry about my husband. He doesn't seem to get that it's my decision how I run my business. Despite my constant reminding!" Mallory smiled. "Just ignore that grumpy old man. I do."

Kinsley let out a sigh of relief. "I'm glad to hear it, Mallory. I feel so much better now that we've cleared the air."

"Trust me, I'm not even a little upset." Mallory squeezed her fingers together in demonstration of how small her upset was, and they all shared a chuckle. "Besides, if my nosy husband is the least bit worried about money, I have enough work to keep me busy clear through the New Year."

"I can imagine. Running your own flower shop must keep you on your toes," Kinsley agreed sympathetically. "Especially around the holidays."

"It sure does. I handle supplying all the poinsettias for the hospital and nursing homes in town. Speaking of that, I need to get motoring. Have a lovely day, everyone." Mallory backed out of the room and disappeared from view.

"See, you were all worried, but it's really only Chris that's a thorn in your rose garden," Becca said with an encouraging smile.

With a nod, Kinsley agreed. "Yeah, I do feel better about it now. My approach wasn't very gracious, but at least now I know."

"Is that alderman still giving you a hard time?" Tilly's brows came together in deep concern, and she landed her hands firmly on her hips. "I'd like to give him a piece of my mind. He needs to leave you alone, once and for all. I don't know what it is that makes him get after you, time and time again."

Kinsley laughed. "No, it's fine. I can handle him. It's just one man, who can be a little irritating. But who isn't a little irritating from time to time? I certainly am!"

"No, you're not," Becca corrected. "You're one of the nicest people I know."

"You have to say that—you're my best friend." Kinsley chuckled.

Becca shook her head adamantly. "Nope. Not true. Wouldn't say it if I didn't mean it."

"I hate to interrupt this sweet bantering between you two, but, Kinsley, did you get the lobster tree decorated down at the marina? Did Peter help you?" Tilly asked.

"Yes, Aunt Tilly, but you know he goes by Pete, not Peter, right? I'm not sure why you insist on calling him by his full name—no one else does."

Tilly pondered this as she looked to the ceiling and then admitted, "He looks more like a Peter to me. Maybe it's because he reminds me of an old classmate from high school I once had a crush on."

"Oh, really?" Kinsley's hands flew to her heart. "Were you in love with this Peter?" she asked.

"'Love' is a strong word. It was a teenage crush," Tilly admitted with a smirk. "He was very good-looking, just like that bar owner down at the wharf. Don't you just love the wave of his hair? He's quite the looker, if you ask me. I'm surprised he's not already taken. Has he ever been married?"

"If he has been married, he's never shared that with us," Kinsley admitted.

"Well, I think Kins has a little bit of a crush on our Pete, too," Becca teased. "Though she won't admit it."

"Is this true, Kinsley? I did notice that you get a little giddy around the boy. Especially when you were crafting those kissing balls."

"Oh, look what you started, Bec. And he's not a *boy*, Aunt Tilly, he's a grown man. Who runs his *own* successful business and puts in a ton of hours down at the Blue Lobstah."

"Sounds like you admire that." Tilly lifted her chin and examined her.

"I think she does," Becca piped in.

"I'm standing right here, you two." Kinsley frowned. "Pete and I have a lot in common regarding how we run a business. But we both work very hard and put in a lot of long hours and don't have time for a relationship," she added with a huff.

"It's okay to care deeply about your business. But there's nothing wrong with taking a little time and having a little fun. Trust me, life passes by quickly. Sometimes when I look in the mirror, I'm shocked at the reminder that I'm in my early sixties. My brain is still locked at thirty-nine." She grinned. "My mind definitely hasn't hit the forties yet."

"Well, you certainly run circles around us, Aunt Tilly," Kinsley said admiringly. "You put in a lot of hours and, frankly, I can't keep up with you."

"Oh dear! Speaking of that . . . I forgot I have cheddar

biscuits in the oven. I need to get back to the kitchen, stat!" Tilly turned and rushed out the door.

"Oh no! Don't burn those biscuits!" Becca exclaimed. "Those are a favorite of mine, too. Count me in for dinner!" But Tilly was already out the door and long gone.

Chapter 5

The weekend had finally arrived for the town's annual boat parade and fireworks event. The evening was balmy by Maine standards, the temperature hovering around thirty-one degrees, with a light wind. Kinsley was thankful for it, because so much preparation had gone into the decor that she wanted it to go off without a hitch. In previous years, a nor'easter had taken the festivities completely off the calendar. But this was not to be one of those years, evidently. Which was a huge relief.

Kinsley looked out over the cliff walk in the direction of the marina, where the yachts were already lining up for the parade. Most were decked out in Christmas lights from bow to stern, and one even had a full-sized Christmas tree lit inside the bridge, where the captain was navigating. Sounds of laughter and jubilation echoed from the boats across the water. It seemed a festive mood was in full swing, and the party hadn't even technically begun.

"Hey, there you are. I was looking for you."

Kinsley turned at the sound of Pete's voice. "Me?"

"Yeah! You're the talk of the town. You're the *It girl*!" he added with a wink and a cackle.

Kinsley's jaw dropped. "I am?"

"Everyone loves the lobstah-trap tree! I wish you could've been there to hear all the nice comments that have been floating across my bar. They've been pouring in all afternoon! I'm telling ya, people are all over it. We did good." He grinned, which lit his face afire, like the upcoming fireworks. He really did have a winning smile. So much so that Kinsley had to turn away from him, as he was causing her stomach to erupt with butterflies.

"I'm glad." Kinsley met his eyes again and mirrored his smile so as not to seem rude. She leaned her hip on a nearby post and turned her attention back to the yachts. "Looks so pretty out there, all those lights sparkling on the water. Beautiful evening for this. I'm really glad the weather held," she said, searching to say anything to settle her jitters around him. Part of her really wanted to nip her growing attraction in the bud, because the fear of losing him far outweighed taking their relationship to the next level, but her growing feelings were undeniable. Kinsley apparently hid it well, though, as he continued chatting along as if nothing were amiss. And completely oblivious of the nervous energy that was bubbling up inside of her.

"Yeah, it's too bad we couldn't afford one of those yachts." He waggled a long finger between them. "Then you and I would be partaking in the parade. It's still fun to watch, though." Pete then jutted a thumb over his shoulder. "Hey. You comin' into the bar? I have a glass of wine with your name on it. It might help you warm up before the big party is in full swing." He rubbed his hands together in excitement.

"Sure, I'll come in for one. I think Becca was planning to meet me, too. Have you seen her yet?"

"Yep, sure did. That's the other reason I came out lookin' for ya. Shall we?" He gestured to the door as if he were a butler greeting her at a grand estate. Kinsley grabbed ahold of his arm after narrowly slipping on a patch of ice. He then looped her tightly by the arm to protect her from a repeat fall, and the two headed in the direction of the back door.

Inside the Blue Lobstah, the bar was packed with patrons, almost too crammed to walk through the crowd. The upcoming boat parade was good for Pete's business, and Kinsley was glad for it.

Becca was perched on a stool in their usual spot at the end of the bar, talking to Raven. She waved Kinsley and Pete over as soon as Raven had pointed them out.

Kinsley greeted her friend with a squeeze. "Don't you look nice! I love your sweater, is it new?" she asked as she slipped onto the adjacent stool.

Becca was wearing a Nordic-looking navy sweater that showcased white snowflakes along the neckline. She looked down at it and pulled it taut, to take her own peek. "Thanks. I just bought it online. It looks very ski bunny to me, which is sort of funny since I don't ski. But hey, it's warm and seasonal." Becca lifted her glass of wine in cheers and Kinsley turned toward the bar to see Pete sliding a glass in front of her before moving on to help the next customer.

"Thanks," she said to him, and he acknowledged her with a nod and a grin, while simultaneously pouring a beer into a tall mug.

"Any word on your showing appointment?" Kinsley asked.

"Yeah, they made an offer! Fingers crossed it gets accepted. Thanks for giving me the time off to work on it."

"You bet! Here's to believing that the offer will be accepted!"

The two clinked their wineglasses and took a sip.

"Zach said he might stop by tonight, but he mentioned a friend from college was in town that he hadn't seen in years, so he wasn't sure if he'd make it."

Kinsley tried to hide her disappointment. The last thing she wanted was to end up a third wheel on Becca's date night. She squashed her feelings and said, "Things still going well with you and him?"

"Yeah, mostly talking on the phone, though. We've both been busy, but we talked about maybe catching lunch later this week, too. It's hard because he works at the gym as a trainer in the evenings," Becca said, nursing her wine.

"Ahh."

Becca leaned in and whispered, "Look over there—your friend Chris is dressed as the Grinch. How about that?" Her expression morphed into a grin.

Kinsley did a double take. She turned to see the alderman in head-to-toe costume, right down to the green face paint. He seemed in rare form, joking with those who stood beside him at the bar.

Becca bubbled up in laughter. "A bit poetic, don't you think?"

"*How* did you even recognize him?"

"The curly gray sticking out of the Santa hat. Plus, that hideous laugh of his, it's so annoying. Dead giveaway." Becca swirled the liquid in her wineglass, making a whirlpool before taking another sip.

The alderman seemed so preoccupied in conversation that he didn't notice his wife talking with another man and laughing as if she were witnessing a stand-up comedy act. "Who's Mallory talking to?"

"Isn't that Cole Chesterfield? Chris's brother—the one Mallory was looking for at the inn. They kind of have the same features, minus the gray. He must be younger than his brother, I think. Or maybe he's older? Hard to tell. But the two are definitely related."

"Oh yeah. Now that you mention it, I can see the resemblance." Kinsley watched as Mallory moved away from the bar toward a table. Her brother-in-law followed, with his hand along the small of her back. The act, although innocent, seemed almost intimate. "Did you see that?"

"See what?" Becca glanced over but Mallory had already been swallowed into the crowd.

"Nothing," Kinsley replied. She realized she'd been a little too judgy, and since she didn't like gossip, decided to crush it. "Never mind."

"Hey, there's your aunt."

When Kinsley caught sight of her, she beckoned Tilly over to their side of the bar. Her aunt moved in their direction but stopped to chat with friendly faces along her journey.

"Your aunt is the cutest. Does she know everybody in town, or what?" Becca asked.

"Yeah, pretty much." Kinsley smiled.

When Tilly finally made it to Kinsley's side, she was flushed and instantly removed her coat. "It's warm in here! What a turnout! This is terrific," she said, fanning a hand in front of her animated face.

Kinsley took her aunt's coat and tucked it onto her lap. "I'm so glad you made it out tonight. You never get to enjoy anything because you're always tending to your guests."

"Yes, that's certainly true," Tilly agreed with a nod. "But all my guests were happy to either partake in the boat parade with friends or come and enjoy the fireworks with the rest of us. When I left, the inn was eerily empty. Which is quite rare."

"Rare indeed!" Kinsley exclaimed.

"Can I order you up something from the bar?" Becca asked.

"How about a glass of pinot to celebrate your night off? I'll put it on my tab," Kinsley offered.

"Oh, I suppose it wouldn't hurt for me to sip on it." Tilly sighed. "I'm a bit warm—and thirsty, too."

Kinsley waved Pete over and gave the order. Before long, Tilly had a wineglass in her hand, and her nose was growing as bright as Rudolph the Red-Nosed Reindeer's on Christmas Eve night.

"Whoa! This is going right to my head." Tilly giggled. "I feel so warm inside." Her smile radiated as she took another sip.

Tilly wasn't the only one feeling the holiday cheer. Kinsley noticed Chris drop his Santa hat and stagger while trying to put it back atop his green head before heading toward the table to join his wife and brother. He didn't make it that far because he walked smack-dab into someone, spilling his drink. That person gave him a shove backward and the Grinch fell completely on his backside, a wave of shock rippling across his face before he sprang to his feet like a cat. Kinsley didn't realize the older man had it in him to be so agile.

"That guy is such a jerk, he gets all handsy and rude when he drinks," Raven said, leaning toward them from the opposite side of the bar. "I'm not even a bit surprised that he's causing a scene. Honestly"—Raven lowered her voice to a whisper—"I'm not sure which voters he's kissing up to that keep him in office. I think it's just because nobody else wants the job," she continued before Pete summoned her back to work, asking her to take the trash out and then grab a bottle of tequila from the back room.

"Guess you're not the only one who has a beef with him," Becca said with a raised brow. "Sounds like Raven's not a fan of the alderman, either."

"Yeah, I'm not sure if that's good news or bad news, considering he makes decisions for the town," Kinsley uttered before turning to her aunt, who had finally taken a seat on the stool beside her.

Before long, punches were flying between the alderman and the unidentified man. And the entire crowd was watching.

Out of nowhere, Pete was dragging the two of them by the collar toward the door. The sound of Pete's voice bellowed above the crowd noise. "Get outta my establishment! And sober up before you walk through my doors again!"

Mallory and Cole soon followed the drunken Grinch out into the cold and didn't argue with the bar owner. Instead, Mallory looked mildly embarrassed as she hung her head.

Pete addressed the crowd. "Sorry for the interruption, folks! That's the last you'll see of them tonight!" he said as he washed his hands of the matter, stepped back behind the bar, and began pouring drinks as if nothing were amiss.

Kinsley and Becca shared an inconspicuous smile before turning their attention back to Aunt Tilly, who was giggling like a schoolgirl. The wine had clearly gone straight to her head.

"Hey, I saw the lobster-trap tree you and Pete put together out there. Impressive!" Becca said.

"Thanks! Yeah, I think it really adds a nice touch to our town's decor. And you saw the big red lobster on the top? That was Pete's doing."

"Yeah, that's terrific! It really adds to the tree. I love it!"

"Me, too. I think we'll use it every year going forward. It's a statement piece, for sure."

"Thanks for reminding me, Becca." Tilly hiccupped. "I'll need to go over there and check it out. I ran from the parking lot. It was so cold I didn't lift my head to see it. But I'll make a point when I go outside."

Kinsley was on the precipice of saying something when Raven barreled through the door and shouted, "Is there a paramedic in the house? Someone fell in the water!"

Pete cupped his hands around his mouth and yelled back, "Has anyone called 911?"

"Yeah, outside! But time is of the essence! We need help now!" Raven shrieked before doing a 180 and running back outdoors.

Chapter 6

Kinsley tossed her aunt's coat off her lap and back into Tilly's arms. She leapt from the barstool, sending it to teeter on its side. After catching the stool with one hand before it hit the floor, she steadied it and then abandoned the bar area completely. She eased her way through the crowd toward the door and sensed Becca on her heels when she heard her friend's voice carry over the din of chatter behind her.

"Wait!"

Becca reached her side breathlessly. "I'm not sure we ought to go out there. That screaming sent chills down my spine. You know I have a weak stomach for blood! What if the person who fell in is someone we know?" Becca then grabbed ahold of Kinsley's shoulder to spin her around.

"You don't have to go with me, but I can't let it go, Bec. I need to see what's going on out there. *Especially* if someone we know fell into the sea!" Kinsley answered resolutely as she threw open the door, letting a rush of cold air hit them like a rude awakening after their time spent inside the steamy bar. She zipped her coat and threw on her hood before dodging patches of ice and navigating as quickly as possible toward a crowd that was quickly forming at the base of the pier, which led to the marina. She forced her way through the gathering to see what they were looking at. All were staring in one direction—toward the Atlantic.

A woman pointed with an outstretched arm. "There he is! See him bobbing in the water!"

It was then Kinsley did a double take. Chris's Santa hat had been carried away with the tide and was hung up on a nearby rock. Green face paint floated to the top of the water like eerie fluorescent algae. The Grinch costume clung to the alderman's limp body like wrinkled wet laundry, where he lay crumpled and wedged between a large jagged rock, at the base of the pier. His head was struck with crashing waves as the tide relentlessly rolled into shore.

Becca gasped.

Kinsley had been so preoccupied with what she herself was witnessing that she hadn't even noticed her friend had reached her side.

Waves were now crashing over the Grinch, fully engulfing his body, and two men quickly jumped into the icy water to his aid. One of the men lifted Chris up under his arms, while the other unwedged his body from the boulders. They dragged him out of the water and onto a flatter surface, but the alderman hadn't moved. Within moments, one of the men solemnly shook his head, after he'd checked for a pulse.

"Oh nooo. Aren't they at least going to administer CPR?" Kinsley threw her hand over her mouth. "It can't already be too late. We need to do something!" she cried helplessly.

"This can't be happening," Becca murmured. "He must've drowned. Did you know it only takes forty seconds for someone to drown? And it can happen with as little as half a cup of water?"

"You mean to tell me I was that close to death when you saved me in swim class and became my water wings?"

"Yep."

"That's awful!" Kinsley exclaimed. "I really didn't think a drowning could happen that quickly!"

Becca and Kinsley had met when they were kids and attended the same swim class, where Becca had quite literally saved Kinsley's life.

Pete was now at their side and said, "What happened?" before he glanced to the sea and let out an expletive. He then ran his hands nervously through his hair.

Tilly also followed them to the marina, where the restless crowd continued to expand. When her aunt reached Kinsley's side, she gripped her arm and held it tight. "Oh my goodness! Did anyone see how this happened?" Her eyes doubled in size, and she clutched a protective hand to her heart.

Pete ushered them away from the main crowd. When they were out of earshot he said, "Chris had a lot to drink tonight. And honestly, it's not because he was overserved. I think he was drunk before he even stepped into my restaurant. You think he just fell in?"

"I saw him staggering, too. That's probably what happened," Kinsley agreed with a nod. "How awful!"

"Where's that guy from inside the bar who pushed him?"

Becca asked. "You don't think the argument continued outside, do you?"

They all scanned the crowd but didn't locate the man and no one said another word regarding the bar fight.

Pete broke the silence when he murmured, "The poor guy! And his wife . . . This is awful. Especially around the holidays."

They all nodded their heads solemnly.

"We're going to have to support Mallory any way we can," Kinsley said. "Somehow, we need to make sure she doesn't feel isolated and alone at Christmas."

"You're absolutely right," Tilly said. "The community will have to gather around her and be her strength right now."

Pete rubbed his jaw and had a worried expression on his face.

"What?" Kinsley asked.

"A small part of me is worried the family could blame the bar for overserving him. Not to mention the altercation that led me to kick him to the curb! You don't think they'd sue me, do you?"

"I highly doubt it. Mallory is a very kind woman and she'll see the truth in all of this. It's all going to be okay." Kinsley rubbed his shoulder to soothe him, but her efforts did little, as she could literally feel the tension growing in his muscles. She really hoped that, for his sake, she was right.

Just then, Detective Rachel Hayes, Kinsley's brother's ex-girlfriend, entered the scene. Kinsley didn't notice if the lead detective from the Harborside Police Department had been inside the bar earlier but wasn't at all surprised by her presence. Most of the department was there to enjoy the festivities, too, and some were there to provide crowd control. Kinsley noticed Rachel talking to the men who had carefully lifted Chris out of the water. When his body reached the shore, the detective moved to examine him from head to toe.

Before long, the Grinch was covered with a sheet. It was then the stark realization hit Kinsley hard once again: Mallory was a widow. She looked to the crowd in search of Chris's wife, but Mallory seemed to appear out of nowhere and run to the sheet, where the lead detective lifted it for her inspection. Where was Cole? Hadn't they left the restaurant together? Mallory put her head in her hands and wept. Kinsley felt an urge to go and console her but didn't think it was her place, as Mallory was now being led away by another officer and taken to the back of an ambulance, where the attendant handed her a bottle of water and covered her shoulders with a blanket to stop her from shivering either from the cold or from the shock of it all.

Kinsley, Becca, Tilly, and Pete didn't utter a word as they watched the stretcher with Chris's lifeless covered body roll past them. Shock littered their worry-filled faces and Kinsley was left to wonder what had really happened. She looked over to see Chris's brother consoling his sister-in-law. And she could have sworn she saw Mallory give him a weak smile. Kinsley couldn't help but think her expression seemed a bit inappropriate or untimely.

Rachel had stepped away from her coworker momentarily, and Kinsley darted from her group of friends to catch her.

"Rachel!" Kinsley waved her hand frantically to gain the detective's attention.

Rachel spun on her heels to greet her. "Hey, Kins." She blew out a breath. "Tough night, I don't have a lot of time to talk. Perhaps we could meet for a coffee sometime soon and catch up. Shoot me a text and we'll figure out a time."

"Yeah! I can't believe what happened here tonight! It's awful!" Kinsley exclaimed.

"Sure is." Rachel hung her head.

"Yeah, especially around the holidays."

A sullen lull came between them.

"Have you heard? My brother is planning on coming home for Christmas!"

"Yeah, he mentioned that might be a possibility the last time we spoke. Sounds like he booked the trip, then?"

"Yeah, I think he might be home for a month this time."

Kinsley watched Rachel register this information before saying, "Is that right?"

"Yeah. Isn't that great?"

"That'll be wonderful for you, quality time with your brother instead of a quick visit. I'm glad he's coming home for longer this time. It'll be good to see him. I'm looking forward to it, too." She smiled warmly.

"Yeah, I'm really excited," Kinsley continued, hoping to keep the investigator's attention just a wee bit longer.

"I'm sure. Anyhow, I have to get back to it." Rachel began to pull away and Kinsley stopped her again by reaching for her arm.

"You think Chris fell in because he was drunk?" Kinsley asked, closely studying the detective. She knew by the look on Rachel's face that there was more to it than that.

"I probably shouldn't divulge . . ."

"Rachel, please?" Kinsley whispered. "I might be able to help."

"Blunt-force trauma to the top of his head. That's all I'm going to share," Rachel said quietly.

"How do you know it's not from his fall? He could've hit his head on impact, those rocks below the pier are incredibly jagged and sharp. And I didn't see any blood on the ground. Surely, we would have seen a trail of blood since the ground is covered in a fresh dusting of snow. Wouldn't we?"

"The blood washed away from his time in the water. But there was a strike to the top of his head. And I know . . . it wasn't from the rocks. Seriously, Kinsley, that's all I can share. You understand."

"You know Chris was wearing a Santa hat, right? Wouldn't that prohibit a chance of leaving a specific mark on his head?" Kinsley asked.

Rachel looked as if the wheels were turning rapid-fire in her brain. "Yeah. I think the hat hit the water before he did. It had to. Maybe it fell in during the initial altercation, I'm not exactly sure. But I know what I saw."

"Do you know who you're bringing in for questioning?"

"I'm putting a list together right now," Rachel admitted, chewing the side of her cheek.

"Well, I shouldn't point fingers, and I didn't see him initially, but—"

"What?" Rachel's brows narrowed. "If you know something, you need to tell me."

Kinsley cleared her throat. "Nothing, never mind." The last thing she wanted to do was implicate someone who could be completely innocent of a crime. Just because Cole and Mallory seemed to disappear and reappear at a moment's notice didn't mean they were involved. Did it? Or the man who fought with Chris inside the bar—he seemed to play the disappearing act, too. Nothing was conclusive, merely speculation.

Rachel studied her further before finally letting it go. "All right, then, if you think of anything, you have my number."

"By the way, it's going to come back to you that the alderman and I had issues with each other. I may as well just bring that to your attention right now, before someone else mentions something." Kinsley put up both hands in a defensive stance and stated firmly, "But I assure you, I was sitting inside the Blue Lobstah and had nothing to do with this. And you know me, right? I would never hurt anyone . . ." She trailed off, hoping for a life preserver. Unfortunately, the detective didn't toss one.

Instead, Rachel breathed deeply. "I'll need to know the details, so you and I will probably need to talk down at the station at some point."

"Should I follow you, right now?" Kinsley asked nervously. She had hoped being transparent about her issues with the alderman would be helpful, but unfortunately it seemed to backfire. Perhaps she shouldn't have brought it up at all.

"No, but I'll be in touch soon. Don't disappear on me."

"Of course not." Kinsley didn't like the tone of the detective's voice. It had quickly grown sharper and less friendly than she was used to hearing from Rachel.

"Look, I gotta get back to work and meet up with the medical examiner. Let me know when you find out the dates of when Kyle flies in. I'd love to see him. And I'll be in touch about your issues with Chris," Rachel said before quickly moving back in the direction of the ambulance.

Kinsley returned to her small group of Aunt Tilly, Becca, and Pete, who continued to murmur among themselves. They immediately stopped talking when she beckoned them to step even farther away from the rest of the crowd.

"Whatcha find out?" Becca asked finally when the group was out of earshot.

"It wasn't an accident. He suffered some kind of blunt-force trauma," Kinsley whispered.

Tilly gasped and her eyes doubled in size, her expression laced with obvious fear.

Pete leaned in and lowered his voice. "Wait. You mean someone offed him?"

"Sounds like it," Kinsley said, letting out a slow breath.

Becca shook her head slowly. "Oh wow, that's not at all what I was expecting you to say. I thought he fell in because he had too much to drink."

Kinsley agreed with a nod. "I know, right? Looks like someone just made Santa's naughty list."

Chapter 7

When Kinsley had made that offhand comment about Santa's naughty list, the last thing she'd imagined was that that she might actually be on it.

"Yes, it's unfortunate your name has come up several times during questioning. I know you had given me a heads-up about this the night of the murder, but I wasn't expecting the sheer volume of fingers pointing in your direction." Rachel folded her hands on her desk, but her eyes narrowed in on Kinsley. "Can you explain that?"

Kinsley found herself staring blankly back at Rachel. Sitting across from the lead detective, she was still in shock that she had been summoned to Rachel's office at the Harborside Police Department to begin with. She was reeling that all this was even possible, so she asked pointedly, "Really? Who all brought up my name?"

"I can't tell you that."

"What about the guy that fought with Chris at the bar? Why aren't you questioning him instead of me?"

"Don't worry. We're following any and all leads at this point. I assure you, everyone that needs to be questioned will be."

Kinsley's gaze traveled over the muted tan walls, where she noted all of Rachel's achievements, neatly framed and hanging, perfectly level across the room. Each award, including a few from her time in the Air Force, were set in matching black one-inch frames. The seriousness of the conversation, and the confines of the office Rachel held, did not go unnoticed. In fact, it made Kinsley squirm in her seat.

"Come on, Rachel. This is me you're talking to," she pleaded.

"Yes, and I'm handling an ongoing homicide investigation, where your name has inconveniently come up, repeatedly. How do you expect me to handle that? Give you special privileges? While the chief is breathing down my neck looking for the number one suspect in this case? We're talking about a high-profile elected official from Harborside who was brutally murdered by someone from this town. I'm sorry, but I have no other choice than to ask these questions."

"Wait. So, you really think that someone is me?" Kinsley gripped the wooden armrests of her chair to try and settle herself.

"No." Rachel put up a quick hand of defense. "That's not what I said. But I can't just explain you away without some answers. Especially when your name keeps coming up." She shuffled a few papers around her desk and stacked them before tucking them aside and facing Kinsley squarely. "Give me something to work with here, Kins. A little help would be greatly appreciated."

"But you know I have an alibi, right? I was inside the Blue Lobstah with my friends at the time of the murder. You can ask any one of them! Heck, even Aunt Tilly was there that night!"

"Yes, I understand that, and I'll confirm it. However, I still need to hear what issues you had, if any, with our victim. I'm just doing my job."

"Of course." Kinsley shuffled her feet beneath her on the ugly gray carpeting. Suddenly she was struck with how badly the police department needed a remodel. The carpet was well worn and even spotty in places, and it didn't match the tan walls. Working in the gardening field, Kinsley was always playing with complementary colors and texture combinations in her mind. Such as pairing white marigolds with blue hydrangea and pink geranium, or pink begonias with red and orange ones and maybe a hint of blue delphinium, for added contrast. Gardening was her escape, it was her life breath, and suddenly she felt like SeaScapes could be in jeopardy if clients thought she had even a hint of involvement in a murder investigation. Just the mere *thought* crossing her mind made her head spin.

"Kinsley?" the detective prompted.

Kinsley met her eyes evenly. "Look, Rachel, I want you to understand something. I didn't have a problem with Chris. He seemed to have a problem with me, because I accepted a few floral pieces from his wife to add to the kissing balls we were crafting for the town. But honestly, it doesn't matter if it was about Mallory's donation or something else, Chris has *always* been right up in my business. Don't you remember last summer, when he blamed me for all the carnage up and down Harborside? Those dead flowers were part of the last investigation I assisted you with. He wanted to replace me back then, too. The guy has had it in for me for a long time now. Who knows why he liked picking at me like a spent flower? I sure don't!" Kinsley threw up her hands in frustration. "I really wish he were still alive to ask him, because honestly, I was nothing but kind to the man."

A knock at the door interrupted their conversation and Kinsley turned toward the sound. A young, uniformed officer who looked barely out of high school stepped inside and said, "Pete O'Rourke is here to see you. You want me to tell him to come back another time? Or . . . ?

"Tell him I'll need a few more minutes. You can offer him a cup of coffee while he waits. There're also pastries in the break room if he'd like—you can offer that, too."

Kinsley frowned. She wasn't offered coffee *or* pastry and her mouth was growing increasingly dry from this conversation.

"Sure," the officer answered before he slipped away and closed the door behind him.

And that wasn't all that crossed her mind. Kinsley fidgeted with her fingers in her lap. Pete was here? Was he *asked* to come by the station? Or had he stopped by on his own accord? Had he thought about things and decided to put his two cents in?

The barrage of questions in her mind kept rolling until Rachel interrupted them by saying, "Go on."

"I don't even know what else to say at this point," Kinsley admitted in defeat.

"At the scene, you alluded to the fact that you might have a suspect in mind. But you didn't divulge. Refresh my memory." Rachel leaned back in her chair casually but held Kinsley's gaze in challenge.

The last thing Kinsley wanted to do was throw someone else under the bus, especially with no justification for what she was thinking. "Yeah. I don't exactly want to point fingers. I'm beginning to see what that feels like, and to be honest, it's not giving me the warm fuzzies. I'm uncomfortable. I don't think I wanna be here anymore, answering these questions."

"Well, in order to clear your name, you must," Rachel said. "I need answers to share with the chief. And I'd like those answers to lead me far away from you. Understand?"

Kinsley cleared her throat. If she didn't speak her mind, her own neck would be on the line. She hemmed and hawed before giving it up. "I know that law enforcement typically looks at the spouse and the persons closest to the victim first. And maybe you should consider that route. I admire Mallory, she has a thriving floral business downtown and she's a very kind woman. But even good people make wrong choices, right? What I'm trying to say is . . . I might've seen something that gave me pause. I mean, it's just that Mallory and Chris's brother, Cole, seemed a little inappropriately close the other night. If that makes sense. It was enough that I took notice anyway."

Rachel leaned forward in her chair and steepled her fingers, bringing her in closer across the hard steel desk. "Go on . . ."

"Not much more I can tell. Mallory came to the inn looking for her brother-in-law as soon as he arrived in town and asked that we not tell Chris that she had stopped by. I saw some touching that was a little too familiar at the Blue Lobstah the night of the event. She was laughing a little too hard at his jokes . . . that sort of thing."

Rachel's hazel eyes, the color of "Sweet Tea" heuchera leaves, widened in size. "Familiar touching? Can you expand on that?"

Now that Kinsley was being cornered, she wondered if she was reaching. "I dunno. This feels wrong." She kneaded her forehead with her fingers. "I don't feel comfortable implicating people. Especially when I have no clue of their involvement . . . If any at all."

"Let me be the one to sort that out," Rachel said bluntly. "Please continue," she added with a roll of her hand.

"I saw Cole put his hand on the small of Mallory's back. I dunno, it seemed intimate somehow. But maybe I'm just over-thinking it," Kinsley admitted as she bit on her thumbnail.

"Okay. Anything else?"

"As soon as I found out that it was Chris that had landed in the water, I looked for Cole and Mallory and I didn't see either one of them."

"Ahh, I see. So, you noticed they were missing."

"Yes, I did," Kinsley confessed.

"And when did you first see them back on the scene?"

"I'm not sure I remember . . . Maybe talking to you?"

"Okay. Anything else you want to add?"

"I don't think so."

"All right. I'll dismiss you—for now."

The way Rachel said "*for now*" was unnerving to Kinsley. So, she threw out a joke to ease the tension. "You're not going to tell me not to leave town or something like that, are you?" she teased with a chuckle.

"Technically, unless charged with a crime, that's illegal. The department has no jurisdiction over you."

That wasn't exactly the answer Kinsley was looking for. It seemed Rachel wasn't in a joking mood.

Chapter 8

The kissing balls that hung from the light posts in downtown Harborside were holding up nicely, Kinsley thought as she reached away from the ladder and tugged on one to double-check that the branches were stiff. Adam was away at an out-of-town hockey game, while Becca was working on a counteroffer at the Realtor's office, across town. The two had decided they'd meet up early in the afternoon, at Edna Williamsburg's estate to decorate. Kinsley's neighbor, and Tilly's best friend, had hired them for an entire Christmas makeover—which included a twelve-foot balsam fir for Edna's grand entrance. Kinsley had already had the tree delivered to Edna's garage so that the limbs would relax before being ornamented. This sizable job needed an assistant, otherwise it would go until the wee hours of the night, and Kinsley was more than happy to wait for help from her bestie. Besides, this gave Kinsley the time she needed to recheck a few things. And that included

verifying to see if the overnight subzero temps had helped, and
it did because after rechecking more than five kissing balls, she
concluded they officially held together as planned—the limbs
solidly frozen inside of the florist Oasis. So, unless an act of
God happened, the branches should stay intact throughout the
entire holiday season. One less thing to worry about.

Kinsley descended the ladder and was met by Cari Day,
walking a dog.

"The downtown looks great; it's so nice to see our handiwork everywhere! Now that I know how to make them, I'm
considering crafting one for my house, too. It would look so
nice hanging from my front porch," Cari said as she adjusted
her sunglasses, but still tented her eyes to look at one of the
balls.

"They are fun, aren't they? I agree, they turned out beautifully. Thanks again for volunteering!" Kinsley smiled warmly.

"Absolutely! And be sure and sign me up for next year, too.
It was fun, and a great way to jump-start the spirit of the season. The added bonus was that it was nice to visit with a few
other Harborside residents, too. I hardly ever get to see Jackie
anymore, she's so busy with her kids. And she's really nice. I
enjoyed spending a few hours talking with her."

"Yeah, isn't she a sweetheart?"

The dark Lab that was dancing at Cari's feet seemed to be
waiting for a greeting from Kinsley, which she more than
obliged, with a scratch under the dog's chin. "Oh, what a
sweet pup."

"He's a love!" Cari gushed. "Meet Shadow."

"Hi, Shadow," Kinsley cooed. She then noticed a scar on the
top of the dog's right ear. "Oh no! What happened to him?"

"He was attacked by my neighbor's pit bull. Some people

just don't know how to train their dog. It makes me so mad!" Cari clicked her tongue, irritably. "People like that shouldn't be allowed to have pets—it's wrong."

"Oh, that's awful!" Kinsley said as she turned her attention back to the dog and stroked the top of Shadow's head gingerly. "You poor thing!"

"Oh, you don't know the half of it. I was threatening to sue because he refused to pay the vet bill, and it happened on his property. You know, my neighbors should be liable for that!" She shook her head angrily and then continued, "That's the law. But some people in this town seem to think they're above the law. They also think they have power over the rest of us."

"I'm sorry to hear that, sounds like a terrible thing to go through."

"Well, we won't have to worry about that happening again, will we, Shadow?" Cari knelt by the dog and adjusted the leash around him, as he'd quickly danced about and tangled a leg in it.

"Why is that? Don't tell me your neighbor put the dog down after the attack?" Kinsley asked hesitantly.

"No. But didn't you hear? His owner died at the boat parade! I doubt that Mallory will hang on to the dog. I don't think she was very fond of her husband's pit bull from the get-go. She complained about the dog *all* the time. It's sad, really, it's not the dog's fault."

"Wait. Chris Chesterfield was your neighbor?"

"Yeah." She lowered her voice to a whisper. "Good riddance, if you ask me. The ornery cuss," Cari added under her breath.

Kinsley was taken aback that others in town besides Pete and her had disagreements with the alderman. This was news to her. Especially after her conversation with Rachel, as the detective hadn't alluded to anyone else having issues. But she could understand how an animal being injured due to Chris's negligence would turn someone sour.

"I do feel badly for Mallory and what she's going through. I mean, she's still my neighbor. And she's a nice person, I just don't know what she ever saw in the man," Cari continued. "Maybe the volunteers that came to the inn the other day would be willing to make meals? Or help her some other way? What do you think?"

"Yeah, that's a good thought. She might need help with plowing her driveway, too, or other things around the house, that sort of thing." Kinsley looked to the sky. As if on cue, snow began to fall softly, like the heavens were shaking craft glitter over everything. It immediately began to stick to Shadow, the dog's fur collecting an even coat of snow.

Cari wiped the snow from the dog's back and then shook out her glove. "Snow's starting to stick," she said. "Anyhow, let me know if you'd like me to organize something. But right now, I need to keep moving. I need to get Shadow to the vet for his shot and checkup before heading back to the humane society. I'm running late! But it was nice to see you, Kinsley. Have a great day!" she added with a backward wave of the hand.

"You, too. And don't worry, I'll organize something for Mallory. I'll be in touch!" Kinsley then folded her ladder and loaded it in the back of her pickup before driving over to the Blue Lobstah. Perhaps Pete would be willing to donate a few meals? Besides meals, she needed to poke Pete about what he had discussed with the Harborside Police Department. After what felt like an interrogation from Rachel, Kinsley had gone in search of him at the police department, but never caught sight of him before leaving for home. And despite having her decorating business to take care of, this was one thing she needed to do, if only to clear her own head to be able to move on with her day.

Kinsley found Pete restocking glasses behind the bar, and she slid onto a nearby stool to catch his attention. She was glad only a few customers were seated farther down, as she really wanted to talk to him privately. "Hey, you."

Pete grinned when he caught sight of her. "What are you doing here this early? Must be having a rough day if you're looking for glass of wine already." He wiped the outside of a wet glass with a thin drying towel before setting it carefully on a nearby shelf.

Kinsley laughed and leaned in closer. "No, nothing like that. I just wanted to stop by and ask you a few things." She drummed her fingers along the top of the counter while she waited for his undivided attention.

"You want a hot chocolate?" Pete jutted a thumb toward the door located behind him. "I have some in the back, I could snag a mug for you. Or how about a coffee?"

"Nah, it's okay. But . . . any chance you got a minute to chat?" Kinsley slipped off her coat and set it on the stool beside her, getting more comfortable, and hopefully making the decision for him to officially stop loading glasses onto the shelf and give her his full attention.

"Sure, what's on your mind? Should I be worried?" Pete continued to stack the last of the glasses. Finally, he tossed the towel aside before focusing on her fully. "Must be serious since you didn't just call."

That comment made her second-guess herself. Why *didn't*

she just phone him? Was she looking for excuses to see him? She could feel the heat rush to her cheeks, and she reached to cool them with her cold, bare hands.

"*Kinsley?*" He rolled his hand in the air, waiting for her to continue.

"Right. I was in the neighborhood and, to be honest, I wanted to see your expression. You tend to wear your thoughts on your sleeve, so yeah, I guess I needed to see you."

"Fair enough. Shoot."

"Did Rachel call you in for questioning? Or did you just decide you needed to go to her office and share your statement? I overheard you were there—we literally just missed each other."

"Oh." Pete dropped his hands from his hips to his sides. "Rachel called me."

"Did she interrogate you?"

"Nah, I didn't feel that way about it. She was actually pretty nice about everything. Kinda eased my mind when I mentioned I was afraid I might be sued over this."

"Oh well, that's good, I guess. So out of the two of us, it seems I'm the only one with my neck on the line," she replied.

"What do you mean?" Pete's eyes doubled in size. "You're not considered a suspect. No way! I don't believe that Rachel would even entertain that." He shook his head adamantly as if refusing the thought.

"Well, you weren't interrogated over this, but I certainly was." Which made Kinsley wonder. Even though she had an ironclad alibi . . . Did people from Harborside actually think she was capable of hiring someone to murder Chris? She hated the fact that there had been animosity between her and a dead man. It gave her the worst feeling in her gut. She pushed aside the horrible thought and returned to the matter at hand. "What did Rachel want then, if not to question you? I'm just curious."

"She wanted to ask my expertise on bottles and glass, stuff like that."

"Really? What do bottles and glass have to do with the case? Did she tell you?"

Pete scanned the restaurant as if checking to see if anyone else had entered before he leaned closer. Lowering his voice, he continued, "She actually wanted me to identify a shard of glass."

"Huh?"

Pete pointed to the top of his head and a grim expression followed. "They found glass embedded in Chris's head. That's why they are certain it wasn't an accident that he fell from the pier. They think he was pushed after being hit over the head with a bottle. That's the growing consensus anyway."

Kinsley's jaw dropped.

Pete winced. "I know—crazy, right? Ouch!"

"This is *very* interesting information indeed!" Kinsley sat up higher on the stool. "Did Rachel think the perp swiped the bottle from your bar to do this? And did you come to any conclusions? About the shard of glass, I mean."

"Oh boy, here she goes with her twenty questions," he said, laughing, but his comment didn't deter him from talking. "It looked to me like it could've come from a Grey Goose bottle. There was a frost to the shard of glass, so that was my suggestion. They're planning to do further testing, I guess, to see if I'm right." He shrugged.

"Were you missing an entire bottle of Grey Goose from the bar?"

"Not that I know of," Pete declared. "But you remember, it

was crazy that night. I honestly don't know if it came from my bar. I asked Raven and she said she didn't think so." He threw up his hands in frustration and then frowned, causing Kinsley to prod further.

"*What?*"

"Look, I'm terrible at inventory. I can't say for *sure* it didn't come from my bar. I'd really hate to think that it did," he said defensively.

Kinsley tapped him lightly on the hand, which was now resting on the bar, to comfort him. "It's not your fault. That's not what I meant."

Pete didn't look overly convinced. "How would you feel if the murder weapon potentially came from your establishment?"

"I dunno. How would you feel if you were the one interrogated like I was because the guy was always up in my business?"

"Come on now."

"I'm serious! How would you feel? Pete, I need to solve this thing. I can't have my name connected to any of this. It's awful!"

"I really can't imagine Rachel would think that. She *knows* you, Kinsley."

Kinsley smirked. "Doesn't matter. According to our detective friend, she must do her 'due diligence.'"

Kinsley kneaded her forehead to think.

"What? Your silence is killing me," Pete teased.

"I do wonder if that would make the murder premeditated. If the person stole the bottle from here beforehand?" Kinsley pondered.

"Great." Pete hung his head and shook it. "That doesn't exactly make me feel better."

"I'm sorry." Now Kinsley was the one to grimace.

"Don't share this information with anyone, okay? Put it in the vault. I shouldn't have even told you; I was told to keep my own mouth shut about it and here I go." Pete nervously ran his hand through his hair.

Kinsley zipped her lips and then stuck out a pinky for a pinky promise in response and they shook on it. "This is me you're talking to. You have my word."

Another lull came between them before Kinsley said, "Oh, I have another reason I stopped in today."

Pete looked up. "What's that?"

"How do you feel about providing a few meals for Mallory, you know, while she's going through a tough time? She just lost her husband; she could use the support from all of us."

"Of course, I'm always on board to help or encourage a community member in need. I only have one hesitation."

"What's that?"

A furrow rippled across his forehead. "I dunno . . . Again . . . I'm all for chipping in . . . but would it bother Mallory?"

"Why on earth would you think that?"

"Maybe Mallory is mad and thinks I overserved her husband? You know, if he weren't drunk that night maybe he would've been able to ward off his attacker. Not to mention the bottle most likely coming from my bar."

"You don't really believe that she would hold that against you, do you? You were the one who mentioned he was tipsy before he even walked in here! I wouldn't worry."

"I dunno. I can't help but feel *somewhat* responsible if the bottle came from here. Wouldn't you?"

"Pete, don't do that to yourself. I promise you; Mallory is not like that. She knows the choices her husband made were his alone. It wasn't your fault he was hit on the head and dumped into the Atlantic. That was all his doing. Maybe it's a little harsh to say but, knowing him, he probably provoked it."

"I suppose."

"But—if you help me solve this case, it might help clear my name and find the real perp who's currently running free on the streets of Harborside. And we should help Chris's wife as much as we can. That's just the right thing to do."

Pete didn't look overly convinced. In fact, he still looked worried. Which made Kinsley want to dig in even further. But he conceded when he said, "I'll have an order of fish and chips ready at the dinner hour, if you can deliver it. I'll be too swamped to step away, as things usually pick up around here for happy hour. Sound fair?"

Kinsley nodded. "Fair enough."

"As far as the rest of it, I suggest we keep our noses out of it and let the police handle it. Do we have a deal?"

Kinsley wasn't ready to make that deal. The delivery of the food, yes. The dropping of the investigation into the death of the alderman? Not a chance.

Chapter 9

Later that afternoon, after the twelve-foot balsam fir was moved from the garage and set into place in the grand entryway of Edna Williamsburg's estate, Kinsley and Becca went straight to work. The expansive height of the ceiling almost made the tree look small in comparison, and Kinsley hoped they'd made the right decision.

"Do you think it's too short?" Kinsley asked finally, landing her hands on her hips and chewing the side of her cheek.

Becca brushed the question off with a flick of her hand. "Nah, it's fine."

"'Fine' isn't really what I'm going for here. I was hoping for magnificent! This tree needs to be perfect for this space! Edna hosts one of the most elite holiday parties in all of Harborside, so this entrance needs to be absolutely jaw-dropping."

"Are you going to go all *fir crazy* on me? It's a beautiful tree, just look at it!" Becca took a few steps backward to examine the tree further, and Kinsley followed.

"'Fir crazy'? Hitting me with more gardening puns, I see." Kinsley giggled.

Becca followed suit with a chuckle. "I know you love your job, Kins, but this is supposed to be fun. Don't be so serious! Once we trim the tree, I think you'll be happy with it. If I didn't think it would work in this space, I'd be honest and tell you." She gave Kinsley a comforting squeeze before moving over to the box filled with Christmas lights. "Don't forget I also stage houses for a living before I list them," Becca reminded with a schoolmarm finger wag.

Kinsley didn't move but continued to admire the tree. If she were to choose again, she would've gone a few feet taller. The girth of the tree somewhat made up for it, though, as the balsam fir seemed almost as wide as it was tall and adequately filled the space beside the stately staircase.

They had decided to go classic with the tree's decorations, using mostly whites with hints of soft blue and teal to add a coastal flair. Kinsley decided a lighted garland along the winding stair railing, along with artificial white starfish and glittered seashells, would look great. Maybe a few potted urns with blue poinsettias spray-painted with glitter, too.

While she contemplated all this, Kinsley worked the cord around the tree from the top of the ladder while Becca fed the strings of white lights to her.

"Hey, what do you think about placing a few urns of blue poinsettias on top of some tall pedestals in the corners? I could add some white hydrangeas around the base, too." Kinsley finally voiced her thoughts from the top of the ladder.

"I love that idea! Can I ask a rather stupid question?"

Kinsley stopped wrapping the tree with lights for a second and looked down at her friend, giving Becca her full attention.

"How do you grow those blue poinsettias? Special seeds or something? I mean, I know florists add the glitter spray because I've seen them glittered, and I know they don't grow that way. I'm not that dumb," Becca snorted.

"Poinsettias naturally grow in hues of white, pink, red, and even green. The off-color ones are spray-painted shades of blue and purple. To further answer your question, though, poinsettias are grown from cuttings and placed in rooting hormone. They're typically not grown from seeds," Kinsley corrected.

"Learn something new every day. Thank you." Becca grinned. "Now, if anyone asks me, I can give an educated answer and not feel like a complete idiot."

"Hi, ladies. That tree smells divine! I can't wait to see it fully decorated."

Kinsley and Becca turned their attention to Alice, who had entered the room.

"Hey, Alice. I didn't know you were working today," Kinsley said. "I thought you had to take Adam to his hockey game."

"His dad had to take him because I got called in. It's all hands on deck here to prepare for the upcoming party," Alice replied, opening a nearby closet door, and returning with a feather duster in her hand.

"Do you think Edna would mind if we borrow you for a bit? I hate to steal you away from your work, but I was thinking of adding bows to the garland and since you make the best bows . . ." Kinsley hinted.

Alice's eyes gleamed with joy. "I can certainly ask. I'd love to help! It beats dusting," she said with a smile.

Just then, Edna entered the space and looked on in delight

at all that was unfolding. Her eyes, the color of forget-me-nots, shone with childlike wonder as she clasped her hands in excitement.

"I'm so happy to have you ladies spreading your Christmas magic. Luke didn't want to get involved with decorating this year, and I don't understand it. He used to love putting up the tree and decorating the house for me." She frowned. "My grandson claims his work is keeping him too busy for it this year. How can you be too busy for Christmas?" she added with a huff.

"It certainly is a busy time of year," Kinsley conceded. "We have a booked schedule ourselves, with a ton of new decorating jobs in the queue. I'm guessing Luke isn't the only one feeling overwhelmed this season."

"I do hope you're both planning to attend the party. I realize the event is a bit early in the afternoon, but most of Harborside will be in attendance," Edna continued as she wrapped her sweater tighter around herself as if she'd been met with a sudden chill. "It would be good for you to meet some folks. Plus, it might help expand your business."

"Speaking of business, do you mind if we steal Alice here for a bit to craft us some bows to add to the decor?" Kinsley asked, putting her hands in prayerlike position. "Pretty please?"

Alice looked to Edna with a hopeful expression and the homeowner obliged warmly. "Whatever you need! Just do your magic!"

"Your wish is our command! Thank you," Becca said brightly, and Kinsley nodded her assent.

Alice immediately got to work after Becca handed her a roll of ribbon and a pair of shears.

"I know we're in good hands with you ladies handling the

decor. I can't wait to see it all come together." Edna gazed around the space and pondered. "Yes, it's going to be lovely indeed for this town-wide event."

Kinsley knew "town-wide" really meant that all the "important people" of Harborside would be added to the guest list. And the majority of those lucky enough to make it onto that list would make it a point to be in attendance. Edna had deep pockets, knew most everyone, and was very generous when it came to her community. In fact, Kinsley thought maybe she could prod the woman about the alderman and his unfortunate demise. Perhaps she would have knowledge of something amiss in Chris's life.

Kinsley descended the ladder and met Edna at the bottom, where she beckoned the older woman to come closer.

"Yes, Kinsley dear? Something I can help you with?" Edna asked. "Do you need more lights? I may have more in storage, or you can add it to my tab down at the hardware store if you need to purchase more. They have me on file over there."

"No, it's not that. I was just wondering why you didn't come out for the boat parade. I was surprised I didn't see you that night. Did you go, and I just didn't catch you there?" Kinsley looked to Becca, who quickly picked up on what she was doing. "Aunt Tilly even made it out for a bit of time, if you can imagine."

"It's too cold along the waterfront during the winter months for these old bones. I stay close to home until spring now, otherwise my arthritis acts up. I'm not one of those snowbirds who likes to travel south, either. Why would I leave Maine? All my friends and my grandson are here!" Edna brushed her hands up and down her arms as if she were freezing just thinking about it. She pulled a stylish-looking silk scarf closer to her neckline. "It's a lovely event that Harborside provides, dear—just not for me."

"But you heard what happened that night? Right?" Kinsley asked.

Being as she was so influential, Edna *must've* heard something. There's no way the events that unfolded that night had not yet reached her ears.

The dots seemed to connect for her neighbor as she suddenly stiffened her spine and began to wring her hands. "Oh yes, of course I heard. What a travesty! I don't understand why someone would want to harm that poor man! He was a gift to this town, if you ask me."

Kinsley was not surprised Edna thought fondly of the alderman. She had heard Chris was accustomed to "sucking up" to those with money in Harborside. Knowing him, he probably had Edna wrapped around his pudgy little finger. She inwardly chastised herself for thinking ill of the dead. But seriously.

"Terrible, isn't it?" Becca said cautiously, and moved closer to Kinsley, where she secretly bumped her a warning with her elbow. Kinsley took it to mean Becca thought she should *tread lightly* regarding her questions about the alderman.

Edna's expression remained crestfallen. "It was quite a shock. Honestly, I'm not sure the news has sunk in yet."

"Not as shocked as I was to be hauled in by Rachel for questioning!" Kinsley admitted. "You know me, Edna. I couldn't hurt a fly in my own garden!"

"You? Why would the police question *you*?" Edna's eyes narrowed. "I will have none of that. Don't you worry, I will have a talk with the chief, there is no need for that kind of nonsense." Edna lifted her chin in defiance. "I've never heard anything so ridiculous! *You!* Of all people."

Kinsley was touched by Edna's love for her, and her immediate defense.

Edna continued fiercely, "I'm sure there is a long list of suspects besides the likes of you! I mean, Chris was always very gracious to me, but I'd be lying if I said I wasn't aware he rubbed a few people wrong."

"Really, like who?" Kinsley asked, unable to resist the opportunity to prod further.

Becca's eyes also flew to Edna in search of answers.

"Well, dear, I honestly don't know if I can actually pin the blame on someone specific." Edna sighed, and a faraway look washed over her. "But what I do know is, you shouldn't have been made to feel like some sort of criminal! That, I'm one hundred percent sure of. What a waste of taxpayer dollars, questioning you like that." She pursed her lips in annoyance.

Kinsley deflated. She had been hoping for a lead in the case, and instead came up with nothing. It was like looking forward to a firework exploding vivid colors in the sky and instead watching the firework misfire.

"I guess with him gone I don't have to feel responsible anymore . . . for some of his financial decisions," Edna added with a sigh. "I tried to warn him."

"What do you mean? Warn him about what?" Becca asked.

"I do think I might have misled him a little." Edna smirked. "But I wasn't the only one."

Becca's eyes narrowed in on Edna. "*Misled* him?"

Kinsley leaned in closer to hear as Edna had lowered her voice to an almost inaudible tone.

Edna laid her hand against her cheek and frowned. "I may have given Chris some bad investment advice."

"Investment advice?" Kinsley asked. "For the town of Harborside, you mean?"

"No, for his personal investments." Edna hung her head. "It's sort of my fault. You see, I'm the one who convinced him it would be wise to come on board with this particular investment to add to his portfolio, but I think he took it too far. At least that's what Luke told me after we learned of Chris's death."

Kinsley knew Luke worked in the financial arena, but she didn't have any specifics regarding his employment. "Invest in what exactly?" Kinsley pushed.

"I suggested he purchase stock in an advancement in medicine that was going to heal the world as we see it. A new pill that would be life-changing for so many who suffered. But . . . the prototype. Well, I won't bore you with the details, but it was just too early. So, I called Chris and encouraged him to hold out and wait, but instead I think he put all his eggs in one basket. Never a wise thing to do when making investment decisions, but that man sure could be stubborn with things like that. He was too busy seeing dollar signs to listen."

"What is it?" Kinsley pressed. "This pill?"

"I shouldn't say . . . We're learning it was a bit of a scam. But . . . like I said, I warned him not to overinvest," Edna stammered. "I've probably said too much. Anyway, there was to be a lawsuit down the line. It would take years, I'm sure, but he may have been able to recoup some of the losses. Though, perhaps not in his lifetime."

"Would Chris have had to testify about it? I mean, share in a courtroom how he invested in a scam?" Kinsley wondered aloud.

"I'm sure we all would, at some point," Edna answered pensively. "Anyhow, I just hope his wife has a good life insurance policy. Because after all that, I think the man was close to broke."

Kinsley suddenly understood why Chris was so weird about money with his wife and how she handled Precious Petals. It sounded like his life savings had been sucked dryer than an unwatered poinsettia. The question was, Did his empty bank account lead to his murder?

Chapter 10

By the time Kinsley and Becca had wrapped up the decorating at Edna's estate it was well after five o'clock. Although they were close to the Salty Breeze Inn and Kinsley could easily pull the truck into the driveway and call it a day, that's not what she planned.

"Follow me?"

"Next door?"

"Yeah, you can leave your car in my aunt's parking lot, and then you can jump in mine, and we'll head over to the Blue Lobstah."

Becca shook her head. "Nah, I'm too tired. I don't feel like sitting at the bar tonight. You go," she said, nudging her friend. "Pete can keep you company tonight."

"No, we're not going for drinks. We're going to pick up takeout for Mallory."

"Huh?"

Kinsley explained the earlier deal she'd made with Pete and reminded Becca, "Didn't you hear what Edna said? She hopes Mallory has a sizable life insurance policy."

"So?"

"So, we need to find out how Mallory is doing financially. It could provide a motive, couldn't it? If they were hurting for cash. I'm just sayin'."

"Now you're *really* going fir crazy!" Becca exclaimed.

"Just get in the truck. You're coming with me," Kinsley demanded with an eye roll. "We need to get some answers."

"So pushy, geesh." Becca complied with a chuckle before ducking her head and settling into the passenger seat of the SeaScapes vehicle.

B efore long, the two found themselves seated at the end of the bar at the Blue Lobstah, sipping on cinnamon-and-clove Christmas tea while they waited for Mallory's fish and chips take-out order.

"So, how're things going with Zach? You haven't mentioned him lately."

Becca sighed heavily.

"Oh no! What?" Kinsley readjusted herself higher on the stool. "Don't tell me it's over already? You barely started dating."

"Yup, it's over already. You were right, he's just too into himself. Our conversations seemed to always revolve around him and his life and his workout schedule. I was getting the impression our connection was based on physical attraction and nothing more. I need something deeper than that, you know?"

"Yes, and you deserve something deeper than that," Kinsley stated resolutely.

Becca leaned in and whispered in Kinsley's ear. "Hey, speaking of losers, isn't that the guy Pete threw out of the bar? I mean, the one who pushed Chris the other night?" She pointed out a man who was leaning against the bar nursing a beer, with his focus on the overhead television.

"I think so. Honestly, it all happened so fast, I don't think I'd be able to pick him out of a lineup. Would you?"

"I'm pretty sure that's the guy. Are you gonna go over there and give him the third degree?" Becca teased while she toyed with the tea bag inside of her mug.

"And say what exactly? *Did you take your altercation outside and kill a man by beating him over the head with a bottle?* I'm sure that'll go over well!" Kinsley snorted.

Becca shrugged. "Dunno. That's your department."

Kinsley responded with an eye roll.

"You know, this tea is really warming me up," Becca said, removing the tea bag with a spoon and setting it aside on a napkin. "You mind if I order another?"

"Yes, in fact I do mind. We're on a mission," Kinsley said. She was relieved when Pete showed up with a wrapped brown paper bag emitting a tantalizing scent. Becca must've caught wind of it, too, because she added, "Where's ours?"

"I can get another order ready if you'd like?" Pete offered. "It'll take a few minutes, though; the oil's being changed in the fryer as we speak."

"No thanks, we gotta go." Kinsley practically dragged her friend off the stool and nudged her in the direction of the door. While Becca was gathering her coat in her arms and before they were about to exit, Pete stopped them with an outstretched hand.

"Wait."

Kinsley turned to face him fully.

"Got some news on the alderman," he said.

"News? Do tell!" Kinsley set the take-out bag atop the bar and waited for an explanation.

Pete summoned them in closer and Kinsley and Becca leaned into the bar to catch the latest gossip. "I heard the guy was darn near broke. And there was even talk that he might've needed to sell his house over it. He was one mortgage payment away from losing everything!"

"How'd you hear that?" Kinsley whispered.

Pete rolled his finger around his head like an imaginary lasso. "You wouldn't believe what I hear within these walls," he mouthed with a chuckle. "People think I can't overhear their conversations, but you add a little liquid truth serum and people get pretty loud."

"Edna alluded to their money problems, too, when we were working at her house," Becca murmured. "She said that Chris was hurting for cash, but I guess I didn't realize he'd lose his house over it."

"Yeah, that's rough." Kinsley grimaced. "Poor Mallory. I wonder how she'll keep Precious Petals going if she has that hanging over her."

Pete leaned his weight farther on the bar and called them in even closer and whispered, "And that dude, over there . . ." He pointed with a discretionary finger and waited. The two turned to sneak a peek at the man who Kinsley and Becca had already suspected was the man who had the altercation with Chris the night of his murder.

"Yeah?" Kinsley wondered if Pete would confirm their suspicions.

"He's the one that I kicked outta here with Chris. I can't

believe he'd show his face in here after that. And talk so boldly about it."

"Talk boldly? What did he say exactly?" Becca asked.

"That he's glad the man's dead."

"You're kidding."

"I wish I was."

Kinsley was not sure what to make of that bit of news. Especially having learned the alderman had aggravated others besides herself. Certainly, alcohol could lead a person to shoot their mouth off when drunk and say something inappropriate, like wishing a man dead. A drunken man's words didn't exactly convict a person. But they certainly gave Kinsley more to mull over as she gathered the list of suspects in her mind.

Chapter 11

The Chesterfield home stood in stark contrast to the other houses in the neighborhood, which were all decked out for the holidays, when Kinsley eased the truck into the recently plowed driveway. Only one light emitted from the lone brick Cape Cod window, and the matching dormers were caked in snow. Kinsley couldn't help but think if the house were outlined in white lights, the cape would mimic a glittery Christmas card. It was odd to think that Chris would never again pull his car into this driveway. Never shovel the path. Never walk his dog on the nearby sidewalk. Never decorate the house for the holidays. The fleetingness of life hit Kinsley harshly.

"Do you think Mallory's home?" Becca asked, interrupting her reverie.

"Only one way to find out," Kinsley replied, turning off the ignition and plucking her leather purse from beneath her feet.

"Well, if she's not home, I've got dibs on the fish and chips."

Kinsley quickly opened the driver's-side door before she changed her mind and allowed her friend to convince her to rip open the bag for the two of them to share. Her stomach was also beginning to rumble from the tantalizing scent of fried food that now filled the truck.

The two traversed the winding shoveled path that led to an evergreen-colored front door and Kinsley stomped her boots to remove any remnants of snow before ringing the doorbell.

They waited what seemed like an eternity before Mallory opened the door. Kinsley hoped they hadn't woken her from a nap. The racoon rings around her eyes were deep but surprise washed across her face, making her look more awake. She wrapped her sweater tighter around herself as if to shield her from the sudden chill seeping in from the open door.

"We brought you dinner from the Blue Lobstah, compliments of Pete O'Rourke," Becca said.

"Oh, how thoughtful! Thank you." Mallory opened the door a little wider as if she planned to welcome them in out of the cold.

A dog started barking, growling, and scratching against a door somewhere inside the house. Kinsley and Becca must've shared an uneasy look because Mallory took a step backward and said, "Can you just give me a minute? I need to let Vixen out into the backyard before you come inside. He'll attack if you have food in your hand. Just give me one second," she repeated before slipping out of sight.

A cold wind sent a shiver down Kinsley's spine, and she danced from foot to foot to stay warm. She lowered her voice to a whisper and said, "I'm glad she's taking the dog outside. Did I tell you I heard Vixen bit another dog and they are on the verge of being sued over it?"

Becca grimaced. "No, you hadn't mentioned it. Based on how he sounds, I can't say I'm surprised. His bark is a bit menacing."

Before long, Mallory reappeared and encouraged them to enter the house. They removed their coats and boots before following her down a narrow, dimly lit hallway. A warm glow welcomed them into a small living room, where a gas fireplace was fully ablaze and an artificial Christmas tree, devoid of lights and ornaments, stood in the corner. A large box, topped with abandoned lights, was tucked beneath it like a half haphazardly opened gift.

Becca handed Mallory the take-out bag.

"I can't believe you two delivered this for me. It's so kind of you. Remind me to call Pete before you go to thank him. I don't have much of an appetite, though. Do you mind if I put it in the kitchen and reheat it later?" Mallory asked.

"Totally understandable, you eat it whenever you're ready," Kinsley said before Mallory left them alone again in the room. "I feel so bad for her. To have lost her husband over the holidays. I'm sure the Christmas season will be difficult for her, moving forward," Becca said.

"Yeah, I feel for her, too." Kinsley gestured a hand toward the corner of the room. "I think we should offer to decorate the tree for her. Maybe with everything going on, she no longer has the heart for it, but it might just cheer her up a little. You think?"

"Yeah." Becca's glance traveled to the bare tree. "You're right, that might be a great way to help lift her spirits. The poor thing is probably still in shock. How could she not be, everything happening so suddenly?"

Mallory returned and encouraged them to take a seat on the nearby sofa. Kinsley sank deep into the plush ruby cushions, almost losing her balance.

"How are you holding up?" Kinsley asked tentatively as she tried to get comfortable in the seat.

Mallory slowly rocked back and forth in a glider rocker across from them as if she was soothing herself with the motion. "I'm okay. It's weird, it's like I still think he's with us and Chris will just come home from work, as if nothing's amiss. He was such a big presence here. It's eerily quiet, even with the dog." Her gaze traveled the room almost as if she were expecting Chris to reappear at a moment's notice.

"I'm sure the dog misses him, too—it's good you can comfort each other," Kinsley said sadly.

"That dog of his has brought nothing but added stress to this household," Mallory replied under her breath.

"I'm sorry to hear that. I heard about the accident with Shadow," Kinsley said hesitantly, hoping she wasn't being too forward in bringing it up.

"Oh? You did?" Mallory turned her attention from gazing at the fireplace back to Kinsley. "I suppose with a small town like Harborside, that makes sense. I'm sure everyone knows about it. Cari was pretty upset with us. I'm still trying to smooth things over with my neighbors. Hopefully in time, I can make things right."

Kinsley cleared her throat. "Oh, I hope you don't think that everyone is gossiping about it. I met Shadow when I was working downtown and happened to see the scar on his ear when I was petting him. I was the one who prompted Cari to explain. I don't think she would've brought it up otherwise." The last thing she wanted to do was cause more angst between the neighbors.

"Ahh, I see. Yes, the whole thing was awful. Chris refused to handle the vet bill and we argued about that for days. I guess

I'll go ahead and pay it. Nothing is preventing me now . . ." Her voice lowered to a mere whisper. "I guess I'll be making all my own decisions from here on out, won't I? And I'll have Chris's life insurance money to get our bills straightened out finally," she stated more to herself than to the two seated across from her. "Boy, it's uncanny sometimes, the way things work out."

Becca tried to soothe Mallory's growing tension by asking, "We'd love to help somehow. Would it be presumptuous if we offered to decorate your tree for you?" She pointed to the bare tree that seemed to scream at them, *Light me up!*

It was almost impossible for Kinsley to see an unornamented tree in front of her and not do anything about it. She was glad that Becca had finally voiced it for the both of them.

"You would do that for me?" Mallory asked with a hint of surprise to her tone. "You all did such a fine job at the Salty Breeze Inn, how can I say no?"

"Of course," Kinsley said. "If you're up for it, we'd be glad to help."

"The lighting of the Christmas tree is one of my favorite traditions. I love to wake up in the morning and have a cup of coffee by the fireplace with the tree lit. Chris always thought I put it up way too early and wanted to wait until Christmas Eve, as was custom for his family growing up. Personally, I really enjoy having it decorated all season long."

"Me, too," Kinsley agreed with a nod. "It's amazing how a little light can lift the spirit."

"Yes, let's do it, then. I don't need any more convincing," Mallory said with a little more pep in her tone.

Kinsley unearthed herself from the depths of the sofa cushions and moved over to the box of Christmas lights. "If you find there's anything you need help with in the next few weeks, just say so. We can organize a few more meals to fill your freezer for when your appetite returns, too. Whatever you need, Mallory, please don't hesitate to ask. We have a tight-knit group here in Harborside that would jump at a moment's notice to assist you," Kinsley said, and she meant it. Especially since Chris had been a member of the common council, she felt he was owed at least that respect.

"Oh, I appreciate it, but I think I have everything I need for now. Cole is running some errands for me and will be stopping over at the inn, too. He's canceling the remainder of his reservation and coming to stay with me for a little while. I have plenty of room here." Mallory's eyes scanned the room. "No reason I should be in this house all alone. Cole mentioned he'll help me make the proper arrangements for Chris, too. It would just work out better for us to have him here with me now instead of at the Salty Breeze."

"But I thought you said Cole was allergic to your cat?" Kinsley asked as she looked beneath her own feet as if one should appear.

"I don't have a cat," Mallory corrected. "I must've meant Vixen. But I've already been looking for a new home for the dog, somewhere in the country, where he can run freely. I have a friend who has a farm, and she might be interested in taking him. I'm sure my neighbors will be thrilled with that idea, too."

"Oh, I must've misunderstood," Kinsley said. But she couldn't help but think it strange. She was *sure* Mallory had said he couldn't stay with them because of a cat. Maybe there was more to why Cole wouldn't stay here while his brother, Chris, was still alive. Had the brothers been at odds?

Chapter 12

Before long, Kinsley, Becca, and Mallory were sitting back to admire their handiwork. The tree was now fully lit with strings of colorful lights and packed tight with ornaments. An angel, as white as the newly fallen snow just outside the window, hovered over the top branch. Hot chocolate, homemade caramel corn, and a plate of shortbread cookies, which a neighbor had dropped off earlier in the day, waited on a nearby coffee table to enjoy when they finished their task. Kinsley snagged a treat and handed it to Becca, who had been eyeing the snacks ever since Mallory had placed them there.

Becca whispered, "Thank you," and immediately popped a piece of sugary popcorn into her mouth.

Kinsley then took a shortbread for herself.

Mallory smiled warmly. "It's beautiful, thank you both so very much. I didn't realize how much the Christmas tree could lift my spirits. And it really has." She beamed as she moved to adjust an ornament to a different location, away from a heat vent that was causing the glass orb to sway precariously.

Kinsley typically chose to decorate her own Christmas trees with more natural elements, like dried flowers such as hydrangeas, roses, and the like. She also tended to use dried berries, or items gathered from the sea. However, Mallory's tree was adorned with handmade things and various ornaments clearly purchased from tourist attractions such as Disney World, Mount Rushmore, or the Empire State Building. The ornaments gave the tree an eclectic, homey feel.

"No problem, we rather enjoyed helping, didn't we, Bec?" Kinsley said.

"We sure did." Becca nodded, reaching for another handful of popcorn off the table.

Kinsley turned to Mallory and said, "You mind if I ask you something?"

"Sure. What is it?" Mallory turned to pour herself a cup of cocoa and took a sip before setting the mug back down on a narrow table beside the glider rocker.

"Have you heard if there are any leads in the investigation? Do you know the man that Chris had the altercation with at the Blue Lobstah?" Kinsley was afraid she would upset Mallory, but she hoped to clarify some things. Was it possible that the man's anger followed Chris out of the bar, and he had killed him in a fit of rage? Especially considering what Pete shared with them when they picked up Mallory's order of fish and chips, Kinsley couldn't help but wonder.

Mallory nodded. "Yes, that's Jackie Horn's husband, Tim. You haven't met him?"

Kinsley shook her head. "Nope. However, I did meet Jackie when she came over to help with the kissing balls at the Salty

Breeze. She's a sweetheart of a lady. I think she might be a friend of Adam's mom, Alice."

"Oh, I remember Jackie. Doesn't she have a bunch of kids? She was so nice!" Becca chimed in between popcorn chews.

"Do you know what the fight was about?" Kinsley urged. "It looked like it resulted from more than just a spilled drink."

"I'm not really sure. I know that Tim wanted to open a new restaurant in downtown Harborside, and the project was denied a few weeks ago. Chris's impression of the matter was that Tim thought my husband was the one who cast the final vote, which kept the project from moving forward. But that just wasn't the case."

"What would lead Tim to think that Chris had the final say in the matter?" Becca asked.

"Mostly I think because the vacant retail space is located in the storefront directly next to mine," Mallory said, taking a seat in the glider rocker.

"Did you have a problem with it?" Kinsley asked.

"Nah, it didn't bother me. He wanted to open a bar with a restaurant attached and I would have quite liked it, because maybe it would be a place I could easily grab lunch during a workday. However, Chris didn't see it that way. He thought it would become too rowdy having a bar downtown. He wanted Harborside to have that quintessential New England feel to it, like Martha's Vineyard or Nantucket. He was hoping for something a little classier for our area, like a wine bar." Mallory rocked slowly back and forth in the chair, using the heel of her foot to keep cadence. "I dunno. Now we'll never know, as the whole thing was given the kibosh."

Becca bent at the waist before Kinsley could comment and plucked a wad of tissue paper from the carboard box beside her. "Oh, looks like we missed something. Seems there's one more ornament in here to add to the tree." She smiled, handing Mallory the find.

Mallory removed the tissue paper and held a sailboat ornament toward the living room lamp, and a bright smile formed across her lips. "Oh," she said, sighing happily. "I didn't know I still had this one. That's too funny." She rose from the rocking chair and moved toward the Christmas tree to place it.

Kinsley couldn't help but notice the immediate change in Mallory's demeanor. "Does that ornament hold a special memory for you?"

Mallory turned to Kinsley and nodded. "It sure does. It's from a trip north of here, at a little place I'm sure you've heard of called Bar Harbor."

Becca handed her a hook for the ornament and said, "A special trip to northern Maine that you and Chris took, I presume? How lovely! I love when ornaments hold special meaning."

Mallory chuckled. "No, to be honest, this one was from a trip Cole and I went on together. I've collected Christmas decorations since I was a small child and my parents took us on vacation. My mother always collected one from our family vacations and I continued on with the tradition whenever I would go somewhere," she admitted, biting her lip as it started to tremble.

Kinsley and Becca shared a look of disbelief.

"I'm sure it might come as a surprise to you to hear that Cole and I dated when we were in high school. It's how I met Chris, actually. Chris was much older, wiser, and had already graduated. He had a good job . . . He was the responsible one . . ." Her voice trailed off.

The bombshell, however, left Kinsley speechless.

"Oh?" Becca said as she shifted from foot to foot and averted her eyes, clearly uncomfortable. She moved back over to the treats on the table and aimlessly poured herself a cup of cocoa and took a sip as if avoiding the conversation altogether.

Mallory continued, "My mother refused to allow me to go anywhere with Cole, as he was always getting into trouble in school back then. He was a bit of a class clown but he's since grown up and has become quite successful in the computer programing arena. If my mother were still alive, she'd never believe Cole's bank account far surpassed Chris's." Her lips curled upward, and her gaze traveled back to the ornament as if reliving old memories.

Kinsley and Becca exchanged another look, which Mallory must've caught.

"Oh, don't seem so surprised! You must have noticed the age difference between Chris and me?" Mallory asked with a furrowed brow. "Haven't you? I can't possibly look that old!" she teased as she rubbed her hands through her hair, which was obviously dyed an unnatural shade of auburn. "I'm sure it's strange to hear I dated Chris's brother in high school. But it was such a long time ago," Mallory mused. "It's almost as if we never had a relationship. Cole wasn't the type to settle down. Never has, even after all these years, so I guess I made the right decision. My mother's push to keep me away from him was probably the correct one."

Kinsley's mind was racing. What if after all these years, Cole still had eyes for Mallory and decided to take matters into his own hands? She was reaching but it could be a potential motive. She had to add this little tidbit to her mental notes.

"I made the right decision. Chris was such a valued member of this community, after all . . ." Mallory said almost to herself.

Kinsley had no idea how to respond so she looked to Becca for help, but her friend remained deeply concentrated on her cup of cocoa and averted her eyes once again. The only thing to do was to push through the sudden awkwardness in the room and change the subject.

"You know . . . my family had a tradition sort of like yours. My parents made a point to purchase an ornament from each new Air Force base we were stationed at. Now that I think about it, I wonder what ever happened to all of those. I think Aunt Tilly put them away somewhere because one year, soon after they'd passed away, she brought them out to decorate the Christmas tree and I burst into tears. I think I may have freaked her out over it," Kinsley confessed. "I felt bad about that since my aunt was only trying to be nice and I reacted rather strongly."

"Oh, I'm sorry you lost your parents so young like that. How old were you when they died?"

"It was right before my thirteenth birthday," Kinsley replied sadly.

"I apologize if I tripped a hard memory for you," Mallory said, the tone of her voice thick with empathy. "It's funny how these little things can hold such meaning." She lifted the sailboat in her hand again, and then carefully found one last open spot for it on the tree and slipped it onto the branch.

"No, that's okay. I kind of forgot about it until you mentioned collecting ornaments from your travels," Kinsley said earnestly. "I'll have to ask my aunt if she still has that box packed away somewhere. I'd like to see them again, now that I'm older."

"Maybe when your brother comes home on leave," Becca suggested. "I bet he'd like to see the collection, too."

"Yeah, that's a great idea." Kinsley smiled.

Becca changed the subject, saying, "Anyhow, thanks for sharing this time with us, Mallory. We probably need to get going. Please let us know if there's anything else we can help with. Anything at all . . ." Her gaze rose to the clock on the wall, and her eyes narrowed in on Kinsley as if to say, *Take the cue and let's get moving.*

"I do hope this tree brings you some comfort during this difficult time. And if we can help you or Cole with anything, in any way . . . please don't hesitate to let us know," Kinsley said empathetically.

"I appreciate that. More than you'll ever know," Mallory said genuinely.

Mallory's kind demeanor made it tough to see her as a suspect in her husband's murder. Could someone so nice have the potential to kill?

Chapter 13

K insley, please be a dear and hand me that whisk?"
Aunt Tilly was bustling about the kitchen, where a myriad of bowls, cookie sheets, and utensils were spread across the countertop and powdered sugar filled the air like a cloud of snow. The scent in the space was heavenly, though, so Kinsley dared not say a word as she handed her aunt the kitchen tool. "Anything else I can do to help?"

"Check the oven, would you?" Tilly ordered with a pointed finger, then plunged the whisk into a bowl and began to stir vigorously.

Kinsley opened the commercial-grade wall oven to reveal racks of cookie sheets, where dough was puffing and rising in a variety of holiday shapes. "I think they still need a few more minutes, but I'm no expert. This is your jurisdiction," she teased. "I'm just an official taste tester."

"Did someone say 'jurisdiction'?"

The sound of Rachel's voice caused Kinsley's spine to straighten. She turned and crossed the room to greet the detective with a half hug, though, and joked, "I hope you're officially off the clock and not here with a warrant for my arrest. I'll need to pack up a care package of my aunt's cookies with me if you're hauling me off to the slammer. Maybe I can sway the district attorney's decision with enticing treats. Is that possible? Or is it in bad taste to bribe an elected official?" She hoped she was dropped from the suspect list completely and seriously *not* considered a suspect in the alderman's murder.

Rachel chuckled. "Come on, now, don't be so melodramatic. I'm not here to arrest you. I will, though, if you burn those cookies, because that, my friend, would be a crime!" she teased, holding her at arm's length. "I feel like I just stepped into Santa's village. Just look at this place." She turned from Kinsley and spun on her heel to take it all in, and her smile widened. "Every countertop is covered in Christmas cookies!"

"Please tell me you two are kidding and that my niece was never considered a suspect in Chris's murder!" Tilly said rather sternly as she eyed Rachel carefully and wiped her hands across her powdered sugar–coated apron. "It's not her fault that crotchety old man was a thorn in her side. I guarantee there's probably a line of people who had issue with him!"

Rachel eased both of their minds by saying, "Of course Kins is no longer on that list. We have several eyewitnesses from the Blue Lobstah that night to corroborate that she wasn't outside when the murder occurred. It's all good. And I know you don't mean to speak ill of the dead, you're just defending your niece." The detective winked.

Tilly responded with a cluck of her tongue and a nod. "You got that right. No one is going to look at my girl as if she's some type of criminal. Kinsley couldn't hurt a fly!"

Kinsley took a deep breath and relaxed her spine. "Well, I'd be lying if I said I didn't feel a little bit better knowing that you've officially cleared me."

"Not to worry!" Rachel said with a convincing smile and a dismissive wave of her hand.

"So . . . do you have a prime suspect? Anyone's motive sticking out a little more in your mind?" Kinsley asked earnestly.

"Honestly, I'd rather not talk shop right now," Rachel said, rubbing her temples. "I'm giving my mind a break so I can look at the case with fresh eyes tomorrow."

Kinsley could tell Rachel wasn't going to share her thoughts on the murder of Chris Chesterfield right now, even though she desperately wanted her to. She decided to let it go. For the moment.

"So, what brings you into my kitchen, then? You hungry?" Tilly's tone instantly turned welcoming, and she handed Rachel a frosted sugar cookie covered in red and green sprinkles, which the detective took willingly.

"Ooh, this is so good," Rachel cooed as she licked frosting from the edge of the sugar cookie. "No, it's not your irresistible food that's lured me in here, although, I'm not gonna lie—it's amazing! I stopped by because Kinsley mentioned that Kyle is coming home soon, and I was hoping you could share a few of his favorite Christmas recipes with me. I'd like to help re-create a nostalgic Maine Christmas for him, just like the good ole days," she said, brushing the cookie crumbs from the front of her faded USAF sweatshirt. "It's been a long time since he's taken leave for Christmas, and I was hoping maybe we could all work together to make it special. Remind him of what he's missing back here in Maine."

"Ahh," Tilly clucked with a gleam in her eye. "We'd love your help, Rachel. Thank you."

Since Kinsley and Kyle's parents were often housed on an Air Force base, Aunt Tilly's Salty Breeze Inn was where most of their holiday traditions took place. Even if their parents couldn't make it off the base, Kinsley and Kyle were shipped to Tilly's for a down-home Maine family Christmas, where guests became like family, and returned year after year in accordance with their own family holiday traditions.

Kinsley looked to her aunt. "If I recall, the peanut butter balls were Kyle's favorite. I had to physically fight him if I wanted any." She grinned.

"Yes, he did rather covet those, didn't he?" Tilly said in a faraway voice as if she was trying to remember the special times they once shared. "He also loved my gingerbread cake roll that I used to make for Christmas Eve. I haven't made that in years!" she added with a laugh. "Thanks, Rachel, I'll make a point to bake one when he comes home. I'll add the ingredients to my shopping list while we're talking about it." She moved over to an ongoing list that was always located alongside the refrigerator and began to make a note of it.

"Any other fond memories you'd be willing to share that might help us plan?" Rachel said, leaning her weight against the counter and reaching for another cookie.

"You mean, besides *you*? Despite my brother being stationed in Germany, I know for a fact you're not far from his mind. You realize, he asks about you all the time." Kinsley moved to the refrigerator, pulled out a gallon of milk, poured Rachel a glass, and handed it to her.

"He does, does he?" Rachel said between bites. She then lifted the glass in cheers and added, "Thanks for this."

"Oh, you must know how he feels about you, Rachel. I get the impression my nephew is just being stubborn, hoping you'll be the one to change your mind and reenlist with him. Or at the very least, follow him to Germany," Tilly said as she gathered a few kitchen utensils and tossed them into a bowl to rinse off in the sink before loading it all into the dishwasher.

"Speaking of memories, though . . . I might have an idea. Aunt Tilly?"

Tilly turned to Kinsley but continued with her task at hand, adding a squirt of dish soap to the pile in the sink. "Yes, my sweet?"

"I was recently reminded about the ornaments from the various bases my parents collected over the years. Do you still have those packed away somewhere? Maybe we could put up a small Christmas tree in Kyle's bedroom and Rachel, maybe you can help me decorate it with those ornaments. It sure will be nice to have my brother home for the holidays, and I love the idea of coming together to make it extra special." She rubbed her hands together in animated anticipation. "Now I'm really getting excited. My brother's coming home!"

"Yes, my dear, they're up in the attic. You're more than welcome to go and dig around for them. And by the way, when your brother comes home, are you planning to stay with us here at the inn? I'll save a bedroom for you at the end of the hall."

"Aunt Tilly, my cottage is right across the parking lot. I'm literally living here, right at your back door! It's completely unnecessary for you to give up a paying customer for me."

"Tsk!" Tilly shook her head in defiance. "It's not the same as having all my loves under one roof for the holidays. I'd very much appreciate if you'd stay over here with us. It'll only be for a few days, Kinsley Marie," she added with a decisive nod.

Kinsley groaned inwardly. Her aunt had used her middle name, which meant business. She didn't want to disappoint Tilly, but it wasn't like she had a long commute. She lived right across the parking lot, for heaven's sake! She'd save the disagreement for a time they were alone and could discuss it further. "Do either of you want to go to the attic with me in a little bit and look for those ornaments while it's on my mind? Otherwise, we might get busy with work and forget."

"Right now I have my hands full." Tilly's eyes toured the kitchen and Kinsley could see that her aunt was anticipating her next move.

"I've got a little time now if you're up for it. I can join you," Rachel said.

"Do you mind if we leave you with these dishes?" Kinsley asked. "Or do you want help cleaning before we head up to the attic?"

"I've got this. You two go on ahead. I'll try and remember some other things that were important to Kyle as I'm cleaning up this mess." She turned to the detective. "And I think that's a wonderful idea, Rachel, to make his homecoming special. I wish you two didn't live so far apart. I really do believe you are meant to share a life together," Tilly said wistfully before ushering them both out of her kitchen. "Go on now, go have a look in the attic while I finish my tasks. I have guests that need attending to as soon as I'm finished up in here."

Kinsley didn't argue. Ever since she was reminded about the ornaments from her youth, nostalgia begged her to seek them out. She was glad to hear that her aunt hadn't gotten rid of them.

Kinsley and Rachel abandoned the kitchen, trudged up the

stairs and down the long hallway that led to the painted
wooden door of the attic at the far end of the inn. It had been
years since Kinsley had stepped inside the space.

As they made the upward climb into the attic, the temperature dropped significantly. The drafty rafters allowed the harsh
Maine gusts off the Atlantic to seep through the aged boards
and curl around them. When she got to the top of the stairs,
Kinsley reached above her head and pulled the string for a
hanging lightbulb to illuminate the space. Boxes, crates, an-
tique furniture, and her parents' footlockers from their military
days lined the walls. At first glance, the boxes weren't marked
and Kinsley realized they had quite the job on their hands. No
wonder Aunt Tilly didn't join them—trying to find the ornaments could take hours. Kinsley sighed audibly before saying to
Rachel, "You sure you're up for this?"

"A lot of history here," Rachel said, rubbing her arms vigorously as if warding off the sudden chill.

"Yeah, I don't even know where to begin," Kinsley admitted.
She leaned over and opened a random cardboard box to reveal
a stack of clothing, which looked as if it had belonged to her
aunt at one time, as a familiar-looking fuchsia blouse topped
the pile. She closed the flap of the box and moved on. Kinsley
unlatched a footlocker to reveal military awards, caps, and a
pair of well-worn combat boots. "I haven't looked at this stuff
in *years*," Kinsley chuckled as she plucked out her mother's Air
Force service cap and plopped it on her head and turned to smile
at Rachel.

"That looks good on you," Rachel said. "I'm surprised you
didn't enlist, like your brother."

"Yeah, no thanks. Military life isn't for me, though I highly respect those who choose to serve our country and protect us. It's just that I like being planted in the same garden . . . like a perennial flower." Kinsley removed the service cap and reverently set it back inside the footlocker. "You know, I wish I knew what really happened to them," she added quietly.

"What do you mean?" Rachel asked, lifting her arm to lean her weight against a wooden beam located above her head. "I thought you knew about the accident."

"I mean, what *really* happened. I get the impression that there was more to it than what we were told when we were kids. The military sealed the records and refuses to tell us anything, other than my parents died in an accident, somewhere on the base. That's not enough information for me. Something in my gut tells me there's more to it than that." Kinsley flipped open another box and shook her head and laughed when met with Barbie dolls and books from her youth. She couldn't believe her aunt had held on to these toys.

"Oh."

The tone of Rachel's voice gave Kinsley pause. She turned and faced the detective head-on and searched her eyes. She was met with an expression she couldn't quite gauge.

"What?" Kinsley asked finally when Rachel remained tight-lipped.

"It's nothing." Rachel shrugged and moved away from her as if she didn't want to be caught in the hot seat. Had Kyle given Rachel information about her parents' death that Kinsley herself wasn't aware of?

"Rachel," Kinsley pressed. "Do you know something? If you do, please share it with me!"

"What were you told, exactly?"

"I was told that they were in an armored vehicle during a training exercise and that the Humvee flipped and crushed them both. I had to beg my aunt for years to share even that with me."

"Ah."

"Why? From the way you're acting, I'm missing something here. If you know something, please, Rachel—tell me." Kinsley lifted her hands in a praying position and held them there until the detective responded.

"It's not for me to tell," Rachel said quietly, and then turned her back. "You need to talk to your brother about it."

"Wait a minute. You can't leave me hanging with that! That's not fair. I know what we were told doesn't jibe with what I know. The Air Force doesn't usually allow a married couple with kids to work on the same jobsite in case one of them gets hurt. It's a known fact. They do that to protect the kids from losing both parents in a wartime situation, and it wasn't even wartime."

Rachel turned to her then. "It's complicated, Kins. Just ask Kyle about it when he gets home."

Kinsley threw her fingers up in air quotes, "Is my aunt aware of this 'complication'?"

Rachel adamantly shook her head. "I don't think so. Not that I'm aware of."

"Then what *are* you aware of exactly? What do you know that I'm not privy to?"

"Let's just say, I'm aware that your brother is just as much of an amateur investigator as yourself. And I know he's been looking for answers regarding your parents' death for many years. He just doesn't have the security clearance to prove his theory."

Kinsley felt an uneasiness wash over her. Why wouldn't he

have told her? She felt with more urgency than ever the antici-pation of her brother returning home. If Kyle knew something about their parents, she wouldn't let him return to Germany until he shared whatever he'd uncovered. There was no use pressing Rachel on the matter, as the detective clearly wasn't going to budge.

Chapter 14

When they finally found the ornaments located in the back of the attic, and a three-foot artificial tabletop tree that looked as if it had been rolled over by a snowplow, Kinsley convinced Rachel to stay just a little bit longer and help decorate it. She refused to let the investigator go without answering a few more pointed questions. Either about her parents' deaths *or* the investigation into Chris's murder. One way or another, she wasn't about to let Rachel get off so easy.

They went into the Clipper room, located at the end of the upstairs hallway, as that was typically where Kyle stayed during his extended leave. Aunt Tilly rarely rented the room out when Kyle had plans to be in town. Tilly was especially proud of his service to their country and always made his visits extra special by spoiling him as much as she could. Her aunt also kept the Ferry room across the hall open for Kinsley to be close to her brother. Kinsley knew that she probably wouldn't win that battle and should just give in to her aunt's wishes. Tilly didn't ask for much, but when it came to family, she was keen on her expectations.

Rachel was wrestling with the haggard branches on the artificial tree when she asked, "Are you sure you want to use this? It looks like it's seen better days!" She laughed. "I'm not even sure it'll hold an ornament. Maybe I should go and buy a new one."

"I was just thinking the same thing," Kinsley said with a frown, setting down the box of ornaments. "But for now, it's a time-crunch issue. Unless you have time to go to the tree farm with me and cut one down, we really have no other choice."

"Nah, I really don't. I guess this will have to do."

"We'll fix it, don't worry. A string of lights, a few ornaments, and Kyle won't notice the difference anyway. I think he'll appreciate our efforts."

"You think he'll like having a tree in his room?"

"Yup. He loves Christmas trees. When we were kids, after we would decorate the tree, we would lay beneath it and look up at the lights and make wishes that we'd secretly share with each other. Kyle can be quite sappy when he wants to be," Kinsley reminisced with a wide grin. "My brother is far more sensitive than most guys I know, he just keeps things close to the vest. I miss those days. He and I were tight back then."

Rachel nodded assent. "Yeah, I've seen that side of him, too. He was a very attentive guy when we were dating and would surprise me when I would least expect it."

"Really? Like what? I'd love to hear it."

Rachel smiled. "Like, one time he bought me this." She lifted her sleeve to reveal a metal bracelet with a name engraved on it. "It's a POW bracelet. It has the name of a prisoner of war on it whose body has never been recovered. I told him I always wanted one and one day out of the blue, he surprised me with it," she answered, covering the bracelet back up with the sleeve of her sweatshirt.

"That's sweet." Kinsley removed a set of white lights from the cardboard box and began to untangle them. She moved to the electrical socket to see if the unraveling was even worth the effort before continuing and was surprised to see them illuminate. "Ha!" She grinned. "They actually work!"

"I have to admit, I wasn't expecting them to light." Rachel chuckled.

"Yeah, me, either. These look pretty ancient. Aunt Tilly has a bad habit of keeping everything, including things that most people would toss in the trash. She always insists one day it 'might get fixed.'"

"Yeah, that sounds like Tilly."

While Rachel was straightening out the branches and Kinsley finished untangling the lights, Kinsley said, "We stopped by to see Mallory Chesterfield yesterday and brought her a hot meal. Are you aware that Mallory dated Chris's brother in high school? Before she and Chris were married."

"Is that so?" Rachel said lightly. "I guess I'm not surprised, seeing as you mentioned they seemed rather close the night of the event."

"Yeah, well, I was surprised to hear her admit that they'd dated in the past. You think money, such as a sizable life insurance policy, could be the motive in this case?" There. She finally shared the nagging feeling that had been bothering her ever since she stepped out of Mallory's house and learned about her past relationship with Cole.

"Uh-huh. Could be."

"Also, Edna mentioned to me that Chris had a problem with a bad investment on some type of medical advancement that sounds like it didn't meet the FDA requirements in the testing phase, or something prevented the drug from moving forward. He lost a ton of money over it. Do you think that could be motive? I mean, it sounded like the investors might have to testify down the line."

"It could."

"And did you know that Jackie's husband, Tim Horn—the one Chris had the altercation with at the Blue Lobstah the night of the murder—thought that Chris had thwarted his plans to open a bar in downtown Harborside? Tim thought the alderman was the one to blame for holding him back."

"You heard that?"

Kinsley dropped what she was doing and turned to ask the detective pointedly, "You're not going to give me much, are you?"

Rachel shook her head and snorted. "What do you really want to know, Kins?"

"Do you have a suspect? Are you leaning heavily on one motive more than another? Or . . . I guess what I'm asking is, Are you anywhere close to solving this murder?"

"Not yet."

Kinsley strung the string of lights carefully inside the branches, hoping for it to hold. As she did so, artificial needles fell onto the floor, making it look more and more like a Charlie Brown tree. She resisted the urge to hum the tune. Instead, she pressed, "Then what would you say? I feel like I'm pulling teeth here! Have you cleared *anyone* from the suspect list?"

"You mean, besides you?" Rachel teased.

"Touché."

"Mallory and Cole were nowhere near the victim at the time when Chris fell into the Atlantic."

"So, you cleared them, then? Is that what you're saying? Because they could've hired someone. The stakes for them seem high, in my opinion. The life insurance payout, the unrequited love story . . ." Kinsley stated matter-of-factly. "I mean, come on . . . it's textbook. As we discussed earlier, isn't the spouse or love interest typically the number one suspect? That's where all the true crime shows seem to point. The only problem with it is Mallory is so nice. I'm having a hard time wrapping my head around that. But it's still possible. Right?"

"I agree. But we don't believe the crime was premeditated, do we? This seemed to happen in a fit of rage."

Kinsley laced her arms across her chest and pondered. "Why would you say that?"

"The Grey Goose bottle. Sounds like it was already in the perpetrator's hand, or at least, close to it. The bottle was probably used as a weapon because it was handy during an argument. Whoever it was that did this clearly didn't think through their actions. But maybe that's just me." Rachel shrugged.

Kinsley dropped her hands to her hips. "Or, playing devil's advocate here, the person or persons took advantage of the 'right opportunity' to do what they had already been planning. What if the fight at the bar gave Cole and Mallory the perfect opportunity to place the onus on someone else? Obviously, everyone in the bar that night assumed the fight continued outside. Right? What if they lucked out and pushed him in, then blamed it on the guy that fought with him inside the bar? I'm just sayin' it's possible."

Rachel threw up her hands in frustration. "Yes, it's possible.

I just need to keep investigating until I can eliminate suspects one by one because they have an alibi or it's not humanly possible for them to be involved. And right now, nothing is conclusive."

"Someone at the boat parade had to have seen something that night. With so many people around the wharf and the pier, I find it rather strange that no one has come forward. Not to mention all those people lined up in boats. Didn't you hear anything when you canvassed the area?"

"It was dark that night, the overhead light closest to the pier where Chris fell into the water had been burned out for weeks. So, there's that. Yes, there were a lot of people out that night, but you have to remember, a lot of drinks were consumed. It's not uncommon for folks to have a limited memory after a night of drinking. So, people question what they really saw with their own two eyes when not fully in their right mind, if you know what I mean."

"Surely someone had to have seen something," Kinsley pressed.

"Besides that, not everyone is out for the pursuit of justice like you are," Rachel continued.

"What do you mean?"

"I mean, people don't exactly give up a lot of information for many reasons. Sometimes things happen so fast, they're not sure of what they saw. Sometimes it's the sad fact that they don't want to get involved because they'll end up having to testify in a lengthy trial. Or it's a mistrust of the police department. Who knows why people stay tight-lipped. But you'd be surprised; more often than not, people don't come forward. Unless guilt or shame gets the best of them, a lot of times people just leave it up to someone else to communicate things with the hope they can stay out of it. Particularly when it comes to something that happens with a lot of people around."

"Yeah, I suppose. Plus, not a lot of people seemed to be a fan of the alderman, which doesn't help, either," Kinsley added.

"That, Kins, is a very true statement."

"Well, don't worry. I'll help you in any way I can," Kinsley said firmly.

"I was afraid you might say that."

Chapter 15

The following day, after a prompting from a few of the town's residents, Kinsley and Becca returned to the wharf, where a few kissing balls were dangling precariously from the light posts and in danger of washing into the sea. Kinsley was not surprised after the storm that blew through the night before. She had heard through the grapevine that the vicious wind from the ocean had even lifted a few shingles off neighboring rooftops located along the cliff walk. The caretaker's cottage behind the Salty Breeze Inn, where Kinsley resided, had shaken from the gale-force winds. She probably needed to take a walk around her aunt's inn to make sure everything had remained intact after the high winds. She mentally added that to her growing to-do list.

Currently, however, the sun was shining brightly and had melted some of the snow off the sidewalks and the boardwalk leading to the pier. The morning was in deep contrast to the previous night's conditions, and she wasn't complaining, given the task at hand.

Kinsley carefully climbed the ladder while Becca held it steady for her. The higher she climbed, the more she felt the wind whipping around her head.

Becca called out, "You want the jute?"

Kinsley removed a roll of fifty-pound fishing line and a set of fingernail clippers from the pocket of her winter parka. "No thanks, I'm going to try and secure it with fishing line this time around. If it's strong enough to haul in an Atlantic cod, it should be able to hold up a kissing ball, I would think. But we'll see."

"Ah, good idea."

Kinsley wound the fishing line through the chicken wire loop and secured the kissing ball in place once again. She gave an extra-hard tug before feeling satisfied that the line would hold. "I think I've got it," she added before beginning the downward climb. However, before fully descending the ladder, she took a quick look out toward the icy water. They happened to be working not far from where Chris had been pulled from the sea by those two men, and Kinsley shuddered at the recollection. It was still hard to believe the alderman had taken his last breath just a few steps below them. Something red, wedged between the jagged rocks, flashed in the corner of her eye and caused her to do a double take before a wave rose and crested, blocking her view.

"What are you looking at? We need to keep moving, we have five more of these to fix and I'm getting hungry. You promised we could go to Tilly's for the breakfast buffet if we kept up the pace," Becca whined.

"Wait a minute. I just noticed something that might provide a clue in the investigation. I need to go and have a look," Kinsley said as she squinted her eyes to see if she could get a better view. She stepped off the ladder and walked toward the pier. The waves were pounding the shoreline in thunderous cadence, but it didn't prevent her from investigating further. The object was so close to where Chris had fallen in, it might provide insight. Perhaps it was something that had fallen from Chris's costume?

"Where on earth are you going?" Becca asked, trailing behind her. "We have work to do. And it's December, which means your aunt is serving those mouthwatering oversized cinnamon rolls that she only serves this time of year. We'll be lucky if there're any left if we don't get a move on!"

"I think I saw something that might be important." Kinsley scoured the area to find what she had seen from the top of the ladder, but couldn't see it. She carefully lowered her body onto one of the rocks below the pier, desperately hoping she didn't fall. The waves were crashing dangerously close and spraying a mist of icy rain.

"What are you doing! If a wave comes up, you're going to slip, and you'll be washed out to sea and never make it to the hospital! Kins, get the heck out of there, right now!" Becca demanded firmly.

"I need to see what it is! Especially if it might be relevant to the murder investigation," Kinsley shouted back, trying to be heard over the roaring sea. Despite the sunshine, this was not the place to be hopping along rocks. But her inner tenacity wouldn't allow her to stop. This might be the one thing that could lead them to solve the case. Her instinct told her this clue was connected somehow. And she *always* followed her instinct.

Kinsley was sure she saw a spot of red pop up again, so she slowly inched her way closer, careful not to lose a visual of it.

When she finally came upon what she was looking for, she realized it was only a winter scarf that had gotten hung up and wedged between the boulders. She was just about to leave it behind and return to the pier but something in her gut stopped her from doing so. She knelt closer, pushed aside a heavy rock that perilously plunged into the sea, and fully revealed her find. The sun had melted away the ice, allowing Kinsley to pluck the knit scarf from the wet rocks. The red she had eyed from the top of the ladder was from the red and white stripes that covered the garment in a candy cane pattern. A long smudge of bright green was smeared across the scarf, and a trickle of dread rushed down Kinsley's spine. Her instinct had been right. The only bright green paint that she could recall was that of the face paint that Chris was wearing the night of the murder. At first glance, Kinsley wondered if the scarf might've belonged to the alderman, but then remembered a scarf wasn't part of his Grinch costume. She was certain of it.

"Whatcha got there?" Becca hollered between cuffed hands.

Kinsley understood that she might be holding a very important clue. What if the murderer was wearing this scarf the night of the murder? And Chris yanked it off the person in a last-ditch effort to save himself from falling into the sea?

A wave rolled dangerously toward her and splashed the bottom of her winter boot. The frozen spray traveled to her face, where she wiped off the shocking splash with the sleeve of her parka.

"Kinsley!" Becca yelled in a panicky voice. "Get out of there! The tide is rising, you need to come back here!"

After looking down at her feet and noticing the tide was indeed on the rise, Kinsley carefully maneuvered her way back across the rocks, toward the pier. Becca held out her hand for the final pull up to safety.

"Don't ever do that again!" Becca scolded as she pressed her hand to her heart and looped her arm through Kinsley's when she was finally standing safely next to her. "You could've died in there!"

"I'm fine, no worries," Kinsley said sheepishly, but then held out the scarf for Becca's inspection.

"You almost drowned in the icy sea for that? If you want a new scarf, girlfriend, I'll buy you one!"

"No. I think I just found an important clue in the ongoing investigation. I think this scarf might've belonged to our killer."

"*Really?* What makes you think that?"

Kinsley pointed out the eerie smudge of bright green paint that streaked across the scarf, and Becca's face turned as white as snow brought on from a Maine blizzard. Her friend's re-action only confirmed to Kinsley that she might be onto some-thing.

"Who was wearing that striped garment the night of the murder? Do you know?"

"That, my friend, is the million-dollar question. It could be anyone, really."

"So true . . ." Becca let out a slow whistle. "Almost everyone seemed to be wearing holiday attire to show their festive side the night of the boat parade."

Kinsley held out the scarf to view the length. "Whaddya think? Is it too short to belong to a man, or no?"

"I think the scarf could go either way. I honestly don't know, Kins." Becca shrugged. "I'm not sure you're going to be able to narrow that down."

"I think we need to call Rachel."

"I'm not getting one of your aunt's cinnamon rolls today, am I?" Becca asked with a long, drawn-out sigh.

Kinsley knew this isn't what her friend wanted to hear. "Doesn't look like it."

Chapter 16

D ue to a conflict in her schedule, the detective couldn't join them that morning, so Kinsley and Becca had no other choice than to go back to their SeaScapes tasks with an intention to return to the pier later that evening. Rachel planned to meet up with them at the Blue Lobstah to discuss their finding, because Kinsley wanted to point out exactly where she had discovered the scarf to show its relevance to where the murder had occurred.

Later, while decorating a Christmas tree at the Schneider residence, Kinsley proposed a plan to host a stakeout, using the scarf as a ploy to sift out a suspect, and Becca had readily jumped on board.

"How about this . . . ?" Kinsley asked while stringing the garland. "We send an email to the list of top suspects: Cole, Mallory, Tim Horn, maybe even Jackie, because she's Tim's wife, and Cari. Tell them we've been cleaning up after the boat parade event, and we're hanging lost-and-found items on the lobster tree this evening for owners to pick up at their leisure. I suspect the owner of the scarf is not going to want a piece of evidence hanging on the town's Christmas tree for everyone to see. The owner would rush to retrieve it! Right? And if one of them does . . . bam! We catch the person trying to hide evidence by picking up an item they know could potentially implicate them in a crime!"

A new spark had shone in Becca's eyes. "So, you think if the person is *not* guilty, they wouldn't rush to retrieve it, they'd just take their time coming to collect it? Or not even show up at all?"

"Exactly!" Kinsley exclaimed. "What do you think?"

"It's a long shot, but I like where you're going with this. It's not such a bad idea," Becca said with a slow nod of her head and a raised brow.

"This could work," Kinsley pressed. "I mean, if you're guilty, and you know the scarf was hanging on your neck the night Chris pulled it off of you in an attempt not to fall in the sea . . . and you'd been looking *everywhere* for it . . . wouldn't you want to come and get it, if only to dispose of the evidence?"

Becca agreed with a nod. "If it were me, I'd be going crazy right about now looking for it."

"And then Rachel will show up, and we'll just hand the suspect and the evidence over. Easy-peasy."

"Exactly. Easy-peasy."

So, with the plan in place, and Rachel due to join the scene after the fact, it was settled.

However, when the time to execute the strategy finally arrived, Kinsley's confidence began to wane. She realized it might not have been such a good idea sending an email out to all the suspects and alerting a potential murderer to their little side investigation. But it was too late to backtrack now. Because everyone on their list had been emailed and the plan was in forward motion.

"You really think this is gonna work?" Becca asked, her tone skeptical.

Kinsley didn't like hearing the trepidation in her friend's voice. She certainly hoped they'd made the right move, but she needed to appear confident for Becca's sake. "If I didn't think it could provide more intel, I wouldn't have suggested it. Besides, we have to try something."

The two huddled behind a snowbank and watched as the candy cane–striped scarf blew back and forth from the wind off the ocean. Kinsley had hung the scarf with an oversized knot, low enough on the lobster tree so that anyone of limited stature could reach it if need be. The sun had set hours ago, causing the temperature to drop quite significantly. She blew into her gloved hands and flexed her fingers in an effort to warm them, to no avail.

The sound of the dumpster lid closing shut behind the Blue Lobstah caught their collective attention and then Raven walked over to greet them. "What are you guys up to?" she asked. "You lose something?"

Becca downplayed the situation and said they were hoping to find additional clues regarding the alderman's case, and they were just looking around the area for anything potentially missed.

Raven rolled her eyes. "Well, good luck with that. I doubt you'll find anything out here in the dark, but that's certainly your call. Just make sure and head inside before you freeze to death out here. In any event, I'm done for the day and going home. Have a great night."

"You, too," they said in unison before Raven left them.

"She's right, I hope someone shows up before I have to carve this snowbank into an igloo," Becca said as she hunched closer to Kinsley. "Have you seen those restaurants that have igloo-style dining options? We should have a few domes here in Harborside. You know, real estate is my jam, I could sell those under the right conditions."

"Shh!" Kinsley warned with an uplifted finger toward her lips. "Someone's coming!"

Becca responded with a zip of her own lips, and then huddled in a little closer, so as not to be seen.

"There's two of them," Kinsley whispered. She wondered then if it was Cole and Mallory, as the couple moved toward the lobster tree, arm in arm. The hoods of their parkas were up over their heads so all that could be seen was the height difference between two people.

The couple moved closer to the wharf and stopped to admire the lobster tree before their collective gaze shifted to the moonlit Atlantic. They then turned to each other and kissed.

"Who is that?" Becca asked as she squinted her eyes.

"I'm not sure, but it doesn't look like they are interested in the scarf, more like our mistletoe kissing balls," Kinsley uttered quietly.

"Hey," Becca said, chuckling, "at least our efforts in crafting those kissing balls are having a positive impact on this town."

The two shared a giggle. Then watched as the make-out session ended and the couple, oblivious to the scarf, moved farther down the pier.

"Ugh." Becca sighed. "I was kind of wondering if that was Cole and Mallory. But if it was, they certainly weren't interested in removing evidence, were they?"

"Yeah, my thoughts exactly," Kinsley whispered. "If it is them, maybe they're just playacting to see if anyone is watching."

Becca pointed out another shadowy figure off in the distance. "Shh, someone else is coming!"

They zipped their lips and held their breath in anticipation.

From Kinsley's viewpoint, the individual was of average height and had broad shoulders. Something about the person appeared to be male. The hood of his dark sweatshirt was pulled over his head, though, concealing his identity. He held the strings of the hoodie tightly, at the nape of his neck, with ungloved hands. He moved closer to untie the scarf from the lobster tree and Kinsley leapt from the snowbank and ran toward him with Becca on her heels.

"Hold it right there," Kinsley said firmly.

Expectation hung heavily in Kinsley's chest as she watched the man lift his hands above his head and slowly turn to face them with the scarf dangling out of one hand, like he was holding a limp garter snake.

Becca gasped.

Kinsley moved closer to the man's side and shook her head in disapproval.

"*Pete O'Rourke?* What the devil are you doing out here?"

Chapter 17

Kinsley wrapped her arms protectively around herself and studied the bar owner. She stared him down until he had no other choice but to explain why he was there.

"*What?*" Pete snapped. "Why are you two looking at me like that . . . all crazy-eyed?"

This caused Kinsley to crack a smile. He mimicked her grin, and his darn smile melted her from the inside out, causing her to momentarily ignore the subzero temps and almost forget why they were there.

"You mean to tell me that holiday garment belongs to you?" Becca asked, pointing to the scarf that now touched the ground as it hung lifelessly from Pete's hand. "We never sent you an email—how'd you know it was even out here?"

"Are you kidding me?" Pete replied, looking at the scarf and then back at Becca with disgust. "I wouldn't be caught dead wearing this. Besides, I barely wear a winter coat."

"If it doesn't belong to you, why did you come out here to retrieve it, then?" Becca demanded.

"He's right, he doesn't wear a coat," Kinsley piped in. "I've tried to encourage him, many a time. I even told him I'd knit a scarf for him myself if he'd actually wear one. He runs around like a cantankerous teenager, refusing to wear anything that could actually keep him warm."

"Just drop it," Becca huffed.

Pete put his hands in the air and dropped the scarf to the ground. "Hey, I don't know what's going on here. You guys are acting weird. I'm just trying to be a nice guy and help a friend."

Becca chuckled. "Help a friend? You just destroyed hours of us standing out here in the freezing cold for no reason. You completely blew our stakeout."

Pete planted his hands firmly on his hips and leaned toward them. "*Stakeout?* What are you talking about?" His gaze bounced between them in search of an answer.

"You first!" Kinsley said.

"Someone called the bar and asked that I bring their scarf inside and leave it in my lost-and-found box that I keep by the door. Said they forgot it the other night, after having dinner. All I'm doin' is a favor for a patron, and you're all acting like I committed some sort of a crime! Honestly, I thought it was a joke until I looked out the window and saw it blowing from the lobstah tree like a flag. So, I came outside to get it. What gives?"

"Did you take the call, or did Raven take it at the bar?" Kinsley asked.

"I did. Raven just headed out. Why?"

"Did you happen to recognize the voice on the other end?" Kinsley asked expectantly.

A new light shone in Becca's eyes as she nodded approval toward Kinsley, and then they gave him their full attention.

Pete's brows furrowed, he rubbed his chin intently, and then he said, "Now that you mention it, the person sounded a lot like Rudolph. That's why I thought this was some sort of joke! But then I looked out the window, saw the scarf, and decided to play along. I thought I was gonna be caught on candid camera," he admitted with a shrug.

Kinsley bubbled up in laughter. "Rudolph. As in . . . *the Red-Nosed Reindeer*? Now, that's funny!"

Pete agreed, throwing his head back in laughter. "Did I ever tell you that was my favorite cartoon as a kid? I watched it every Christmas! Dare I admit, I still watch it every holiday over a bowl of Lucky Charms first thing Christmas morning. Ahh, the memories . . ." His face suddenly flushed as if he were embarrassed about sharing he still watched cartoons. He cleared his throat and puffed up his chest. "Yeah, I'm sure of it—the voice sounded just like Rudolph. But seriously, I thought it was just one of my patrons pulling a prank on me. Some of my regulars do that sort of thing. Heck, last week one of them left an oversized stuffed lobster with a beer bottle in the claw on top of the bar. These guys act like kids leaving toys at my bar!"

"You've got to be kidding." Kinsley deflated and then quickly recovered. She looked to Pete warmly. "I mean, not about the tradition of you watching the show—that's supercute. But about the voice . . ." She trailed off. "I mean no offense, Pete, but how are we gonna figure this out if you didn't recognize the sound of the caller? How would someone disguise their voice to sound like a cartoon character?"

Becca interjected, "It sounds silly, but our friend here is

probably on point with what he heard. I bet the voice did sound like Rudolph the Red-Nosed Reindeer."

"Wait. What?" Kinsley turned to face her friend.

Becca gestured a hand to Pete. "Yeah! I just saw a commercial for this toy on TV last night. They're all over social media, too."

Kinsley looked at Becca with confusion.

"What are you talking about?"

Becca continued, "You can buy a toy, a microphone thingy, that disguises your voice to sound like various Christmas characters—including the animated reindeer. I'm guessing the caller on the other end of the phone used a voice-changing microphone to stay on the down-low."

Kinsley blew out a frustrated breath. "Looks like we're in for a rough holiday season if Rudolph the Red-Nosed Reindeer is to blame."

The three shared a laugh.

"Seriously, though, now what?" Kinsley asked, swiping the scarf off the ground. "There must be something else we can do to figure this out. This can't be the end of it, right?" With a smile she turned her attention to Pete. "Hey, I'm already too far into this thing to let it go now! You don't know the half of it— I risked my life for this clue!" she added with a grin.

Before she uttered another word, Becca pointed out the detective walking swiftly in their direction. "Perfect timing. Looks like Rachel is here."

"Pete," Kinsley mouthed under her breath. "Not a word. Do not tell Rachel what you're doing out here. You understand? I'm having second thoughts about my idea of hosting a stakeout. She might get upset."

"Got it." Pete zipped his lips and tossed an imaginary key.

"Hey, so what's this? You found something that might be relevant to my case?" Rachel asked when she reached Kinsley's side. "How is it that none of my people from the Harborside Police Department picked up on an important clue? I had them out here canvassing for hours! And yet you claim you found something that might help with the investigation?"

"In all fairness, I wouldn't have found it, either. The only reason I happened to see it was because I was up on a ladder fixing a kissing ball and had just the right angle to catch it. The scarf was wedged between the rocks. I'm pretty sure if it wasn't sunny today, the ice and snow would've kept it hidden."

"Well, I certainly appreciate you standing up for my fellow officers. Lemme see." Rachel slipped on a disposable glove and reached for the scarf to examine it with her own two eyes.

"Doesn't that look like the face paint Chris was wearing for his Grinch costume that night?" Kinsley asked. "It's the same chartreuse color, isn't it? And look, it's streaked all the way across."

"Listen to my gardening friend, she knows her summer bloom colors," Becca said proudly, sharing a fist bump with Kinsley. "What do you think, Rachel? Is that paint?"

"Yeah, it definitely could be," Rachel said as she squinted her eyes to study the stain further.

"Kinsley's theory is that the killer was wearing the scarf the night of the murder and Chris grabbed onto it in a last-ditch attempt to save himself from falling off the pier. Which, unfortunately, as we all know, didn't occur, because the man met his fate. Perhaps the scarf drifted out to sea but then the waves brought it back in when the tide returned," Becca said.

"Or the wind off the Atlantic blew it onto the rocks that night," Pete added with a nod.

Becca's pencil-thin eyebrows narrowed in question. "I'm guessing you can't extract DNA off it since the scarf has been swimming in the salt water since the night of the boat parade."

"Yeah, I agree, the salt water probably did some damage in regard to collecting any DNA," Kinsley piped in. "I'm kinda surprised the green paint smear is still on it, to be honest."

"It looks like the green paint is embedded into the knit fabric, and if it's oil-based it wouldn't wash out so easily. In any case, it certainly matches the color of the paint Chris was wearing on his face that night," Rachel uttered quietly.

"Well . . . then . . . it's a clue that could potentially help move the case forward," Kinsley said eagerly. "If we find the owner of the scarf, it could link us to the killer. Right?"

"Yes, but unfortunately, we can't exactly canvass the hundreds of people who were here the night of the boat parade to see if they remember anyone wearing this exact scarf. It's likely more than one person wore something similar because folks were dressed in holiday attire. And there are no outdoor cameras by the marina, so it's not like there is video surveillance or CCTV we can look at. As a matter of fact, after this incident I've reached out to the chief to get the ball rolling and encourage the town to have cameras installed out here. In this day and age, I don't see why we don't have them. The technology exists, we may as well use it." Rachel slipped the scarf into an evidence bag that she had plucked out of her winter jacket and then zipped the evidence bag up tight.

"So now what?" Kinsley threw up her hands in frustration. "That's it? You're just going to stuff it away in the evidence pile? Are you saying this won't provide any help in solving the murder?"

"No, I'm not saying it's not helpful, and I appreciate you

reaching out to me. I'll add it to the evidence and maybe down the line it will provide some help. But as far as I can see, at this moment it's unlikely," Rachel admitted with a frown.

Becca's shoulders sank. "Well, that sucks," she said.

"Wait. I might have an idea." Kinsley let her mind play out the thought a little further before sharing it with the others. "How about if Pete puts the scarf in the lost and found inside his restaurant and we see if someone picks it up?" she suggested with an uplifted finger. She shared a conspiratorial look with Pete to remind him not to mention that the caller had suggested this in the first place. The detective didn't need to be privy to her and Becca's little stakeout escapade. The last thing she wanted was to be pushed out of continuing with her own investigation.

Rachel pondered a minute before turning her attention to Pete. "Where is the lost and found located inside your restaurant?"

"By the door. Why?"

"So, the killer probably frequents the Blue Lobstah and most likely will come back looking for it. Right?" Becca suggested.

"Yeah," Kinsley said to convince Rachel further. "Especially since it's close to where the big event was held. The person would know they can slip in and out of Pete's restaurant and remove the scarf from lost and found easily without being seen. Oh. That might prove problematic."

Kinsley held back that Pete had a conversation with a suspected killer who disguised his voice like Rudolph. Rachel might lose her candy canes if she got wind of what they had been up to. Best to keep that little nugget out of the conversation.

"Ah, problem or not," Pete interrupted, "I can't sit around

babysitting to see who picks it up. It's been busy. Folks don't like to cook much right up until the holidays are upon us," he added with a grunt. "Please don't add anything to my to-do list."

"Let's put a camera on it!" Becca suggested. "I'm sure we can hide one discreetly. Can't we?"

"That's a good idea," Rachel said thoughtfully. "Do you have any objections to that?" she asked Pete.

Pete shrugged. "I guess not, if it'll help in your investigation. Anything I can do, Detective. As long as you're the one responsible for it. 'Cause, like I said, I'm barely keeping up with demand around here."

"It's settled, then. I'll have a camera on it by the end of the night. I just need to run back to the station and get one," Rachel said with a nod.

"Well, excellent, at least all is not lost." Kinsley shrugged. "How about a round of fish and chips, on me? Who's hungry?"

Becca threw her arm around Kinsley. "Yesss! I do believe that's the best idea you've had all day." She grinned.

"Rachel, you in?"

The detective nodded. "I could eat."

Pete waved a hand for them to follow. "Let's get out of the cold, then, ladies, so I can feed ya. I might even throw in a hot toddy on the house. I'm freezing." He rubbed his hands vigorously to warm them.

"Maybe you should dress for the weather up here. You know, you're not in Boston anymore. You live in the north now," Becca teased, following closer on Pete's heels.

He replied with a shrug and a dismissive wave of his hand. "Ah, Boston gets wicked cold, too, ya know."

"Yeah, but not like here," Becca defended.

"Rachel, do you want to go and grab that camera and meet us back here? Your food should be ready by then. We'll wait for you," Kinsley suggested.

"I'll be back in a jiffy," Rachel said as she hurried away from them in the direction of the parking lot.

Kinsley hoped this camera idea would work. Whoever was behind disguising their voice was also owner of the candy cane–striped scarf—and most likely a killer.

Chapter 18

I'm so glad we decided to do this. I think we should make it a yearly tradition," Becca said, adjusting the elf ears on her head and then smoothing her long dark hair. "Besides, it's for such a good cause."

"I couldn't agree more!" Kinsley said with a grin as she swung the bell, causing it to ring out in a merry tune. She, too, was wearing elf ears, though hers were crafted of red sequins and Becca was wearing green ones.

The two had volunteered to collect donations for the Salvation Army in front of Toby's Taffy for a two-hour-long shift. And both smiled as a passerby stuffed a folded bill into the kettle. They had chosen the perfect day to volunteer, as the town of Harborside was hosting the Twelve Days of Christmas, which was twelve days of holiday sales and freebies to lure customers to the downtown shops in mid-December for their final holiday push. The growing crowd was helping fill the Salvation Army kettle, too, which was a very good thing.

"Thank you! And Merry Christmas!" Kinsley and Becca said in unison as another passerby stuffed money into their kettle. They shared a laugh at their synchronicity.

"And please help yourself to a piece of peppermint taffy before you go," Kinsley offered. She reached for the red bucket located behind them on the wooden bench in front of the window outside of the taffy shop. Toby wanted everyone to feel welcome at his candy store year-round and refused to put the bench into storage during the winter months and would often be seen clearing it off with a shovel. Not that anyone sat on it until spring thaw, save a random bird now and then.

The man plucked a piece of saltwater taffy from the bucket, tipped his hat, and smiled before continuing along Main Street.

Kinsley looked proudly at the kissing balls that hung from the light posts above the active sidewalk and traveled along Main Street. She thought the seasonal decor certainly added to the ambience of the event. The businesses that had window boxes or flowerpots outside of their storefronts during the warmer months, and were current SeaScapes customers, had also been decked out with emerald green boxwood, red dogwood branches, and glitter-dusted dried hydrangeas. Kinsley had also added colorful orbs and solar lights, which would flicker on after dusk.

Becca began to sing "A Holly Jolly Christmas," and Kinsley joined in the singalong. The sound caused more than a few heads to turn, and a clap of approval now and then. It also helped stuff their kettle with donations and prompted them to sing louder.

"Well, don't you two embody holiday cheer! I'd be honored

to donate." Cole Chesterfield seemingly appeared out of no-where. Kinsley hadn't noticed which shop he came out of or if he had come from the rear parking lot located behind the build-ing. In any event, she did a double take when he reached into his pocket and plucked out a crisp one-hundred-dollar bill from his wallet and neatly folded it in front of them, as if he were a magician showing off his tricks, before pushing the money deep into the kettle with his thumb.

"Thank you so much, that was so generous!" Becca said with a grin.

Kinsley agreed that Cole was being generous but couldn't help but think it a little odd that the man had made an extreme effort for them to witness just how *much* money he had pushed inside of their kettle.

"Oh, would you look at that, it's starting to snow. How fes-tive! I just love a white Christmas, don't you?" Cole said, lifting an ungloved hand to the sky and then brushing the flakes off his thick hair. "However, I best get moving, I didn't dress for the weather today." He chuckled as he flung off the snow with a shake of his hands.

Kinsley held out the bucket of saltwater taffy for him to take one. "Before you go," she offered.

Cole plucked one from the bucket and immediately removed the wrapper and popped the sugary treat into his mouth. "De-licious," he said between chews.

"There's more inside, and a host of other holiday flavors, if you would like to purchase some," Kinsley suggested, gesturing toward the entrance of the taffy shop.

"I'll be sure and hit that up on my way back through," Cole said with a smile, and then licked the sticky sugar from his fin-gertips.

Kinsley made direct eye contact before she said, "Mr. Chesterfield, we're so sorry for your loss. Your brother was instrumental in helping the town of Harborside run smoothly and he will most certainly be missed. Especially down at the town council meetings. It'll be quite a change without him there."

"Yes, we're so very sorry," Becca added solemnly.

"Well, I do appreciate your kind words." Cole's tone lowered to a whisper before he uttered, "From what I've heard, though, I'm not sure how much he'll really be missed around these parts. My brother was a little too self-righteous and believed his way was the only way." The volume in his tone rose when he added, "And I'll be stepping in for him just as soon as I move back to Harborside permanently and can run in next year's election."

Kinsley couldn't help but agree with his assessment of his brother, but was surprised by his response, and bit her tongue to keep from saying the wrong thing in reply. Until this moment, she hadn't really thought about who would step in for Chris at the town council meetings until the next election.

Becca was busy with the next person who had arrived at their kettle, greeting them with a smile and began a brief side conversation about a sale going on and the free candy cane the person had picked up at the nearby gift shop.

Kinsley moved closer to Cole and asked, "You'll be moving back to Harborside, then?"

"I think so."

"Who will be taking over for Chris until the next election?"

"The board will have to appoint an interim alderman. I'm hoping that I can be the stand-in. Or Mallory might be appointed if no one else is willing to do it. Either way, the interim will have to be approved by the common council. Many times, it's often hard to find someone to step in midterm."

"I see."

Cole waited until the passerby who was chatting with Becca moved on their way before adding, "Have a good day, ladies, and keep singing!" He turned and hurried away in the direction of Precious Petals.

Kinsley leaned in and whispered, "Cole's sure in a chipper mood for someone who just lost his brother. You think he's on his way over to Mallory's shop?"

"Sure looks that way, and I overheard him tell you that he's moving back here. That's interesting news, to say the least," Becca said out of the side of her mouth as the two watched him step into the flower shop, as they'd predicted. "It's almost as if he's stepping directly into his brother's shoes."

Suddenly, it seemed as if the heavens opened and shook a snow globe, as glittery powder fell harder onto the sidewalk below their feet, where it quickly began to accumulate.

Becca happily sang "White Christmas," and Kinsley joined in once again.

Toby, juggling two disposable coffee cups where steam was rising from the lids, stepped out from the taffy shop. They stopped singing and Kinsley moved to hold the door for him.

"I brought you both some cocoa," he said as he handed the cups off to them.

"That's so sweet of you, Toby," Kinsley said, taking a sip that instantly warmed her to the core. She didn't even realize she was cold until she held the drink and it defrosted her gloved hands like Frosty the Snowman melting inside the poinsettia greenhouse.

"Yeah, the snow just started to pick up and it's getting a little chilly out here. Thanks for the cocoa," Becca said as she lifted the cup in gratitude.

"It's no problem at all. I'm so happy you friends are doing this—it's wonderful that you chose to volunteer," Toby said, wiping what must've been a little spilled cocoa onto his apron and then removing a tissue from his pocket and blowing his nose, which seemed to instantly drain from the cold the minute he had stepped outside.

"Yeah, Bec and I were just talking about making this an annual tradition. Everyone seems to be in a good mood, we're having so much fun out here!" Kinsley looked to Becca, who agreed with a grin and another sip of her cocoa.

"I'm glad you're both enjoying your time. It certainly is a great cause. Can I share something with you?" he asked, and then cleared his throat as if preparing for a big speech. "I'm not sure if you know this but my father was a deep-sea fisherman. Just like his old man, and my great-grandfather before that. My father sailed right up this coastline, all the way to the tip of Nova Scotia for Atlantic cod." Toby gestured a hand north to be sure they'd get the point of how far he'd traveled, before continuing. "And he shared with me once that during the war, when money was tight and the shipping vessels weren't paying enough, the Salvation Army fed the sailors on more than one occasion when they'd dock into port. Instead of using the money they had earned from fishing, which all went to keep their families afloat, the fisherman would often choose to go hungry. My father always told me, if I ever had any extra money in my pocket, to donate to the Salvation Army, as they had quite literally saved our lives."

Kinsley's jaw dropped. "Wow, Toby. You never shared that

story with me. I mean, I knew your dad was a fisherman, but you never shared the sacrifices he'd made on behalf of your family. That's awe-inspiring."

"Well, now you know." He shrugged. "It's probably why, to this day, I stockpile my food. It's a generational habit." He rubbed his ample tummy and gave a hearty laugh before his expression turned serious once again. "For what it's worth, I just wanted you both to know that what you're doing out here is important to our community. And my patrons have been sharing that you've been serenading them as they pass by, as well. Keep up the good work, ladies! Now I must get back inside before my Jenna returns from running errands and finds I'm not keeping up like I promised and decides to fire me. We wouldn't want that, now, would we?" he teased with a Santa-like twinkle in his eye before slipping back into the taffy shop.

"I'm so glad he shared that with us—it makes what we're doing out here seem that much more real," Kinsley said before taking another sip of cocoa and saying, "Heart of gold, that man."

"He's as sweet as his taffy, that's for sure!"

The two were interrupted with another donation to their kettle.

"Thank you! And Merry Christmas!" they said in unison.

After the person had walked away, Kinsley asked, "What Cole mentioned about someone stepping into Chris's position on the town council got me thinking. What if Chris's ordinances and policies *were* the tipping point that prevented Tim Horn from setting up shop? Do you think Chris preventing Jackie's husband from starting that business in downtown Harborside is enough motive to kill? Is there a chance that could change and be pushed through now that Chris is no longer with us?"

Becca shrugged. "I dunno. It would be kind of a big deal if Tim was counting on the new business to move forward to support his own family. Don't they have, like, a houseful of kids?"

"Yeah, they have three. That's expensive nowadays and a lot of mouths to feed."

"Sure is."

Kinsley turned to set her cocoa down on the bench but Becca grabbed her eagerly by the arm and spun her back around, causing the bucket of taffy to fall from the bench and tip onto its side.

Kinsley shrieked. "What the—"

"Look!" Becca exclaimed, pointing a finger across the street.

Kinsley saw she was pointing to someone off in the distance with the hood of their parka covering their head and a striped candy cane scarf wrapped tightly around their neck.

Chapter 19

"It's the scarf! The exact same scarf as the one you found down by the dock!" Becca exclaimed. "Didn't you see it?"

"Yeah, it looks like the same one, but that scarf is under surveillance down at the Blue Lobstah, remember?" Kinsley reminded her as she gathered the saltwater taffy that had fallen to the sidewalk. She dried it off by brushing it against her coat before placing it back inside of the bucket.

"Yes, but one of us needs to go after that person and find out where they purchased it. And quick, because they're getting too far away!"

That got Kinsley's attention. Becca was right. If they found out where they purchased the scarf, or which shop was selling them, maybe they could narrow things down a bit. "I hadn't thought of that. Good call."

"You go," Becca said with a slight shove toward the edge of the sidewalk. "I'll stay here with the kettle."

"Are you sure?"

"Yes! And hurry! Our target just turned down Maple Street."
Becca pointed to a side street that led to only a parking lot.

Kinsley handed off the bucket of saltwater taffy to Becca
and darted off in the same direction as the person who had
disappeared. She quickly looked both ways and had to wait for
two cars to pass, before sprinting across Main Street. When she
finally made it across, a tall gentleman who had just stepped
out of the town hall smacked right into her, causing her to lose
her balance on the snow-covered sidewalk and topple to the
ground.

"Heavens!" the man exclaimed, helping to her feet. "Are
you okay?"

"I'll be fine." Kinsley didn't recognize the older gentleman,
but the biggest thing hurt was her ego, as a small crowd was
quickly forming around them. She wiped the snow from her
backside to show that she was not injured.

"Do we need to call a doctor?" someone asked. "Or dial
911?"

"No. I'm okay—I'm fine, really. Thank you, everyone," she
said, waving the concerned citizens along. "Gotta go," she said
to the crowd before limping away.

Kinsley searched for her target, but the person had already
disappeared around the brick building. She hobbled toward
Maple Street and as soon as she reached the edge of the sidewalk, her head swung right and left, but the person had simply
vanished. Just as she was about to give up, she noticed someone
in the adjacent parking lot pop their head out from the trunk
of a car and proceed to dust the snow off the car with an ice
scraper. He or she was wearing the scarf! She darted over to the
car and exclaimed, "Excuse me!"

The person turned and smiled.

"Jackie? Is that you?" Kinsley asked, moving closer to get a better view.

"Hey, Kinsley, how you doin'?" Jackie adjusted the hood of her parka so her eyes could be fully seen beneath the fur lining of her thick coat. "Cold out here, isn't it? This weather has me wanting to stay home with a hot cider by the fireplace. I'm freezing! Where's your truck?" Jackie chuckled as she eyed the parking lot in search of it.

Kinsley waved a hand of dismissal. "I still have a few errands to run, but I thought I'd catch you before you head off."

"Ah well, I was just Christmas shopping for the kids and got some good deals. What's up?" She set the ice scraper on the side of the windshield and turned to face her fully with a smile.

Kinsley mirrored her smile. "Tim's home with the kids, then?" she asked.

"Yes, he always takes one day off from work so I can take advantage of the Harborside sales."

"There are some great sales going on, aren't there? Speaking of . . . May I ask where you bought that scarf? It's so festive and cute, I'd love to buy one for Becca for Christmas."

Jackie looked down at the scarf, which now hung limply from her parka. "Oh? This? I don't think you can get these anymore. Come to think of it, I think Toby's Taffy was giving them away a few years ago for the December sale. One of those first-customer-through-the-door deals, if I recall correctly," she mused. "Well, anyway, I happened to be one of them." She smiled brightly.

"Oh, really?" Kinsley asked. Though it made perfect sense, as the colors of the scarf mimicked the candy cane–striped awning of the taffy shop.

"Yeah, I always thought it was kinda cute, too. And I can wear it all season long since it's not too Christmassy."

"You don't remember who was behind you in line at Toby's that day? I mean, who else was lucky enough to snag one?"

Jackie's smile faded and her expression turned blank. "No, sorry, I can't remember. I was just so excited to get one, and it was years ago. But maybe you can ask Toby where he ordered them from. That's probably your best bet if you want to buy one for your friend."

"Ah yes. Well, thanks so much!"

Jackie's brows furrowed. "Is that all you wanted? Because now that you bring it up, someone from town emailed from an address I didn't recognize and said that they had found a scarf and mentioned I needed to pick it up at the wharf. It was kinda weird. I forgot about it, until just now."

"Oh?" Kinsley put on her best poker face. "Isn't that an odd coincidence. Obviously you weren't missing yours, I see." She chuckled with a sigh. "Well, don't mind me. I completely forgot what I came over here to ask you. I'm sure if it's important, it'll come back to me, and I can reach out to you."

"Yeah, please do. This doesn't have anything to do with the holiday decorations, does it? Personally, I think they turned out beautifully. It was nice to see the kissing balls hung all along Main Street. The downtown looks fantastic. Doesn't it?"

"It sure does, and I also appreciated all the extra hands that made that possible. Maybe that was it—should I put you down for next year to volunteer again?"

"Yes, please do!" Jackie grinned. "I loved being a part of it."

"That's wonderful news. Thanks so much!" Kinsley said with a smile, and was about to turn away when Jackie stopped her with an outstretched hand.

"Hey, have you heard anything about what's going on with the alderman's murder investigation? Any murmurs around town or anything?"

"Nah, not much. You?"

"No, not really. Honestly, it doesn't look great that my husband and Chris were arguing right before he . . . well . . . you know . . . before he . . . took that spill into the water. It really bothers me that some of the townspeople are insinuating that Tim had anything to do with this, because I can assure you, he didn't," she said defiantly.

"I can see how that might bother you, but I personally haven't heard anyone pointing a finger toward your husband." Kinsley nodded sympathetically. She wanted to keep this little share session going.

"In fairness, if anyone should look suspicious to the police it's Cari Day. I don't want to throw a friend under the bus or anything, but if they're going to consider Tim as a suspect, they may as well consider her one, too."

"Oh, are you referring to Chris not paying the vet bill?"

"You know about that?" Jackie asked, studying her.

"Yeah, Cari mentioned it to me."

"Did she also mention that things were escalating between them? She was thrown out of the last common council meeting for being disorderly! Apparently, she brought the issue up in front of everyone, yelling expletives at him from across the room. Let me tell you, Chris didn't like that one bit."

"I'm sure not."

"Oh, it gets better," Jackie continued. "Did you know Chris said he was planning to file a restraining order against her? Honestly, if anyone has anger issues, it's her—not my husband, who was only defending himself that night at the Blue Lobstah," she snorted. "I know her dog was injured and all, but that doesn't give her the right to go all postal at a town meeting."

Kinsley didn't know what to say in response to the allegations that Chris was planning on slapping Cari with a restraining order. That was news to her.

"By the way," Jackie said conspiratorially, "please don't mention to Cari that I shared this with you because I'm sure she'll think I'm just dragging her into this to take the heat off Tim. We know the police are looking heavily at him and we certainly don't appreciate that, but he's innocent. Anyway, there's so much going on over the holidays, my head is spinning and it's getting late. I promised Tim and the kids I'd pick up a pizza on the way home, so I better be going." She looked to the sky grimly. "The roads are going to get slick real soon. Be careful out there."

"Of course! Please, give my best to the family and drive safe!" Kinsley said as she took a step backward and lifted a hand in a friendly wave before heading back to Toby's Taffy, anxious to share with Becca what she had learned.

Chapter 20

By the time Kinsley had returned to the Salvation Army kettle, her side ached and all down her right leg was throbbing. Becca must've noticed her predicament, as her brow furrowed and she reached out to her in concern.

"Goodness! Do you need to sit down?"

"Yeah, I think I will for a second if you don't mind." Kinsley gingerly took a seat on the bench and winced when she rubbed her hand along her thigh, which was sure to bruise, if it hadn't already.

Becca moved the bucket of saltwater taffy aside to take a seat beside her. "What on earth happened? I thought I saw someone fall across the street. That wasn't you, was it?"

"Yep, yours truly!" Kinsley rose a hand as if she were a student responding to a teacher. "However, at least I got some intel out of the deal. Come to find out it was Jackie wearing the—"

The two were interrupted by an older woman who stopped

at the red kettle. "Isn't anyone manning this thing? You're supposed to be ringing that bell!" She scowled, throwing her hands dramatically onto her hips and then waving a pointed finger rather sternly as if scolding a petulant child. "You kids today, sitting down on the job. Let me tell you something, I'm not giving you a dime!" she spat.

Becca sprang from the bench and began to ring her bell. "Sorry about that, ma'am, my apologies. My friend fell on the snow-covered sidewalk and hurt her hip. I was just checking to see if she was okay."

The older woman studied Kinsley as if Becca were lying. Kinsley leaned over and, as proof, showed the woman the side of her jeans that were soaked through.

"Humph," she grunted before stepping past them and moving inside Toby's Taffy.

"Should we warn Toby and Jenna what they're in for?" Becca giggled.

"I'm sure they deal with all kinds of interesting people doing what they do. I should've tossed her a peppermint taffy, though. It may have helped sweeten her up a bit." Kinsley cracked a smile.

"Yeah, maybe." Becca nodded before turning back to the kettle, where she began to sing the popular song "Sleigh Ride" and rang her bell in perfect tempo.

Kinsley scooped up a handful of snow from the back of the bench and formed it into a snowball and interrupted Becca midtune with a light toss of the snowball to her back, and said, "Hey, just so you know, the candy cane scarves came from here."

"Say what?" Becca spun around to fully face her. Evidently, the snowball hit did little to amuse her, as she ignored it completely.

"Yeah, apparently the taffy shop was giving them away a

few years ago for the December sale. I don't remember that. Do you? I feel like I should've, as much as we visit with Toby and Jenna," Kinsley said, rubbing her hip.

"Was that the year your aunt was down with the flu? Remember how sick Tilly was? We had to clean rooms and make beds for her holiday guests. And that's when I learned the secret recipe for that amazing white chocolate peppermint bark she usually makes. You and I made like a dozen batches that year. Remember?"

"Oh, that's right! I totally forgot about that. She *was* so sick, and I didn't get downtown to shop that year, either. I think I bought all my Christmas presents online and had them shipped direct. That was a rough holiday for my poor aunt!"

Becca pulled back the sleeve of her coat to reveal her watch. "We only have a few minutes left on our shift. When we're done here, we can go ask Toby or Jenna about it."

Kinsley gave a thumbs-up. "Sounds like a plan."

A familiar face stepped in front of them and pushed a folded bill into the kettle. "You two having fun out here?" Raven asked with a grin.

"Actually, we are!" Kinsley replied. "What brings you downtown?"

Raven lifted the shopping bags that were looped onto her arms. "Shopping for toys for my niece and nephew. I find the most unique things in these shops and with the Twelve Days of Christmas sale, it's a win-win!"

"And it's a great way to support our downtown Harborside to keep it thriving," Becca agreed.

"Good to see you guys! I gotta run so I'm not late for my shift at the Blue Lobstah. You two stay warm! I'm sure I'll see you at the end of the bar real soon." She winked.

Kinsley and Becca waved good-bye before their singing commenced.

Just then, out of the corner of Kinsley's eye, she thought she saw someone else who looked familiar. She did a double take and despite the pain in her leg, leapt from the bench and ran directly into the arms of her brother, Kyle.

"A little birdie told me I might find you downtown," Kyle said before releasing her from his tight embrace, which caused her to wince just a little.

"Oh no! What's wrong?" he asked, looking her over from head to toe.

Kinsley downplayed her brother's concern with a flick to his shoulder. "Nothing to worry about. Your stupid sister slipped on the wet sidewalk and took a nosedive." She chuckled.

"Ouch." Kyle winced.

"I'm fine, really. But look at you! What a sight for sore eyes!" Kinsley did a once-over to see if anything had changed with her brother during their months apart. He looked a little thinner than she remembered, and his military haircut was showing early signs of receding. His eyes, the color of summer-blooming hydrangea, looked tired, but she could certainly understand that after a long journey from Germany. "I'm so excited that you're home for the holidays!" Kinsley continued as she held her brother tightly on the arm as if she never wanted to let him go. Before she had a chance to ask Kyle anything further, Rachel strolled up and handed him a pair of brown leather gloves. "They were under the seat," she said to him with a smile.

Kyle looked confused so Rachel continued, "Your gloves must've fallen when you got in and you must've kicked them under there by accident."

Kyle's expression morphed into warm gratitude. "Ah, thanks! And thanks again for picking me up at the airport."

"Speaking of which, I'm thrilled you're here, Kyle, but I thought I was picking you up next week?" Kinsley asked. "You never called and mentioned you might catch an earlier flight."

"Yeah, that's what you told me, too," Becca said, and then gave Kyle a welcoming hug. "Good to see you!" she added with a grin.

"Good to be seen!" Kyle turned his attention back to his sister and said, "I heard there's a chance of a nor'easter blowing into Maine in the next few days. The last thing I wanted is to be stuck in Germany alone for the holidays, so I hopped an earlier flight. Besides, I wanted to surprise you and Aunt Tilly. So"—he leaned back and threw out jazz hands—"surprise!" He grinned.

"You win! I'm totally surprised!" Kinsley mirrored her brother's grin. "Have you seen Aunt Tilly yet?"

"No, we stopped here to see you first. Salty Breeze is our next stop. Aunt Tilly said she has a dinner buffet planned for her guests and there's plenty of food to go around." Kyle vigorously rubbed his hands together as if in anticipation of filling his belly. "I can't wait to dig into her cheesy potatoes!" he exclaimed, licking his lips. "Care to join us?"

"Did someone say 'cheesy potatoes'?" Becca stuck her head between them and then jutted a thumb to her chest. "Count me in!"

"Yeah, we can meet you there after our shift. We're just about done here." Kinsley nodded.

"Sounds good," Kyle said.

Rachel gestured a hand toward Toby's Taffy. "I'm going to

pop in there and buy a box of taffy for the station before we go. This is the month when everyone constantly brings in treats for the break room, and I haven't participated enough yet. I'm sure the officers would love something they can take with them while out on patrol. That would really sweeten their shift! I'll be right back," she said before disappearing into the shop.

"Oh, that's a great idea," Becca said. "I think I'll purchase a few boxes for my favorite clients, too." She then leaned into Kinsley's ear and whispered, "And I'll check on the status of the scarf situation while I'm in there." Becca then turned her attention to Kyle. "Can you handle this for a min?" She handed her bell to Kinsley's brother, who took it willingly.

"No problem!" Kyle smiled as he demonstrated a vigorous ring of the bell, which caused the group of three to share a chuckle.

After Becca had disappeared within the confines of the candy shop, Kinsley couldn't help but take the moment to corner her brother privately. With an outstretched hand she stopped him from ringing the bell. "Hey, Kyle. There's something that's been bothering me. You mind if I ask you something?"

"This isn't about that high-profile case Rach is working on, is it? On our ride over here, she mentioned that a city councilman was murdered the night of the boat parade. I suppose you've been putting your Sherlock hat on again," he said with concern. "I hope I'm wrong and you're leaving this one to the authorities."

"Yeah, this is about something else."

Kyle's eyes narrowed. "Sounds serious. What is it?"

"Have you been looking into the accident that caused Mom and Dad's death on the Air Force base? And if so, why now?"

"Where did that come from?"

Kinsley studied him. She wanted her brother to be honest and forthright. But she was surprised to see that he seemed to be hiding something. His eye always twitched when he lied, like when he'd stolen the last cookie from the cookie tin as a kid and would try to put on an innocent face when questioned by their aunt.

He must've caught on that she wasn't going to let this go because he repeated, "Why are you asking me this, right now? I barely made it into town."

Kinsley knew she probably should have waited but she really needed to know what she was missing. "If you know something about them, I have a right to know, too. If you're digging into what happened to our parents—there must be a reason. What prompted you to investigate this now? Tell me," she pressed. "Did you learn something different than what we were told when we were kids?"

Kyle looked beyond his sister to the window that displayed the ribbons of taffy being made in real time. "Did she tell you that?" He pointed to the window where Kinsley assumed Rachel was either standing by the counter or waiting in line to purchase her candy.

"Does it matter?"

"Yeah, it matters," he said, clenching his teeth. "Rachel shouldn't be talking about our folks like that. Especially when she uses them as an excuse for our 'lack of engagement.'" He threw his fingers up in air quotes, causing the bell in his hand to ring. "As if that's the reason our relationship is being put on hold," he added crossly. "Is that what she shared with you?"

The two were interrupted when Mallory approached and shared a friendly wave. Mallory didn't linger, though, and continued walking along the sidewalk. Kinsley couldn't determine if that was because of the strained looks on their faces or if she was just in her own head. In any event, Kinsley was glad not to have to make small talk, because she really wanted to get to the bottom of this.

"Well? Is that what Rachel said?" he pushed.

Kinsley shrugged defensively. "No. What do our parents' deaths have to do with your relationship with Rachel? That doesn't make any sense to me."

"Oh, it makes sense."

"What? How?" Kinsley argued.

"It makes sense because that's why I keep enlisting."

Kinsley breathed deep. "Wait. Hang on a sec. You mean to tell me that your choice to reenlist in the military is because you want answers about the accident that took our parents? Not because you want to serve our country in Germany. Is that what you're saying?"

Kyle held up a hand in defense. "I'm not saying that completely. Of course I want to serve our country. But I could do that here, back in New England or anywhere else, for that matter. However, if I didn't reenlist and take orders to Germany, then I would lose access to the files. And I'd have less than zero contacts with whom to share any new intel. Without any connections, Kins, we're dead in the water."

"I'm not sure I'm following." Kinsley laced her hands protectively across her chest. "You learned something to prompt you to dig into more than what we've already been told. What changed? Why would you investigate this now? After all these years?"

"Right before my reenlistment I learned that Dad had a security clearance."

"*So?* What does that matter?"

"There's no reason why he would have a top-secret security clearance with the job he held in the military. Absolutely, un-equivocally, no reason whatsoever."

Kinsley lowered her voice and stepped closer to her brother and studied him. "Kyle, what exactly are you saying?"

"I'm saying we didn't really know our parents the way we think we did. Not really. They told us that Mom held a job in information management and Dad was an MP, but, Kinsley, that wasn't true. Those weren't their AFSCs—their Air Force Specialty Codes—at least in Dad's case."

"Are you serious?"

"Dead. Serious."

Kinsley kneaded her forehead with her gloved fingertips. "I don't even know what to say. What does any of that mean? It sounds like you think they were involved in intelligence or they were spies or something bizarre like that. And that's what got them killed."

"Trust me, I get it." Kyle rested a comforting hand on her shoulder. "Look, I'm trying to get a top-secret security clear-ance myself so I can gain more intel. But do you realize how hard that is? They don't give those security clearances away like a driver's license, you know. It hasn't been easy. This could take years and a hell of a lot of schooling."

"Does Aunt Tilly know?"

"That I'm looking into it, you mean?"

"No, not that." Kinsley shook her head. "I mean, does she know that Dad had a top-secret security clearance—and why? Have you asked her?"

"Honestly, I'm not sure. It's a conversation that needs to be had. There's a lot here to sift through. But it's not exactly the kind of conversation we want to have with her over the holidays. Is it? I didn't come home to cause family drama. I came home to see you both and enjoy a Maine Christmas. Can we do that? Please?"

The defeat in his voice led Kinsley to believe that their aunt had known more. And if she did, what did that say about their relationship? Didn't they have a right to know what really happened to their parents? Had Tilly been hiding family secrets? Would she tell them the truth, if cornered?

Kinsley squared her shoulders and faced her brother. "You need to tell me everything you know, right this second. I feel like I'm the last one to know something huge and I'm not exactly happy about that."

Kyle held up a hand like a crossing guard stopping traffic for children to cross. "I will—just not right now."

"You can't leave me hanging like this, it's not fair." Her comment came out like a whine, and she hadn't meant it to. She was growing frustrated with this conversation.

Kyle gestured to the door, where Becca and Rachel were talking and laughing as they exited the taffy shop. "Not now," he said under his breath.

Learning that her brother's reenlistment in the Air Force had more to do with finding answers about their parents' deaths than with his service to their country only left her wanting more out of this conversation. Much more. Kyle wasn't going to get off that easy. Nor would Aunt Tilly. Of that, she was certain.

Chapter 21

After loading their plates with a hefty portion of cheesy potatoes, shredded barbeque pork, hot buttery rolls, and seasoned vegetables, the group of four shared a table with Aunt Tilly at the Salty Breeze Inn. It was unusual, to say the least, for their aunt to take a seat during mealtime at the inn. However, being that it was Kyle's first day home on leave, she would make an exception. And most likely this was one of the few times during the entire season their aunt would take a moment for herself. Tilly's face was flushed with joy and her smile radiant.

The dining room of the Salty Breeze Inn reverberated with happy exchanges as guests filled the room as well, but Kinsley was having a hard time being present. She was thrilled to see her brother, but their earlier conversation in front of Toby's left her with a ton of questions.

Becca nudged her on the arm. "Right, Kins?"

Kinsley set down her fork, turned to her friend, and asked, "I'm sorry, I missed it. What did you say?"

"When did we lose you?" Becca teased, giving a quick shake to her arm. "I was just telling your brother and Rachel that they should join us down at the Blue Lobstah before he heads back to Germany. Pete was talking about hosting a New Year's Eve party. We'll have to find out if he's still planning on it. Has he told you if it's still on?"

"Oh." Kinsley forced a smile. "Yeah, that would be fun. Kyle's on leave for a month so we have plenty of time." She sent a weak smile to her brother and then looked to her aunt, who regarded her with a perplexed expression. Tilly knew her well; she wasn't going to be able to hide her emotions from her aunt for long. She didn't like the feeling of these unanswered questions stirring in her stomach. Because of it, she was having a hard time enjoying Tilly's handiwork, instead rolling the cheesy potatoes around her plate with her fork.

"Are you all going over to Edna's party? All the who's who of Harborside will be in attendance," Tilly asked. "I wish I could break away and join everyone, but I just don't see how it would be feasible."

"Edna asked if Becca and I were planning on attending," Kinsley confirmed. "Kyle, you and Rachel should come. Edna would love to see you, I'm sure." She turned to press Becca then. "Did you two learn anything about the scarf when you went into the taffy shop?"

Becca stirred the straw in her glass, looked to Rachel, and asked, "Do you want to share what we discovered?"

Rachel wiped her mouth with a napkin and said, "Sure. Toby said he couldn't remember exactly who received them that year during the Twelve Days of Christmas, but he did think he had a record of it in their files. Normally they take a photo of the winners and hang it in the shop for the entire holiday season. He's pretty sure that year's photo is somewhere in their office and he's going to look for it when the shop isn't so busy."

Kinsley sat up in her chair and then leaned toward the table, excited at the possibility they might learn more. "Oh, that's good. Sounds like that might give us a lead!"

"Yeah, I'm going over there tomorrow morning before they open to see if he found it, if you want to join me."

"I'd love to!" Kinsley exclaimed.

"Count me in, too!" Becca said, sharing her excitement.

"I think I'll stay back, if you're all heading over there first thing in the morning." Kyle chuckled. "I'll take the time to catch up on some sleep. I feel like I'm still in a different time zone." He yawned and then slouched, the chair the only thing seemingly keeping him upright.

"That's probably best." Tilly nodded as she looked to her nephew warmly. "And just so you know, the Christmas decorations in your room were your sister and Rachel's doing. They wanted you to feel especially welcomed for the holiday season." Her eyes darted to the large grandfather clock in the corner of the room. "Speaking of which, I need to get back to my guests, but it was lovely eating with you all—even if it was only for a few minutes," she said with a gleam in her eye as she gathered the silverware onto her plate.

"But you hardly ate anything!" Kyle pointed to her plate, where evidence of shredded pork and cheesy potatoes still lingered. Tilly then playfully stole another bite.

Kyle shook his head disapprovingly. "You need to take better care of yourself."

"Oh, I never eat a full meal, I graze," Tilly admitted, licking her lips. "The experts say that's better for you anyway . . ." Her voice trailed off.

"It's true. The woman barely sits down long enough to eat a complete meal," Kinsley said. "She usually grabs a bite between guests."

"Nor do you, my love," Tilly shot back at her with a wink and a pointed glance to Kinsley's plate, where her food still hadn't been touched.

"Are you going to even try to attend Edna's party?" Becca asked. "Or is it a hard no?"

"I just don't know if I'll be able to break away this year. There's a lot going on." Tilly sighed. "We'll see."

"'We'll see' always meant *no*, growing up," Kyle teased.

Kinsley laughed. "So true, my brother!"

Before Tilly had a chance to walk away from the table, the chief of police, who held a commanding presence, stepped into the room. His eyes searched the dining area until they landed on Rachel. As soon as he locked eyes on her, he waved her over.

"Looks like I'm being summoned," Rachel said, pushing back her plate and rising from her chair. "Sorry, guys."

"I'll take care of your dishes, not to worry. Thanks for joining us, Rachel, and please know you're more than welcome to celebrate the holidays with us. We'd love to have you," Tilly said warmly.

"Thanks, Tilly. I appreciate that. I'll catch up with you all later," Rachel said with a nod before moving quickly away from the table.

Why was Rachel being summoned by her boss? Kinsley wondered.

It must mean there was a break in the case, and she could hardly wait to hear what it was.

Chapter 22

The following morning, Kinsley drove alone to downtown Harborside to meet Rachel at Toby's Taffy. The air was cold and damp when she exited the warmth of her truck. A dusting of snow had fallen overnight, leaving the sidewalks covered lightly in a blanket of glittery white. Kinsley wondered if the nor'easter that her brother had spoken of was soon on its way. The thought of more snowflakes lightened her mood, though. A few inches of fresh white fluff always made the Christmas season feel as if Santa really did exist. She smiled up at the sky before clutching her coat tighter around her neck and ducking into the safety of the taffy shop.

Kinsley was thankful to find that despite Toby's Taffy not yet being open for business, the door was unlocked for them. The indoor lights were still off, however, and the store was lit from only the natural light streaming through the window and the glare from the newly fallen snow. After she knocked the slop from her boots and stepped fully inside, the room was eerily quiet. She removed her winter hat and the static electricity made her hair stand on end, so she smoothed it down with her hand after shoving her leather gloves deep into her pockets. She hung her belongings on a nearby coatrack.

"Toby? Jenna?" Kinsley called out, stepping deeper into the shop. "You in here?" She returned to the window to see if either Becca's or Rachel's car was parked in front of the building and noticed neither had arrived yet. She looked to the oversized clock on the wall and concluded she must've just been the first to arrive. Toby and Jenna typically parked in the rear parking lot behind the candy shop to save the spots out front for customers, so it was no surprise that she didn't see their cars, either. Before stepping away from the window, she noticed footprints in the snow leaving the shop. Perhaps one of them stepped outside momentarily to speak with a neighboring shopkeeper and would soon return.

Kinsley waited what seemed like an uncomfortable amount of time before calling their names out again. When met with no response, she stepped behind the counter and moved toward the back hallway in the direction of the kitchen and the business office. The office light was on, and the door cracked open a hair, which illuminated a path onto the darkened hallway floor. She briefly knocked on the door so as not to startle either of the taffy shop owners, before stepping inside the office.

Kinsley let out a screech.

Toby was lying facedown on the floor with papers littered beneath him. The top drawer of the file cabinet was pulled fully open, folders were askew, and documents were strewn everywhere.

"Toby!" Kinsley cried. She knelt to check for a pulse and

found that his heart was racing. She shook his arm to get him to respond, which caused the injured man to moan.

"What on earth happened to you?"

Toby slowly rolled to one side, put a hand to his head, and moaned again.

It was then Kinsley noticed a small trickle of blood running from his hairline down his neck. Before she had time to examine him further, she heard laughter and chatter coming from the direction of the hallway.

"In here!" Kinsley screamed. "And hurry!" She turned her attention back to the shopkeeper. "My God, Toby, what happened to you?"

His only reply was another moan uttering from his lips.

Rachel entered the room and sprang into action. "Toby! Toby! Can you hear me?"

Toby's eyes fluttered as he grunted and attempted to sit upright. But the shopkeeper seemed to grow dizzy, because he slumped forward, resting his full weight on his knees and holding his head protectively in his hands.

"It's okay, you're going to be okay, I promise," Rachel soothed. "Just sit tight." She laid a gentle hand on Toby for him to stay put.

"What happened?" Jenna squealed when she, too, entered the room, to find her husband on the floor. "Sweetheart, are you okay?" Her lavender-colored eyes grew double in size as she knelt to look him over.

Toby pointed a shaky finger toward a round paperweight that had rolled beneath the desk but was still visible. "Someone hit me with that," he groaned.

"Hit you?" Kinsley exclaimed. "Whaddya mean, hit you? Someone did this to you *on purpose*?" Her glance then flew back in the direction of the paperweight. She moved closer to it and Rachel followed. On closer examination, after rolling it closer to them with her foot, it looked as if the paperweight, which was made from heavy glass and showcased a glittery red poinsettia, was caked in blood. Rachel immediately bagged the paperweight for evidence.

"I must've blacked out." Toby groaned.

"Who did this to you, honey?" Jenna asked as she laid a tender hand to his cheek, which was quickly transforming from a greenish color to fully flushed. Jenna's tone turned irate. "Tell me, and I'll go after them with all the force left in me," she added, clenching her fist.

"I don't know," Toby stuttered. "Someone came up behind me . . . I didn't even know what was happening until I felt this hot red pain in my head! And then I heard the paperweight hit the floor and watched it roll away from me."

"You didn't see anything? Any hint of what the person was wearing? No detail is insignificant," Rachel demanded.

"No, I—" Toby's eyes fluttered, and he held his head again. It was obvious the man was in pain and confused.

Kinsley was bewildered, too. Everything had happened so fast, she could barely take it all in. It was like she was watching a movie in slow motion. Toby and Jenna were the closest people to her on planet Earth, besides her aunt Tilly, Kyle, and Becca, and she just couldn't believe she was witnessing this. The thought of losing either one of them caused bile to rise in her throat.

"We need to call an ambulance and get you checked out," Jenna said firmly, as if she knew her husband would object. Which he did as he immediately argued.

"We can't! It's the Twelve Days of Christmas sale! It's the busiest week of the entire season!" Toby sputtered.

"I'm sorry, Toby, but this office is now an official crime scene. You can't keep the shop open today even if you don't decide to go to the hospital. I know this isn't what you want to hear, but you'll have to remain closed," Rachel said firmly. "I'll have my crime scene investigators here in a jiffy, to collect evidence. You won't be able to open the shop again until after they release it, so you may as well get yourself checked out."

Toby moaned again. This time louder. Kinsley wondered if it was more because of having to close the taffy shop than the injury to his head.

Jenna's glance flew to Rachel with a new sense of urgency. "Yes, we need to get my husband to the ER. And soon."

Toby tried to nod but quickly winced at the pain.

Rachel immediately called the emergency into dispatch, and within minutes paramedics arrived and were wheeling Toby out of the office on a stretcher. By this time, Toby had become a little more alert, and the group could hear the arguing between husband and wife about whether he really needed an ambulance ride to the hospital. Jenna was obviously winning the battle as he was rolled away from them, down the hallway. Kinsley could hear Becca off in the distance, too, and before long, her best friend had joined them inside the office. "What the heck happened? I'm sorry I'm late, I had a few work calls to tend to . . ." Her eyes darted nervously between them. "Jenna said you'd fill me in and that Toby was clocked over the head! Is that true?"

After they shared what had happened, Kinsley ended with, "I just can't believe this. Why on earth would anyone want to hurt Toby? He's like the nicest man in Harborside. I can't wrap my head around it!" she said wearily. "But we need to get to the bottom of it."

Becca was equally astonished and seemed to be at a loss, her mouth set in a grim line.

Rachel moved to the file cabinet, rolled on a pair of gloves that she had plucked from her pocket, and lifted a folder. "This empty folder is marked Twelve Days of Christmas," she said ominously.

Kinsley's heart skipped an uncomfortable beat and began to thump harder. "Please tell me this isn't about the photo we were searching for."

Becca's face grew ashen. "Someone knew we were looking for Toby's photos from the previous year's giveaways and got to it first. How would anyone have known?"

"Did you review the video feed yet from the Blue Lobstah?" Kinsley asked. "Are we getting any closer to our suspect?"

"No, I haven't had time to review it yet. I've been running around like a chicken with my head cut off," Rachel admitted wearily as she continued to scan through the files. "But it's on my list!"

"Please tell us that's not the only thing missing from the files," Kinsley said. However, she knew before the words were out of her mouth that it was likely the only paperwork that would be missing.

Rachel flipped through the files before turning to her. "It sure seems that way. I'll have to confirm with Jenna when she returns. But the rest of these files, even the open ones, have papers that seem to be in order," she added as she continued to read. "Leading me to only conclude one thing: Becca is right."

Kinsley scratched the back of her neck and scanned the floor, looking for answers. "How would someone even know we were looking for that information? It doesn't make sense."

Becca moved Kinsley aside and leaned into her ear so only

she could hear. "Whoever wore the scarf and was emailed to pick it up down at the wharf knew the scarf could implicate them in a crime. We might've tipped someone off with our little stakeout stunt. I'm sure he or she remembered having their picture taken wearing it the year they won it and thought to dispose of any more proof."

Kinsley blew out a heavy sigh. "So, if we never had done that . . . Toby wouldn't be in this situation. That's devastating."

Although they were whispering it seemed the detective was onto them.

"Did you say 'stakeout'?"

Kinsley dropped her head in shame and then proceeded to admit to Rachel exactly what had happened out by the lobster tree. And ended with a very big "I'm sorry!" holding out praying hands for forgiveness.

"This is exactly why I don't like to involve civilians in my ongoing investigations. I think moving forward, you two better stay out of it. As a matter of fact, you probably should get outta here," Rachel said firmly. "Before my coworkers arrive on scene."

Those weren't exactly the words that Kinsley wanted to hear.

Chapter 23

The following afternoon, while slipping into dress clothes for Edna Williamsburg's holiday gala, Kinsley had received word that Toby would make a full recovery from his minor concussion. The relief she felt was an understatement. It felt like she'd been holding her breath since the moment she had discovered him on the floor of his office. She was incredibly thankful to hear the good news that her friend was on the mend. She couldn't help but chuckle, though, when Jenna had shared that she had been tending to his every need and spoiling him rotten. Tilly had pulled a vat of homemade chicken noodle soup from the freezer to send over, and Kinsley was planning to deliver it after making a stop at the party. She wasn't exactly in the partying mood, but due to Becca's insistence, they would still drop in and make an appearance, as planned. The guilt she felt for her part in Toby's injury was something she could not shake and it had kept her awake most of the night. She stifled a yawn and looked into the mirror at the dark circles that hung beneath her eyes. Despite adding coverup, the gray was still evident. Although Rachel wanted her to back out of the investigation, the attack on Toby only prompted her to want to dig into things further.

A knock on her bedroom door stole her attention. "Coming!" She slipped on a pair of high-heeled boots, took one final peek in the mirror that hung above the dresser, and then went to greet her brother.

"Well, look at you! You clean up well for someone who loves to have her hands in the dirt. Sometimes I forget you're no longer a little girl," Kyle teased with a lopsided grin. If he reached out and ruffled her hair, like they were kids again, she would have no other choice than to clock him. Kyle was wearing his Air Force dress uniform, and he looked much more rested than when he'd first arrived in town, which was a relief to see.

"Thanks," Kinsley answered flatly.

Apparently, her demeanor was not lost on Kyle. "What's wrong? Please tell me you're not still mad at me about the Mom and Dad thing. You realize my inquiry into their deaths doesn't change a thing. We've still lost them, Kins—they're never coming back to us," he said sadly. "It's a bit of a moot point to discuss it until I learn more."

"First of all, it's not a *thing*. It's a seriously big deal . . . and we really *do* need to talk about it. But per usual, we don't have time for serious conversation right now because we're running late for the party." Kinsley smoothed her dark slacks with her hands and then buttoned the cuffs on her red silk blouse before looking up to her brother. "Where's Rachel? Is she meeting us over there?"

"She can't make it."

Kinsley removed a set of white gold hoops studded with diamonds from the dresser and slipped them on. "Why not? I thought she said she was joining us. What changed?"

"I'm sure work is preventing her from joining us, otherwise she'd be here. However, Rach cautioned me to keep you safe."

Kinsley looked at him quizzically.

"Because of the blatant attack on Toby, she wants all of us to remain on high alert. And it seems you and Becca are only adding to the problem. She's concerned that one of you might be targeted next." He looked at her closely to see if this was true and she needed her brother's protection. "I had to convince her that I won't let either of you out of my sight," he added evenly. "Are you getting in the way of her job? Just because you're friends with an investigator doesn't give you the right to push her buttons, Kins. You need to let her do her job. And stay out of it."

"I'm not a problem. And I'm certainly not adding to it," Kinsley defended. She hated that ever since her brother came to town, they seemed to be at odds with each other. It was unusual for them, and it was making her mildly uncomfortable. She looped her arm through her brother's and gave a friendly squeeze. "Becca and I will hang close with you, not to worry," she said sweetly.

"You sure you're ready? You need to grab a purse or anything?"

"Yeah, I'm ready. But on second thought I think I'll leave my purse here and just bring my cell along. I don't feel like carrying it around at the party." Kinsley abandoned her clutch on the bed and slipped her phone into her pocket before softly closing the door behind her.

Kyle pointed to her footwear before they even made it a few feet down the hallway. "You might want to wear a more sensible pair of boots and bring those to change into. There's a storm brewing and I'm thinking you probably don't want to be caught over there without your Sorels."

"That's a good idea. I left my winter boots under the bench by the back door, I'll change into them before we go. We should probably walk over to the gala instead of getting locked in behind a long trail of cars in her driveway, though. I don't plan on staying long."

"We haven't even arrived at the party yet and you're already planning your exit strategy? What gives?" he asked with a raised brow. "I thought you were looking forward to this."

"It's not that. I'm just distracted. I need to deliver the soup to Toby and check in on him. I'm not going to relax until I see him with my own two eyes and confirm he's going to make a full recovery."

"Ah. I can go with you. I didn't get a chance to visit with them the other day when you were volunteering. I know I wasn't as close to Toby and Jenna as you were growing up, but I still consider them part of our family, so I'd really like to see them, too. If you don't mind me tagging along."

"I'm sure they'd love that. They ask about you all the time," Kinsley said, patting her brother on the arm warmly.

After donning their winter gear, the two headed in the direction of the cliff walk. A bitter wind circled their heads as they made their way closer to the Atlantic. Kinsley pulled the cords on her hood tighter to her head, and she was pretty sure she looked like a racoon with only her eyes showing.

Kyle laughed. "Hey, need I remind you that you're the one who wanted to walk to the party? I told you a nor'easter was imminent. You sure you don't want to turn around and hop in your truck?"

"Nah, I'm good." Although the wind blowing off the water almost knocked Kinsley from her feet and the lack of sun due to the late afternoon made it almost unbearable. "It sure feels like a storm is on the way, though. Let's hurry."

The two rushed through the back gate of the Williamsburg estate and hurried along the long pathway until they finally made it to the back porch. The immediate rush of warm air lured them inside and the scent of balsam fir welcomed them. Kinsley and Becca had crafted topiaries with evergreens, red dogwood branches, and glittered pinecones, and strategically positioned them at every entrance for the festive scent to welcome all who entered.

Becca was waiting for them by the back door and greeted them both with a kiss on the cheek before declaring, "The decor looks amazing, and we hit it out of the park illuminating this place! Isn't our work stunning?" she said, gleefully clapping her hands together as if it were already Christmas morning.

Approval shone in Kyle's eyes, too, as they moved deeper into the room. "You did this?"

"Yup, Becca and I handled all the holiday decorations," Kinsley said proudly.

"Wow. You've outdone yourselves." Kyle scanned the room and then returned his attention to them once again. "It looks like something out of a Christmas movie. Nice work, you two."

Kinsley felt the genuineness in her brother's words and beamed at him. She was glad they were on better footing now. She decided to tread lightly for the remainder of the afternoon and deal with the heavy stuff later.

The butler greeted them and took their coats before they made it to the main hallway, where rooms fanned in every direction. Cocktail tables with deep blue linens were strategically set throughout the main level, where guests could linger. Moments after the butler had left them, Edna greeted them.

"Welcome!" Edna rushed toward them with cheeks flushed and dressed to the nines. Her diamond earrings reflected the light, almost blinding Kinsley. They must've cost an absolute fortune. While Kyle greeted their neighbor, Kinsley scanned the room and was surprised to find the home wasn't already filled with people, as she thought they had been running late. Harborside citizens were spilling in behind them, however, and the chatter in the room was quickly rising above the harpist who was playing beautifully in the corner.

"Please, head over to the bar area and help yourselves to a cocktail. I'll be back in a moment." Edna rushed past them to welcome the mayor of Harborside and his wife, who clung to his side after removing her coat and handing it to the butler.

"Don't mind if I do. I'd love a glass of champagne!" Becca said, taking the lead and heading over to where a bartender was bent at the waist, reaching for something behind a makeshift bar—a long table covered in a rich linen tablecloth with tall bottles lining the edges.

When they arrived, Kinsley was shocked to see it was Raven standing behind the table, wearing a sleek black sequined dress. She'd never seen her in something other than a Blue Lobstah T-shirt and faded blue jeans. Raven looked stunning with her dark hair hanging silkily down her back. "*Raven?*" Kinsley asked.

"Oh, hey, guys," she said with a growing smile.

"What are you doing here?" Becca asked jokingly. "Did you give Pete your two weeks' notice or something?"

"Nah." Raven chuckled. "Edna called the Blue Lobstah at the last minute and strong-armed Pete into letting me go for the night. She said the bartender she'd hired caught the stomach flu and asked if I wouldn't mind stepping in. Pete and the rest of the staff are covering for me over at the Blue Lobstah, so we thought we'd help Edna out. She sends a ton of customers Pete's way, so I guess he had to do her a solid."

"Oh, how kind of you, Raven," Kinsley said.

"That's nice of you to help Edna out at the last minute," Becca chimed in with a smile. "Can I get a glass of champagne?"

"You bet." Raven reached for a bottle and poured Becca a glass. "Anyone else?" she asked, holding the bottle in wait.

"Sure, I'll take one," Kinsley said.

"Me, too," Kyle added.

"Raven, have you met my brother, Kyle?" Kinsley asked. "I don't think I've introduced you yet, have I?"

Kyle answered for them. "I don't believe we've met," he said, extending a hand to the bartender. "I can't imagine I'd forget a face as pretty as yours."

Raven blushed and then lifted a hand for Kyle to shake. "Nice to meet ya. I've only heard great things," she said with a grin and a nod. "And I'd be remiss if I didn't thank you for your service," she added with a nod to his uniform, and then handed Kinsley and her brother a glass of champagne. "Might I suggest a toast in your honor?"

"To Kyle!" Kinsley said proudly. The three lifted their glasses in cheers and tipped them toward Kyle, before taking a sip.

"Thank you." Kyle grinned and sent a wink Raven's way.

"I'll be back to chat in a bit," Kinsley said to Raven when

her brother and Becca moved deeper into the room to mingle with other guests.

"Yeah," she whispered conspiratorially. "'Cause I've already learned some interesting things while pouring drinks. The gossip is flying tonight and there's something I think you're gonna want to hear."

Chapter 24

Kinsley was about to pump Raven further when she heard familiar laughter coming from the doorway and was surprised to see Jenna moving in her direction. She had no other choice than to return to the conversation later.

"Hold that thought, Raven. I'll be back," she said before abandoning her glass of champagne at the edge of the table and moving with open arms toward Jenna for a warm embrace.

"Yup, I'll be here," she heard Raven say over her shoulder.

"Oh my goodness, I wasn't expecting to see you here tonight," Kinsley gushed.

Jenna, who often seemed to have boundless energy, looked completely exhausted. The light in her eyes seemed dim and her long gray hair lay limp down her back, instead of swept up in her usual bun.

"How are you both holding up? How's Toby?"

"Toby's hanging in there. He's resting finally. The doctors

wouldn't let him sleep because of the concussion so he's been awfully tired. I left him briefly so he could catch up on some much-needed sleep. He said I was hovering too much and he couldn't close his eyes." Jenna laughed.

"And you?" Kinsley held her arms out to her friend and embraced her again. Then, after studying Jenna further, she added, "Looks like you could use a few winks of your own. I hope you're taking care of yourself."

Jenna shrugged. "I'll catch up, not to worry," she answered with a stifled yawn.

"Aunt Tilly took some homemade chicken soup out of the freezer and asked me to drop it off to you. I was heading there after the party. There's enough soup there to last you an entire week!" Kinsley laughed. "You know, my aunt doesn't do anything halfway. I'm sure she's baking biscuits as we speak to go along with it."

"Your aunt is an absolute doll, that's so sweet of her. If you want, I can go over and grab it instead. It will give me a chance to thank her. Besides, I'm not planning on staying long at the party, I just felt I should stop in for Edna's sake. She does so much business with us and sends so many people our way, I had to make an appearance. I didn't want to send any unnecessary alarm bells on Toby's recovery, either. If I didn't show, the whole town would think the worst." She leaned in closer and whispered, "And we're trying to keep the attack private, and just sharing that Toby had an accident. This was per Rachel's request, because if the town knows this has something to do with the murder investigation it might push the suspect further into hiding. She's keeping all intel close to her chest."

"Ah, I see."

Jenna patted Kinsley lightly on the hand. "You stay and

enjoy yourself. Toby really needs the rest, but I'm sure he'd love to see you in a few days when he's feeling better."

"Are you sure?"

"Positive," Jenna encouraged with a nod. "I promise I'll let you know the second he's up for visitors."

Becca and Kyle came over and asked about Toby again. After Jenna had brought them both up to speed she said, "Okay, I'm going to make the rounds and then get going. But I will pass on your well wishes to my husband. I know he appreciates it," she said tenderly.

Kinsley reached to squeeze Jenna's hand one last time before she left them. "You take care."

"Thank you, Bumpkins. We'll be just fine, not to worry, my sweet," Jenna said before finally disappearing in the crowd.

"Oh. Wow," Kyle said with a grin. "I forgot about the nickname the McNeils gave you back in the day," he taunted with a hip bump and a chuckle. "That sure brings me back."

"Yeah, well, don't get any ideas. I only allow Toby and Jenna to call me that," Kinsley cajoled. "It's a little embarrassing at my age, but I don't want to hurt their feelings."

"It's very endearing."

Becca downed the remainder of her champagne and turned to Kinsley. "Where's your glass?"

"Oh, thanks for reminding me, I left it by Raven, and she mentioned she had something to tell me. We should head back over there."

"I'm ready for another, let's go," Becca said, leading the way through the crowd.

"Not working today? No houses to show?" Kinsley asked as they made their way back to the makeshift bar. She was surprised Becca was drinking so early in the afternoon when the potential to show a house might present itself.

"Nope. Nada. My business is freezing up colder than a Maine winter," she said lightly. Kinsley guessed the afternoon champagne was helping with her friend's laissez-faire attitude.

Before they made it back to the bar, they were stopped by Cari Day. "Hey, you two! Good to see you. Happy holidays!"

"Hey, Cari!" Kinsley greeted with a smile. "How've you been?"

Kyle had briefly stepped away from them and begun a side conversation with Edna's grandson, Luke.

"Doing just fine. May I just say, this place looks stunning!" Cari's gaze traveled the room and then back again. "And the kissing balls! I noticed a few of them made their way here, too. I know I played such a small part, but I'm tickled to see my stamp on the decor. How fun!" she said, grinning.

"Isn't it?" Becca agreed with a nod and a scan of the room. "Working on all of this has lifted my holiday spirits this year, for sure."

"Me, too! I already shared with Kinsley it will be a yearly tradition to volunteer on the kissing ball committee, if that's still okay?" Cari asked eagerly, turning her attention back to Kinsley. "I really enjoyed crafting those."

"Yup, I'd be honored to have you help, anytime," Kinsley said warmly. "By the way, how's Shadow doing? Did his visit with the vet go well?" She hoped in bringing it up, maybe she could convince the dog owner to talk about what had happened at the common council meeting, to hear her perspective on the way things panned out.

Cari's eyes lit anew. "Thank you for asking! Shadow is healing wonderfully. And you'll never believe it—Mallory paid the vet bill and all the expenses that were incurred. She confided in me that she had a hidden bank account that Chris was unaware of and knowing his life insurance was on its way, she didn't mind dipping into her private savings." She lowered her voice to a whisper and continued, "Mallory didn't admit it, but I'm wondering if she was planning on leaving him for good and that's why she had a secret bank account. Did you know she already rehoused Vixen to a farmer friend, north of here? Then yesterday I met her out in the driveway and she was loading up all Chris's belongings for a trip to Goodwill. Seems to me, all evidence of the man's life is being removed bit by bit. Anyhoo, I can't believe she thought to pay the vet bill, with everything she has going on in her life right now." She held her hand to her heart before adding, "She really is a kind soul. Not like her late husband," Cari uttered under her breath.

"That's good to hear. Vet bills can be astronomical," Becca said, deflecting from Cari's negative rant. "I know when my Button got sick and I had to put her down, it was the hardest thing in my life! Good to hear your dog is on the mend."

Kinsley remembered when Becca's cat Button had died. It was nonstop crying for an entire week and Becca was barely consolable. Kinsley had encouraged her friend to consider adopting another kitten, but Becca just wasn't ready yet, and she could understand that.

"Yeah," Cari continued. "It's such a relief to not have to worry myself over money concerns this close to the holidays. I'm telling you, it's a blessing. I have so many family members to buy for on my Christmas list."

"I hear you. I'm glad she decided to pay, too, considering how stuff went down with Chris. I heard things got a little heated." Kinsley knew bringing this up was a long shot, but she wanted to gauge the woman's reaction.

"Did Mallory tell you that?" Cari asked.

"I honestly can't remember. I just heard that things got escalated at the meeting, is all," Kinsley prompted.

"Oh, you're referring to *that* meeting. I think Chris was embarrassed that I called him to the carpet in front of his peers. He never would've had grounds to file a restraining order. He was just throwing his weight around so he wouldn't look bad in front of the other council members. Well, either way, it doesn't really matter anymore. Gosh, I need a drink, I'm parched," Cari said, fanning herself with her hand.

"We were just headed for a cocktail; would you like to join us?" Kinsley asked.

"I most certainly would," Cari said. "It's rather warm in here," she added, plucking at her thick sweater. Kinsley thought a warm sweater was probably the wrong clothing choice for a room full of people and was glad she herself had chosen to wear a blouse instead.

The three navigated thorough the crowd and stood in line at the bar. It seemed Raven had her hands full, as drinks were now flowing readily.

When it was finally their turn, Raven asked, "What can I get for you gals?"

Kinsley noticed her champagne was exactly where she'd left it, at the edge of the bar, and moved to retrieve it. She held up the glass, showing that she was good for now, and waited while the others were served.

Becca gestured a hand to Cari. "You go ahead."

Cari turned to Raven and said, "I'll take a dirty martini on the rocks. You got any Grey Goose?"

Chapter 25

The sound of "Grey Goose" hitting her ears jolted Kinsley back to the investigation. Only because a bottle of Grey Goose happened to be the murder weapon that had been used on Chris Chesterfield's head the night of the boat parade. Since Cari seemed to spew some negative musings about the alderman, the drink selection was mildly interesting, to say the least. Because, to Kinsley's knowledge, that pertinent information hadn't been shared with the public, and most believed the alderman was only pushed into the sea. *Did that mean something?* Or was she overthinking, per usual? In any event, she found it a little difficult to concentrate on the party now.

After sharing a raised brow with Becca, Kinsley forced a smile and ushered the three of them away from the crowd that was forming in front of the bar. At this point, she wasn't ready to let Cari leave the conversation and lose an opportunity to ask her a few more pointed questions. But if she brought up the scarf, or whether she had won one from Toby's Taffy a few years back, and Cari *had* been involved, she might blow the case. Not to mention, thus far, the scarf was one of their strongest clues, so she remained mute.

"So . . ." Becca stuttered. "Any big plans for the holidays, Cari?"

"I'm hosting the third annual Christmas party for dogs at the humane society. That's something I look forward to every year. Partygoers bring their pets in costume, and there's a gift exchange. We sure have a lot of fun!"

"That sounds very fun," Kinsley said.

"It really is my favorite event over the holidays. The dogs always look so cute. This year, I've hired a photographer so that we can give participants the gift of a photo with their dog before they leave the party. I think it'll be a nice surprise. I've had this idea on my bucket list for quite a while now."

"People will love that," Becca agreed with a nod.

"Do either of you have a dog?" Cari asked.

"I've wanted a dog my entire life," Kinsley admitted. Growing up at the Salty Breeze Inn with her aunt Tilly meant it wasn't really an option, though. She didn't want to burden her aunt with any more responsibility when she was kind enough to take her and her brother in. "Now that I live in the caretaker's cottage, I wonder if I should reconsider?" Kinsley uttered more to herself than the group.

"Oh, look! There's Jackie!" Cari said, pointing toward the front door.

The three turned to see Jackie and her husband entering the room and removing their coats. And not far behind them were Mallory and Cole. It seemed as though Cole and Tim were laughing it up over something funny. Kinsley thought it notable that Cole was buddying up to the man who had an altercation with his brother at the Blue Lobstah the night he was killed. Another interesting tidbit indeed.

"I'm kind of shocked they're here, though. Isn't it sorta soon to be out celebrating? A little in bad taste for them to show up here at the party—or no? I mean, seriously, the man just died," Cari stated matter-of-factly, and then hiccupped. "Did you hear?" Cari ushered them closer. "Mallory is postponing Chris's celebration of life until after the holidays. She had him cremated," she whispered. It seemed as if the martini was going straight to her head and her loosening lips only added to the proof of it.

"No, I hadn't heard that," Kinsley said, and then turned to Becca. "You?"

Becca shook her head. "No, I didn't hear that, either."

Kinsley didn't know what to think. There was a lot coming at her. Seriously, maybe Cari shouldn't be the one pointing fingers. As the saying goes, sometimes the one to point a finger has three pointing back at themselves.

"Well, do you?" Cari pushed. "Think it's in bad taste, or what?"

Kinsley responded with a slight shrug, and it seemed irrelevant to Cari anyway, as she continued with her ramblings. "I can understand why it didn't take Mallory long to hook up with his brother, though. Out of the two of them, Cole was always the nicer man and better-looking. Honestly, someone in this town did those two a favor. They can finally be together." She downed the rest of the vodka left in her martini glass and looked briefly at the emptiness with a frown. "You know, Chris really embarrassed me at that common council meeting," she continued. "He was mad that I was the one who complained openly in front of his peers about what he willingly let his dog do to mine! And he refused to own up to his negligence and pay my Shadow's medical bills. Then he throws me out of the meeting for being disorderly? And threatens me with a restraining order? I mean, come on!" She hiccupped again. "Who's really to blame here?"

Kinsley looked to Becca, whose gaze turned to the floor as if embarrassed by the venom that had just spewed once again from Cari's lips. It seemed she kept repeating herself for validation from them, but Kinsley wasn't willing to give it.

Jackie caught Cari's attention and waved to her from across the room. "Hey, you two enjoy the party, I'll be seeing ya," Cari said, and abruptly walked away.

Becca let out a hushed whistle. "Well, now. What do you make of that?"

"I really don't know," Kinsley countered. "I find it interesting, though, that Jackie seems to be pulling Cari away from us. Perhaps she's afraid I would share with her what Jackie told me in the parking lot. That she was quite literally throwing Cari under the bus regarding the restraining order issue."

"You know what they say?" Becca lowered her voice to a whisper. "Keep your friends close and your enemies closer." She chuckled. "It seems the suspects are swirling tonight."

"Either way, you and I seemed to get the same impression from her. Cari *clearly* didn't like the guy. But you're right, I don't even know who to consider as the number one murder suspect at this point," Kinsley replied before noticing her brother was dodging guests and heading in their direction.

"I agree . . . Cari's dislike for Chris came out pretty clear."

"Having fun?" Kyle asked when he finally reached their side.

"Oh boy, are we." Becca giggled and then took a sip of

champagne. "This is good, by the way; you should've asked Raven to top off your glass, Kins. 'Tis the season," she added with a grin and a raise of her glass.

Maybe that was exactly what Kinsley needed. Her brain was spinning with potential suspects and motives. So much so that everyone in the room seemed to suddenly close in on her and the chatter in the background became a dulled rumble in her head. "Actually . . . would you mind holding this?" she said, handing her champagne to Becca. "I'll be right back."

Before her brother or Becca could stop her or follow, Kinsley hurried through the crowd and didn't stop moving until she landed outside in the stark cold night.

The brisk air filled her lungs, making her feel instantly better. Snowflakes were falling gently from the darkened sky, and she looked up to take it in reverently. Kinsley closed her eyes and evened her breath to calm the panic she had felt suddenly arise in her chest. The reality of Toby's attack and potentially losing someone she loved dearly and trying to decipher motives of people she cared for and admired, who had crafted kissing balls literally around her aunt's dining table a week prior, sent her reeling. She heard footsteps behind her and a familiar voice spoke.

"Hey, girlie girl! What are you doing out here in the cold, alone? Far as I know, you don't smoke, do you?"

Kinsley's eyes popped open at the sound of Pete's voice.

He was watching her closely.

"No, I don't smoke." Kinsley chuckled.

"Weed?" Pete leaned in closer and took a sniff of her blouse.

Kinsley slapped him on the arm. "Ha! You idiot! I don't smoke that, either!" she said, laughing.

Pete shrugged. "Hey, no judgment if you did."

"Honestly? You wanna know a secret?" Kinsley looked around, but they remained alone, standing outside in the bitter cold. It was so cold in fact that when they spoke, steam came from their breath. "I've never tried either—not even a puff. And that's the truth. If either would settle me down a bit, maybe I ought to try, though," Kinsley poked. "I'm kidding!"

Pete grinned wide. "Well, I was just wondering why you're standing out here in subzero temperatures in nothing but a thin top. Sidebar, I gotta tell you that your perfume is intoxicating." He fanned his hand in front of his face dramatically as if either the perfume scent was too heavy or it was a complete turn-on. With Pete, it was hard to determine.

Kinsley couldn't help but crack a smile and shake her head with a chuckle. She didn't need a smoke; she just needed her friend Pete and his light mood to lift her spirits. The earlier anxiety building from the investigation into Chris's death and the thought that someone from the town of Harborside was surely responsible began to melt like snow on a sunny afternoon from his winning smile alone.

"If you're stressing, I guess it's a bad time to tell you something, then," he said tentatively.

The seriousness of his tone sent a different kind of shiver down her spine.

"Oh no. Tell me what?"

"Hey, look!" Pete noticed the kissing ball hanging from the porch and smiled approvingly. "We made those, didn't we? I think I still have the scar to prove it," he added with a laugh, studying his fingers as if searching for the healing wounds.

"You poor thing. How *ever* did you survive all that blood loss." Kinsley was hoping she'd be in the mood to kiss the man if she ever had the opportunity to stand beneath one, but right now, all she felt were goose bumps crawling beneath her red silk blouse. And stress. Lots and lots of stress. She began to shiver and rubbed her arms vigorously to warm up. "So anyway, what's going on? What were you going to tell me?"

"I hate to be the bearer of bad news. Especially since you seem a little out of sorts. Which is kinda unlike you, to be honest. You're usually quite jovial."

"Just spill it."

By the tone of her voice, clearly he knew she meant business, because he didn't try to deflect again.

"The lost and found is no longer, um, how do I say this?" He rubbed his five-o'clock shadow attentively.

"Oh no."

"Yup."

"The scarf with the green paint smear is gone, isn't it?"

"Yup. And everything else I had in that box. The whole darn thing is missing. All of it."

Kinsley was incredulous. "And not *one* of your staff members saw who took it? How is that possible?"

"It's gone."

"The camera?"

"Gone."

"And Rachel knows?"

"Yup, I called her and filled her in. She wasn't exactly happy about the news, either," he answered flatly, placing his hands firmly on his hips.

Kinsley sighed heavily and kneaded her forehead with her fingers. "Well, this night just keeps getting better and better."

"Hopefully they can catch who stole it on remote feed. All might not be lost here. Rachel's looking into it."

"Yeah, hopefully," Kinsley replied, but not knowing how these things work gave little encouragement.

"Sorry." He shrugged. "Figured you'd want to know. Besides, knowing you as I do, you'd be traveling through the nor'easter to see if it was still there. And you'd be wasting your time."

"I appreciate you telling me."

"There's more."

"More?"

"Yeah, the Grey Goose bottle."

"What about it?"

Pete ran his hands nervously through his hair and then cracked his knuckles one by one before answering. "Scotty said the Grey Goose did come from our inventory. He's sure of it because he handled the delivery and did a number count when the bottles came off the truck the day before."

Scotty was a part-time employee whom Pete had recently hired and was working over college winter break. There was no reason for him to lie.

Kinsley needed a minute to think. If the bottle *had* definitively come from the Blue Lobstah, what did that mean exactly? Who had access to it? And where was the broken glass? There was no evidence of it the night of the murder that Kinsley was aware of. Was Cari at the parade that night? She decided to keep these musings close to her chest for fear of upsetting the bar owner further, so instead she was the one to deflect this time.

"What do you make of that?" she asked finally.

"I'm not sure. You?"

"It means someone had access to your liquor or walked behind the bar when no one was looking. The question is, *Who?*"

Pete frowned. "That could be anyone! You know how busy it was that night."

"Yeah, not exactly helpful."

"Anyhow . . . I'm sure Rachel will take that into account when looking at her main suspect."

"Yeah. It probably won't be one piece of evidence that will convict the person. Most likely, it'll be a list of things."

"Exactly."

A lull came between them before the wind blew, causing Kinsley to shiver. "The nor'easter is coming, then?"

"It is." Pete looked to the sky and snow fell on his long eyelashes, causing him to blink.

Kinsley rubbed her arms vigorously and then blew warm breath into her hands. It did little to thaw her, though.

"Seriously, what are you doing out here? You're gonna freeze to death. You should really get back inside." His smile faded and he looked at her intently. "I'm sure everyone is wondering what happened to you."

"I just need another minute."

"Social anxiety?" he asked.

Kinsley shook her head. "No, I'm fine." She folded her arms protectively across her chest and shivered.

"Is this about the alderman?"

"Not entirely, no."

"What is it, then?" He took a step closer and lifted her chin so he could study her. "I can see that something is wrong. Come on, you can tell me."

Kinsley shook him off. She just wanted to sort through her own brain, alone. "I'm just struggling with some personal things. And I guess I'm feeling a bit overwhelmed. I'll be fine."

Kinsley breathed deep and let the air out slowly, as if deflating a balloon.

"Kinsley, I'm your friend. If something's wrong, I wanna help. Talk to me," he said tenderly.

It seemed pretty obvious to Kinsley that Pete wasn't going to let her go without an explanation, so she took another breath of cold Maine air and began ticking the list off on her fingers. "Oh, I dunno. My brother is hiding family secrets from me, which sadly is affecting our reunion. My very good friend Toby was attacked seemingly because of me. Someone in this town, most likely someone we know, is a killer. And it's supposed to be the best time of year. It's certainly not feeling like it. I don't know why I came to this party. I'm just tired of it all, I guess. I'd like to flip the calendar and have it all go away."

Pete's eyes widened in shock. "Toby was attacked?"

"Yeah, keep that information on the down-low, though, will you? He was attacked regarding their Twelve Days of Christmas records, or any proof of winning that stupid scarf. Which feels entirely like my fault since I'm the one who found the scarf and started this trail to the killer to begin with. Maybe you're right, I should've just let the police handle it."

"Oh no."

"Oh yes."

"I'm sorry."

"I'll be okay."

"Anything I can do? I'm only here to drop off a case of wine for Raven, as apparently you people are going through the booze rather quickly at this party," he said, using his thickest Boston accent. "I can walk you home if you'd like. Maybe blowing off this place and sitting in front of the TV or a fireplace with a mug of cocoa and your aunt's Christmas cookies would be a welcome distraction."

"No, thanks. I just need another minute."

"You sure?"

"Uh-huh."

"Okay, then." Pete hesitated before he picked up the case of wine that he had abandoned by the door. Kinsley held the door open for him. "Thanks," he said.

Pete turned one last time before crossing the threshold. "If you want to talk more, you know where to find me."

"I'm a big girl. No worries," Kinsley said, forcing a smile.

"You're a girl who I care about very much and who doesn't need to handle things alone," he said before the door closed softly behind him.

Kinsley took three more methodical deep breaths before re-entering the party.

She was navigating her way through the crowd when Kyle and Becca rushed toward her, their faces riddled with concern.

"Where have you been?" Kyle asked. "We were looking everywhere for you."

"Yeah," Becca chimed in. "I thought you went to the restroom, but you weren't there when I checked. Your brother and I were worried sick. Are you okay?"

Kinsley pasted on her widest smile. "I'm fine . . . I just needed a minute to clear my head."

Luckily, she didn't have to explain further because she found the perfect distraction. Cole and Mallory were engaged in a heated discussion in the corner of the room. Mallory's arms were flailing, and their voices seemed to be quickly rising above the party noise and the harpist. Kinsley watched as Cole took

Mallory by the arm and pulled her farther from earshot. Kinsley discreetly gestured for her brother and Becca to follow her in that direction, so they could eavesdrop on Cole and Mallory's argument.

The harpist finished her set and rose to take a bow. Partygoers began to clap in approval, including Becca. The harpist smiled before Edna commanded the room with, "Attention everyone!" When Edna spoke, the room grew momentarily quiet, allowing Kinsley to overhear the argument between Cole and Mallory clearly for just a moment. She was pretty sure she overheard the red-faced man say, *"I killed my brother for you!"*

Chapter 26

Kinsley was *almost* certain of what she'd overheard but her brain couldn't believe it. Yet when she turned to Becca, whose eyes had grown to the size of sunflowers, and then to her brother, she knew she had heard right.

"You caught what Cole said?" Kinsley whispered. Her heart began to knock in her chest like an overworked jackhammer.

"Yeah," Kyle said. "I'm calling Rachel. I think this is going to trump anything she's got going on right now," he added with a grim expression. "Can I borrow your phone?"

Kinsley plucked her cell phone from her trouser pocket and handed it to her brother, who then made the call.

It seemed that only the three of them had overheard what had been said, though, as the party continued along in full swing, as if nothing were amiss. Cole and Mallory, however, had abandoned the corner of the room and were collecting their coats on their way out. Kinsley wasn't sure she should let them go before the detective's arrival and wondered if she could stall them somehow. But based on the looks on their flushed faces, she wasn't sure she'd be met with a smile, so she held back, not wanting to make a scene.

By the time Rachel had arrived, Cole and Mallory had long since left the party.

The detective was covered in wet snow when they met up with her by the back door, after she texted Kinsley to inform them that she had arrived. "The storm is really gaining speed out there," Rachel confirmed, brushing the snow from her hair. "The weather forecaster is predicting a doozy, and for once I think he might actually be right." She chortled. "No offense, you guys, but I don't think I'm dressed to enter this event." She looked down at her navy blue puff jacket and acid-washed jeans and frowned.

"Honestly, I think I'm ready to head back to the inn before the storm gets worse anyhow," Kinsley said. "I think I've had enough festivities for the night. How about everyone else? I don't want to push anyone to leave if you're not ready."

"Nah, I'm ready to go, too," Becca said. "I'd love a coffee if you're up for it. And I'm quite sure your aunt has a mouth-watering dessert to go with it. The only thing I snagged from here was a handful of shrimp. And the crab rangoon, which was outstanding."

"Yeah, let's all go next door to regroup," Kyle suggested. "We can share what happened when we get back to my aunt's house, if that's okay?" he asked, turning to Rachel for approval. "We probably shouldn't discuss this any further until we get home anyway because I'm not sure it's something you would want to get out to the public, at least not just yet."

Rachel shrugged. "Sounds good to me."

"We walked over. You mind giving me and Kyle a ride? We

can share what we overheard on the ride back. Becca's car is parked in the lot so she can meet us back at the inn. Does that work for everyone?"

Becca agreed with a nod. "Works for me."

"Oh no! I forgot that Raven had something to tell me." Kinsley turned to acknowledge that the bar area was swamped with people. "I guess it will have to wait."

After thanking the host and sharing their good-byes, they gathered their things and then headed out. The snow fell heavily now, as if they lived in untamed Alaska and not southern Maine. The brisk wind felt as though it were slapping Kinsley's face with instant frostbite. She was thankful they were catching a ride and didn't have to take the cliff walk home, which was sure to be coated in ice from the spray off the Atlantic.

When they entered the Salty Breeze Inn and were removing their coats, Kinsley was startled to see Cole Chesterfield standing by the reservation desk and talking with her aunt. She watched Tilly hand Cole a key, and then he quickly took the staircase up to the second floor.

Kinsley rushed over to Tilly, and the others followed. "What's going on?" Kinsley asked.

Alarm swept over Tilly's face when she noted Kinsley's demeanor and the sound of her tone. "What do you mean, 'What's going on'?" she whispered. "I'm tending to my guests! Is there a problem?"

"Cole Chesterfield is a guest?" Kyle asked.

Tilly, clearly not in the know, looked around as if in search of a problem, threw up her hands in frustration, and asked finally, "Yes, why?"

"You mean he's staying here tonight," Kinsley confirmed.

Her aunt was clearly confused by their questioning. "Yes.

He requested a room for tonight. He mentioned something about Mallory not feeling well when they were at Edna's party, and he didn't want to burden his sister-in-law by staying at her house. Why? Did something happen?" Tilly held a hand to her heart expectantly. "Do you think Mallory is okay?"

"Oh boy." Kinsley slapped her hand to her forehead.

"It's okay, Kins," Rachel soothed, sidestepping her. "Now I don't have to search all over town in the middle of a snowstorm looking for Cole. This is actually good; it'll give me a chance to go and question him."

Tilly's brows furrowed as she redirected her attention to the detective. "Question him about what? Are you saying Mallory isn't sick? Will someone please explain to me what's going on here?"

Rachel started toward the stairs. "Not to worry, Tilly, Mallory is fine. I just need to talk with Cole and clear up a few things. Which room is he in?"

"He's staying in Schooner II. When you reach the top of the stairs, it is the third one on the right," Tilly replied before Rachel made the final step and disappeared around the corner of the second floor.

Kinsley wrapped her arm protectively around her aunt. "Nothing too alarming. But come with us, I think we need to go and have a chat."

"What in the world is going on?" Tilly asked. "This can't be about Chris's murder. Rachel doesn't think the alderman's brother is a viable suspect. Does she? I had the impression that he'd been cleared, otherwise they'd have him in custody already, wouldn't they?"

"Let's go and take a load off over by the fireplace, where it's warm. Kinsley's right, there're a few things we should talk about," Kyle said, eyeing his sister before saying, "It might be a long night, Aunt Tilly." He then led them in the direction of the expansive living room with a wave of his hand.

"On second thought, the roads are getting really slick out there. Do you mind if I head out and you all can fill me in tomorrow?" Becca asked, gesturing a thumb toward the exit. "I should probably go."

"Sure, if you think you're okay to drive. Are you?" Kinsley asked, studying her.

"Uh-huh, sober as a judge." Becca held her hand up as if swearing on a Bible. "But if I wait much longer, the roads might get too bad. So, I'm just gonna get a move on."

"I thought you wanted to stay and have a coffee and some of Aunt Tilly's treats?" Kinsley reminded.

"Another time," Becca said with a smile. "We still have plenty of holiday time to come."

The two shared an embrace before they parted ways.

Tilly passed Kinsley on the way to the living room and said in her wake, "Becca had a good thought in mind. I'm going to run to the kitchen to fetch us some cocoa and snacks before we talk. I'll meet you and Kyle in the living room in just a minute."

"Do you need a hand?" Kinsley asked.

"No, sweetheart, you just go and warm up by the fire, I'll be there in a jiffy," Tilly answered before disappearing into the kitchen.

Before long, Aunt Tilly was stepping into the living room with a tray filled with mugs of cocoa topped with whipped cream and a plate full of Christmas cookies. And not far behind her was Becca, caked in snow, with a worried expression on her face.

"What's wrong?" Kinsley asked, rushing over to her best

friend, who was now removing her wet coat and setting it by the fireplace.

"There's no way I'm getting out of here tonight. The plow just came by and blocked me in. I couldn't even get my Acura out of the parking lot if I wanted to. You mind if I crash with you?"

"Oh dear," Tilly gushed after setting down the tray and rushing to Becca's side. "I'm so sorry, but we're fully booked. There's literally no room at the inn."

They all erupted in laughter.

"What's so funny?" Tilly said with a smile.

"I think they're laughing at your biblical reference," Kyle said with a chuckle, which caused Tilly to throw her head back in merriment, and they all joined in laughter once again.

"No worries, we can share a room, just like when we were kids. You still have a blow-up mattress in the attic, right, Aunt Tilly?" Kinsley looked to her aunt for confirmation.

Concern riddled Tilly's face. "A blow-up mattress? That won't be comfortable for Becca! No, that will never do."

Kinsley knew Tilly's guests' comfort were of the utmost concern. "It's fine, Becca can have the bed, I'll take the mattress. It'll be like camping, and we'll have fun with it. Not to worry." She patted her aunt's arm to reassure her.

Becca chimed in. "Yeah, Tilly. She's right, it'll be fun, just like we're kids again."

Just then the lights flickered, and the room fell completely dark. Including all the lighted garland that was electronically powered and wound its way up the staircase handrail and festively surrounded the doorframes of each room. The Christmas tree, which had been lighting the room with a festive glow, was now eerily dark as well.

"Just when I thought this night couldn't get any more complicated." Kinsley sighed.

A look of relief swept across Becca's face. "Honestly, for me, it's good. Looks like I made the right decision to stay over. If the inn is out of power, it probably means half of Harborside is, too. The last thing I want to do is spend the night alone in my apartment in the dark." She reached for Kinsley's hand and gave it a comforting squeeze. "Thank you for sharing your room with me."

Kinsley leaned into her friend's ear so only she could hear. "Yeah, sure. If you're comfortable spending the night in an inn that is quite possibly housing a murderer. Sounds to me like either one is a losing proposition."

Chapter 27

The loss of power at the Salty Breeze Inn wasn't the only thing that was dark. The thoughts coursing through Kinsley's mind were going dark, too. She wondered what Rachel hoped to gain with her conversation with Cole. A *confession*? Was the detective thinking he'd allow her to administer a lie detector test back at the police station? Or was this entire thing going to be chalked up to hearsay? The not knowing was quite literally driving her crazy.

Tilly had left the room and was trying to calm the guests who had frantically gathered at the base of the staircase to let them know she was doing everything she could to restore power. But, unless she was a magician, there was not much she could do. The nor'easter, due to hit Maine full-on, would outsmart anything the power company could handle. Kinsley decided the best course of action was to be of service to her aunt instead of just sitting around worrying.

She turned to her brother. "We should probably help Aunt Tilly hand out candles or flashlights to guests, shouldn't we? Maybe we could convince everyone to remain in their rooms until the power is restored," Kinsley suggested, and then lowered her tone. "Otherwise, aren't we putting her guests in danger by housing a potential murderer? Like, right *above us*," she mouthed as she pointed a finger to the ceiling. "I mean, it's hard to forget the words we heard come out of Cole Chesterfield's mouth. For everyone's sake, I hope I just have an overactive imagination."

"Yeah, that's a good call, a little light won't hurt. Besides, I can't sit here and do nothing," Kyle said, rising from the fireplace hearth. "I'll go look in the closet. She keeps flashlights on the top shelf, right?" he asked as he moved swiftly across the room, not waiting for an answer.

"Yeah. You go and have a look there, and Becca and I will see if there are any battery-operated candles left over from our Christmas decorations that we can use," she replied before her brother stepped over the threshold.

Becca rose from her seat to follow. "Whatever you want me to do, Kins. I'm happy to help. Just point me in a direction."

Kinsley beckoned her friend to follow, and she and Becca moved to another closet where they'd abandoned a Rubbermaid bin full of leftover decorations that they hadn't used at the inn. Kinsley recalled that she had a set of gold battery-lighted candles that hadn't fit this season's decor, as gold wasn't part of the theme. She filled each of the candles with batteries and then gathered as many as she could into her arms and handed the rest of them off to Becca before searching for more.

The two then went and met with Tilly and the guests who had remained at the bottom of the staircase. Her brother had already begun handing out what few flashlights he had found. Which didn't appear to be many, as Kyle had emptied his hands rather quickly.

"Here you go," Kinsley said, handing off a candle to an older woman who looked somewhat distraught. "It's okay, ma'am, the power will be back on before you know it," she soothed. "We're encouraging guests to remain in their rooms until that happens."

"We are?" Tilly asked, turning to her.

"Yes, we certainly wouldn't want anyone to get hurt walking around aimlessly because they can't see."

"But there're battery-operated lighted candles throughout the inn, due to your beautiful holiday decorating," Tilly argued. "That should help guests find their way. They don't have to stay in their rooms if they don't want to."

"We're going to lose heat. Wouldn't it be best for guests to remain in their rooms, where they can at least stay warm beneath the blankets?" Kinsley pressed.

Tilly laid a hand on her flushed cheek; her face riddled with worry. "I suppose . . ."

"Will you please just trust me, Aunt Tilly?" Kinsley said firmly. She couldn't help but fear for the detective's safety in the darkness, even though it was unlikely Cole would attack her. It would most likely remain a civil conversation.

Her aunt responded with a confused expression, which Kinsley decided she would have to deal with later—*away* from guests' ears. Due to the loss of power and coping with that, her aunt still hadn't heard why Cole being a guest at the inn was, in Kinsley's eyes, a bit of a "problem."

Becca had just handed off the last of her candles when she piped in, "Good call, Tilly. I'll go grab some of those candles for those that don't have a light yet," she said before disappearing down the darkened hallway.

Before long, all the guests had been taken care of and only Kinsley, Becca, Kyle, and Tilly had returned to the living room and were keeping warm by the wood fireplace. The orange flames crackled and gave off a warm glow, adding the only comfort to the room. Rachel had not yet returned. They had explained to Tilly their concerns, but it did little to help the unease. If anything, it only added to it. Kinsley wondered if Cole had done something to the detective, too, because it seemed as if she had been gone an awfully long time.

"Aunt Tilly?" Kinsley asked.

"Yes, my love?" Tilly said, turning to her and laying a comforting hand on her knee.

"What do you know about our parents' accident that you haven't already told us?"

"You're bringing that up now?" Kyle huffed from across the room. "Unbelievable timing."

Tilly's gaze traveled between the siblings before she asked, "What's this about?"

"Kyle is looking into the accident and says the records are sealed, like you had told us, but he also discovered that our father had a top-secret security clearance. You know anything about that?" Kinsley focused on her aunt, hoping to see a baffled expression.

Unfortunately, Tilly's glance fell to the floor, and she pursed her lips. Had her aunt been keeping secrets from them all these years? That was something she really didn't want to be faced with. Especially *now*, over the holidays. The last thing she wanted was to create family drama, but she wanted answers.

"If you know something, you need to tell us. You owe us

that much!" Kinsley stated with more fervor than she'd meant, as she slammed a closed fist to her leg.

"*Owe you?* Child, I raised you! Isn't that enough?" Tilly said, her voice rising in defense.

Just then, Rachel, with a rigid spine and blank expression, entered the room. All eyes flew to the detective expectantly.

"Well?" Kinsley asked finally when Rachel took a seat next to Kyle on the stone hearth. Her brother reached for a nearby folded throw blanket and encouraged her to sit on that, instead of the hard rock.

"Cole claims you heard him wrong," Rachel said, leaning forward and resting her weight on her knees and then clasping her hands in front of her as if rethinking everything that had transpired.

"How could that be when we all heard the same thing? That doesn't even make sense," Kinsley defended. "He doesn't know it was us three that brought this to your attention, does he?"

"He inferred that he had a pretty good idea of who had told me, based on your proximity to them when this all happened." Rachel paused and took a deep breath before continuing. "Were you the only people around Cole and Mallory at the time this was spoken? Is there a chance anyone else overheard what he'd said?"

"No, I don't think anyone else heard it," Kyle said. "Cole and Mallory were kinda tucked into the corner on their own."

"This is just ridiculous," Kinsley grumbled, causing the detective to shrug defensively.

"Well, what did Cole say to explain what we heard?" Becca asked. "I mean, we heard what we heard! Right?" She turned to them for confirmation, and Kinsley and Kyle nodded vigorously in agreement.

"He claims he said, and I quote: '*People think* I killed my brother for you.'"

Kinsley sat back into the sofa and let the cushions consume her. "Is that possible? That we missed that?" She looked to her brother and Becca for answers.

"I mean, I suppose it's *possible*, because the harpist was still playing, and it wasn't until after Edna was commanding the room for a speech that we heard him at all," Kyle said. "Perhaps Cole did say, 'people think,' and we just didn't hear that part." He frowned.

Becca sighed deep. "Your brother's right. It's not out of the realm of possibility."

"So, you believe Cole?" Kinsley asked Rachel pointedly. "That's it, then?"

Rachel picked at her fingers absently and said, "What choice do I have? It's not exactly evidence."

Kinsley stood from her seat and began to pace. "I don't know! But we can't just let him stay here, under this roof . . . with the mere possibility . . . I mean . . . what if . . ." Her voice trailed off as she looked at the others in the room. "What if he knows we're the ones who alerted you to question him? We might've upset him by calling the police and pointing fingers."

"If Cole's the perpetrator in this crime, we need proof, Kinsley. Not hearsay," Rachel stated firmly. "There's not much I can do at this point. It's not like I can arrest him based on what you *think* you overheard."

Kyle asked tentatively, "I mean, we're all safe if he spends the night, right? Like Kinsley suggested, we didn't anger him enough for paybacks. Did we?"

"I can't kick a man out into a snowstorm if Rachel doesn't have the evidence she needs for an arrest," Tilly said, gesturing toward the detective. "We'll just have to let him stay the night and review all of this in the morning. Hopefully by then Rachel can gather whatever evidence she needs to clear up this matter. I'm sure everything will work out just fine," she added decisively.

"Tilly's right," Rachel stated matter-of-factly. "And to be honest, the evidence that the department has gathered thus far is taking us in a different direction. So, there's that, too."

"And what direction is that?" Kinsley asked.

"I can't share that with you, yet. I promise you, I will in time."

The detective stopped talking after that.

And that was exactly what Kinsley feared. A potential murderer was literally housed right upstairs . . . above them . . . inside of her aunt's inn—with no electricity. Wasn't that just jim-dandy. Because, in her mind, Rachel had it all wrong. After all, they clearly heard what Chris had said at Edna's party, and the man had a history with Mallory. A strong history. And from what Kinsley had seen with her own two eyes, that relationship could easily be rekindled. It wouldn't be out of the realm of possibility for Cole to kill his brother. Not when there was so much for him to gain.

Chapter 28

Kinsley was so worked up over what had transpired in the last twenty-four hours that she rolled over for the umpteenth time on the air mattress, causing it to groan.

"You okay over there?" Becca asked sleepily.

Kinsley didn't answer. Instead, she punched the pillow and tried to readjust, causing the blow-up mattress to make even more noise than she'd intended. "Sorry," she said finally. "I'm not trying to keep you awake. I'll be more quiet."

"You're fine."

A few moments went by before Kinsley was moving restlessly once again.

"Hey, since it seems neither of us can sleep, should we talk about the case?" Becca suggested. "Perhaps rehashing everything will help clear our minds and we can finally get some shut-eye."

"You, too, eh?"

"Uh-huh. For some odd reason, my brain doesn't want to let

it go tonight. I wonder why." Becca chuckled. "Might it have something to do with a certain guest down the hallway?"

Kinsley flipped onto her back and folded her hands across her stomach and looked to the darkened ceiling. "Right? So what's on your mind?"

"With all the chaos since arriving at the inn, I forgot to tell you something. And it didn't really occur to me that it was important, until now."

"What's that?"

"When we were at Edna's party and I went looking for you during your disappearing act, I ran into Jackie by the bathroom door, and she point-blank asked me about the attack on Toby and wondered if I knew what was stolen. Does the public even know about the break-in? Or were the police keeping that information on the down-low? It bothers me that she knew about it. I mean, how could she know about that already?"

"I was probably the one who blew it when I spoke to Jackie in the parking lot the day we volunteered. She seemed hesitant when I brought up her scarf, but since she was wearing one, in my mind it cleared her because she wouldn't have won *two* of them. But it's something to ask Rachel about next time we see her. I know the authorities were downplaying it and calling it an accident rather than an attack, so it makes sense that they wouldn't tell anyone about the stolen pictures."

"My thoughts exactly."

"Maybe Jackie just happened to be shopping downtown and passed the closed taffy shop and inquired why they were closed in the middle of a workweek? Jenna could've unknowingly tipped her off."

"Yeah, that could be."

"What else have you been thinking?" Kinsley asked.

"That's the main thing that's been bothering me. You?"

"I've been thinking about everything Cari said after all those martinis. She sure was on a rant tonight!"

"There's potential motive there, no doubt," Becca agreed. "The fact that Chris was threatening to slap her with a restraining order sounded like it only escalated the argument between them."

Kinsley tucked herself deeper into the blankets and held them around her chin. "I'm not sure what to think about Cole. Do you believe him, or do you think he was just covering his own butt and is quick-witted enough to come up with that excuse? You think he really said *'People think* I killed my wife for you'? Did we really get that wrong? All *three* of us?"

"Yeah, that's a tough one. I mean, it's a little weird how much Cole and Mallory seem to be getting along, so soon after his brother's death. If anything, Cari's right and, in my opinion, their behavior is in bad taste. I mean, seriously, the guy is barely cold."

"Yeah, I agree. Hey, I forgot to mention that the Grey Goose bottle did come from the Blue Lobstah. I ran into Pete outside of Edna's and he told me."

"I kinda figured. I didn't think someone was walking around the boat parade with a bottle of booze in their hand. I'm pretty sure that's illegal. So . . . the killer had to have access to that Grey Goose bottle," Becca said pensively.

"Yup. I'm not sure that exactly rules anyone out at this point. Do you remember seeing Cari at the parade that night? Her ordering a martini specifically made with Grey Goose vodka tonight, yeah, I'm right back to that again . . . I mean, clearly, she's not the only one to drink Grey Goose, I get that. But coupled with the fact that she had serious issues with Chris over the dog, which, as you mentioned, was getting contentious, there's potential motive there."

"Yeah, I don't recall if Cari was there or not. But her drink of choice just adds one piece to a growing puzzle, doesn't it?"

"Uh-huh."

"Hey, you hungry?" Becca asked. "Things were so chaotic I never did eat that cookie, as promised."

Kinsley chuckled. "I was wondering how long it would take before you'd bring that up."

"Well? Are you hungry? Or is it just me?" This time, Kinsley could hear Becca shuffling around in the bed, as if trying to get comfortable.

"What time is it?" Kinsley asked, leaning up on her elbow.

Becca rolled over and snagged her cell phone from the bedside table. "Three thirty," she said with a yawn.

"Ugh, is that all?" Kinsley covered the pillow with her head, but she could still hear her friend say, "So, I'm guessing a snack is out of the question? You did say we were camping out like we did when we were kids, and if I recall, middle-of-the-night snacks were always part of the equation."

"You're not going to fall back to sleep without something to eat, are you?"

Becca sat up in bed and rubbed her eyes. "Uh-uh. I don't think so."

"Fine." Kinsley tossed the heavy blankets aside and resurrected herself from the depths of the air mattress and then lifted her arms high above her head to stretch her back. "It's freezing in here. I wonder when the power will be restored," she said, rubbing her bare arms, which were erupting in goose bumps. "You stay here under the covers, where it's warm. I'll run to the kitchen and grab us a snack."

"You'd do that for me?" Even though it was still dark, and she couldn't make out anything but a shadowy figure on the bed, Kinsley could hear the smile in her friend's tone.

"You know it," she said, rolling on a pair of thick socks and reaching for her fluffy bathrobe. "Is it just cookies you want, then? Or something else?"

"I could go for a nugget of cheese if there's any. Maybe some crackers . . . or if you can find them, some of those sugary nuts your aunt usually makes around the holidays," Becca suggested. "Whatever you find is fine with me, though."

"You bet. I'll be right back," Kinsley said, leaving the room and closing the door softly behind her. The hallway was pitch-black, and she had to adjust her vision before taking a step forward. After blinking her eyes a few times and catching her bearings, she continued down the staircase toward the kitchen.

When Kinsley reached the door leading to the kitchen, a rattling sound from the inside caught her attention. She pressed her back against the wall momentarily and held her breath. *I'm being ridiculous, why am I'm acting so paranoid?* she told herself before straightening her back, shaking off her fears, and putting her hand on the doorknob. As she slowly turned the knob, the lights flickered briefly above her head, catching her off guard. But then disappointment came when the inn returned to darkness. The power had not been restored. She opened the door and looked up to see Cole Chesterfield's face, lit by the moonlight streaming in from the window. He was holding a butcher knife, and when he caught sight of her, an unnerving expression washed across his face.

Chapter 29

K insley let out a bloodcurdling screech.

This only made Cole throw his head back in laugher. "Sorry! Did I scare you?" he asked, holding the knife up and turning it in the moonlight, causing an alarming glare.

"Please. Put. The. Knife. Down," Kinsley said with as much calm as she could muster. She held up a hand in defense and took one calculated step backward, out of the room.

"You're not seriously afraid of me, are you?" Cole set the knife on the countertop and held her gaze. "Look, I set it down. See?" He then lifted his hands high above his head as if he were being arrested by the Harborside Police Department. He pointed again to the knife. "Not to worry, you're safe."

"What are you doing in the kitchen in the middle of the night?" Kinsley asked pointedly.

"I'm just making a sandwich. Is that a crime?"

"I'm not sure. Did my aunt say you could use the kitchen?"

"Well, no . . ." Cole dropped his arms limply to his sides. "I didn't steal any food or anything, if that's what you're asking. I was just borrowing a knife," he explained. "The sliced turkey and cheese are from my own cooler from when I stopped in at the grocery store earlier today. Is that a problem?"

"I mean . . ." Kinsley trailed off.

"Look," Cole interrupted. "I know it was you who told that officer what you *think* you overheard at Edna's party. And I'm telling you—you got it all wrong." His lips pressed together in a grim line.

His sudden admission caused the heat to rise in Kinsley's cheeks. She hoped the lack of electricity within the room kept her red face hidden. She didn't want to give the man the satisfaction. "What makes you say that?" she defended.

"You and your little friends were the only ones within earshot," he said, taking a bite of his sandwich casually, as if they, too, were now friends. Which, clearly, they were not.

Kinsley didn't know what to say and remained mute. She was quite surprised he actually had the nerve to go there.

"I'm tired of defending myself to this town," he continued between chews. "Mallory and I have a history and I'm not going to let her go this time. Just because I'm friendly with my sister-in-law doesn't make me a killer. It's not my fault my brother died. He just ticked off the wrong person, I guess. It wouldn't be the first time he upset someone enough to want him dead."

Suddenly, Tilly rushed into the room, all flustered and confused with her hair stuck to one side of her head. "I heard a scream! Is everything all right in here?"

"One of your guests decided to help himself to the kitchen," Kinsley said flatly as she gestured toward Cole, who remained steadfast and continued eating his sandwich.

Concern riddled Tilly's face. "Oh. Is there something I can get for you?" she asked. "Would you like something to drink with that?"

Kinsley shook her head in dismay. Only her aunt Tilly would be overly gracious and make a potential murder suspect more comfortable in her own kitchen.

"I just needed to borrow a knife to make a sandwich. I'm sorry if I caused a stir," Cole said, gathering his things and leaving the knife and a trail of crumbs on the counter. "I'll take the rest of this back to my room and get out of your hair."

Just then, the lights flickered again but this time the electricity remained on. The illumination was startling, and Kinsley had to rub her eyes to take it in.

"Oh, thank goodness," Tilly said, clasping her hands in delight. "It's freezing in here. Now the heat will finally kick on again," she added, wrapping her bathrobe tighter around her waist and then running her hands through her hair as if suddenly embarrassed by her appearance in front of them.

"You have yourselves a good night," Cole said, rushing from the kitchen before either one could say another word.

"Well, since I'm up I may as well make a fresh batch of blueberry muffins," Tilly said, reaching beneath the counter for a bowl and measuring cups.

"Seriously?" Kinsley said incredulously.

"What?" Tilly defended.

"Nothing." Kinsley chuckled. "I'm grabbing a snack for Becca and heading back up to bed. I'm exhausted."

"Okay, my sweet," Tilly said, tapping her on the cheek before moving to open a nearby cupboard and pulling out the container of sugar.

Kinsley held back a yawn before opening the refrigerator

and removing some precut cheese and fruit and set them on a tray with cookies and nuts while her aunt bustled about the kitchen as if it were suddenly daylight. She couldn't help but wonder what vitamins her aunt was taking because clearly the woman had more energy than a normal person at this hour. This time she let a full yawn consume her.

Kinsley shook her head and blinked the sleep from her eyes before abandoning the kitchen with food in tow and heading upstairs. She quietly stepped into the bedroom and set the tray on the bedside table.

Becca was fast asleep.

Kinsley rolled over on the leaking air mattress and landed on the floor with a thud. She rubbed her eyes and squinted as bright sunlight filled the bedroom, despite the blinds remaining shut. Becca was propped up with pillows in bed, nibbling on a sugar cookie and scrolling through her phone. At the sound of Kinsley's moaning, she looked up from her phone and said, "Well, now. Look who's back from the dead. Good afternoon, sleepyhead."

"*Afternoon?* What time is it?" Kinsley stood up and then bent over at the waist to a downward dog position with hands to the floor at an attempt to get her body back into workable motion.

"It's twenty past eleven."

After her stretch she stood up and said, "You're kidding me."

"Nope."

"Oh boy, we better get a move on."

Becca tossed the blanket aside and hopped from the bed. "What's on the schedule today, boss?" she asked as she pulled the blankets back up over the pillows in a haphazard remake of the bed.

"We have a few clients for tree decorating today. But before we do that, I'd like to pay a visit to Toby and see how he's healing. I'll text Jenna first to see if it's okay." Kinsley walked to the blind and opened it to reveal a glaring scene of stark white below. "Looks like the storm is over. We've got quite a few inches out there."

"You think we can get out? We probably have some serious shoveling to do," Becca said, joining her at the window.

"Well, if it's almost noon, I'm sure the plow has already swiped the back parking lot. I might have to help Aunt Tilly with the walkway, though, if Kyle hasn't already gotten to it. Sometimes the gentleman who plows for us handles the walkways, too, but I'm sure he's swamped trying to get the rest of Harborside plowed out and back to business as usual."

"Gotcha. Thanks for the snacks, by the way," Becca said with a smile, returning to the bedside table and taking a few nuts from the tray and popping them into her mouth.

"Sure! That reminds me, you missed all the excitement last night."

"Excitement?"

"Cole was in the kitchen with a butcher knife and scared the life outta me."

Becca's eyes doubled in size, and she stopped chewing to give her full attention. "And . . ." She rolled her hand for Kinsley to continue.

"And he was pretty adamant he didn't kill his brother."

Becca's eyes grew even wider. "You asked him?"

"I didn't go there—but he sure did."

"Do you believe him?"

Kinsley chewed her lip and pondered before she said, "Honestly, I don't know what to think anymore. My head is spinning. You?"

"I'm with you on that," Becca said with a laugh. "Since it seems we have a big day ahead, I'm going to grab a shower before we go, okay?"

"Yeah, please hurry, because after we get cleaned up, maybe we can finally get some answers to all of our lingering questions."

Chapter 30

Snow covered the bushes, trees, and the community's holiday decorations in a thick blanket, making the town of Harborside look like a sparkling winter wonderland. *Anything* that had been left outdoors was now dipped in sugary white and the sunlight caused it all to twinkle joyously.

"It's so pretty!" Becca swooned as her gaze remained fixed outside the passenger window of the SeaScapes truck as they bounced along the plowed roads, which still were thick with slush and ice buildup.

"Sure does look like a Christmas card now, doesn't it? It's amazing how a fresh snowfall can bring the magic back to the holidays," Kinsley said, gripping the steering wheel tight to prevent the truck from landing in a ditch. "I absolutely love it!"

"Me, too, but ask me again in February how I feel about the snow and ice," Becca joked.

When they exited the truck, Kinsley looked up to see that the kissing balls had a new coat of white as well, making them look like frosted cupcakes. That would surely melt soon enough, as the sun was out in full force, giving the town an almost shocking glare. Kinsley had to tent her eyes to look at the kissing balls.

"Toby is working today? And not home resting?" Becca asked as they opened the door of Toby's Taffy and kicked the excess snow off their boots so as not to drag the slop inside the candy store.

"Yup, that's what Jenna said in her text. Can't keep that man down for long!"

They wiped their feet on the oversized mat inside the door as well, before moving deeper into the space, which smelled of sugary goodness.

"Hi, ladies!" Jenna greeted from behind the counter. She tossed a rag behind her and then turned and gave them her full attention. "Glad to see the roads are good enough that you could make it out today. The rest of the town seems to be still hibernating."

The taffy shop was unusually empty due to the storm. "Yeah, it sure is beautiful out there," Kinsley commented. "It's like a winter wonderland."

"Indeed! Have you heard, some in town are still without power?" Jenna asked. "We're the lucky ones. I'm sure it'll take the power company some time to have everything restored."

Just then Toby emerged from the back room and met them with a smile. "Now, there's a sight for sore eyes," he said with a twinkle in his eye. Kinsley immediately ran to greet him with a bear hug. She held him tight as if never wanting to let go.

"You okay?" she asked, looking Toby over and holding him at arm's length. "I was so worried."

"Of course! You know me, I'm tough." Toby winked at her and then lifted an arm to show his biceps, which caused the group to share a laugh. He then gave a half hug of greeting to Becca.

"Kyle sends his best. He wanted to tag along to see you, too, but he's helping Aunt Tilly dig out from the storm. He said he'll catch you soon, though," Kinsley said.

"Oh, tell him thank you. We'd love to see him—right, Jenna?"

"We sure would," Jenna replied with a smile.

"Any word of who did this to you?" Becca asked.

Toby slowly shook his head, which remained bandaged. "Not a peep. And we're telling folks who ask that I fell and banged my head." He lifted a finger to his lips for them to remain hushed and keep the secret.

"Were you missing anything other than the records from your Twelve Days of Christmas file?" Kinsley asked.

Jenna moved out from the counter to join the group. "Not that we can tell. All the other files seem intact, and there was petty cash still left in the drawer," she said, wiping her hands on her apron and planting them firmly on her hips.

"And you still can't remember who won a scarf that year, huh?" Kinsley asked.

"No, it was a few years ago and we host a giveaway every single year. This year we gave away a Harborside mug with a cocoa bomb," Toby said, pointing to the wall where an enlarged photo depicted this year's winners with gleeful expressions.

Kinsley moved closer to the photo to investigate. "Is this the only place you display it? I mean, has the local paper ever done a write-up about it or anything?"

"No, it's never been in the paper, but we usually post it on our social media page," Jenna replied.

"Why didn't we think of this before?" Kinsley asked eagerly, plucking her cell phone from her winter coat and logging into the site. She scrolled the yearly posts until she came upon a group of people standing with bright smiles and wearing the now very familiar candy cane scarves.

Kinsley, with Becca standing close over her shoulder, noted: Jackie, Mallory, Raven, and two older folks whom Kinsley didn't recognize standing proudly in the photograph. The only missing person on her suspect list was Cari Day, who was the one person she was currently leaning toward the most as the potential culprit.

Kinsley couldn't exclude any of them. Jackie, Mallory, and Raven were all present the night Chris Chesterfield was pushed into the Atlantic Ocean. Which meant any one of them could be implicated in the crime. And *one of them* had a connection to the murder.

Chapter 31

The next day, Kinsley planned to work solo for a few hours while Becca handled a pressing real estate deal, and Adam spent the morning at the orthodontist having his braces removed. Between decorating jobs, Kinsley decided to pay Raven a visit to see what she knew about the other two women who had stood beside her in the photo and had won a candy cane–striped scarf from Toby's Taffy a few years back. She also wanted to know what Raven had planned to tell her at Edna's party.

When she pulled the SeaScapes truck into the Blue Lobstah parking lot, Kinsley noticed Raven on the far side of the lot alongside the dumpster, tossing in a bag of garbage. Raven had already reentered the eatery via the south side of the building, where the staff commonly entered, before Kinsley had even exited her truck. She held her coat taut at the neck and bent her head to avoid the brisk wind rolling off the ocean as she quickly moved to follow Raven. When she opened the door to the storage room, which connected to the back of the bar, Kinsley was met with a surprised look upon Raven's face.

"Oh, hey, Kinsley," Raven said, relief washing over her face. "You startled me."

"Sorry about that," she replied, reaching out a hand to calm her.

"No worries. You know we're not open for another hour, right?" Raven asked as she turned to move a crate of beer bottles to a different location inside of the storeroom and stack it on top of another.

"Yeah, I know. I was just passing by on my way to a job and thought I'd pop in."

"You looking for Pete, then?"

Raven continued to shuffle items around inside of the storage room until Kinsley said, "No, I was actually looking for you. You got a minute?"

"Me?" Raven turned to her then and gave Kinsley her full attention. "Sure, what's up?"

"Do you remember at Edna's Christmas party; you mentioned you had something to tell me? I meant to go back and ask you about it, but the night got away from me. And when I looked over, I noticed you were swamped. What was it? Do you recall?"

Raven's brow furrowed and she laced her arms protectively across her chest. "I said that?"

Kinsley examined her closely when she replied, "Yeah, you mentioned that you'd overheard something that might be relevant to Chris's murder. Something important that you wanted to share with me. Don't you remember?"

Raven's neck flushed, and the heat crawled up to her face. She toyed with her ponytail as if suddenly uncomfortable with the direction the conversation was heading. "Honestly, I don't remember." She averted her eyes and looked hard at the floor.

"Really?" Kinsley prompted.

"Oh, wait a second. I know what I was going to share with you that night," Raven said, and Kinsley waited with bated breath.

"I overheard another city councilman, Jack, mention that with Chris out of the way, Tim is planning to move forward with his plans and try and open a new business again. But I don't think it really means anything. It's probably just gossip."

"You sure?"

"Uh-huh. I should've never brought it up." Raven turned away from her and stepped deeper into the storage room, and Kinsley followed.

With Kinsley on her heels, Raven continued, "Hey, I'm sorry, I can't help you more. I'd love to stop and visit but I really must get back to work," Raven said, officially dismissing her.

Something hard caught beneath Kinsley's boot, causing her to skid and almost lose her footing on the concrete floor. She looked down and saw something that looked like rock salt used to melt snow on the highway. She decided to crush it with the toe of her boot so that Raven wouldn't slip on it, either. But the rock salt didn't break down when she pressed on it once again. She attempted to crush it beneath her boot one more time, to no avail, so she bent and picked it up to throw it in a nearby trash can. It was then she realized that it wasn't rock salt at all. It was a shard of glass. A piece of frosted glass. Raven noticed and asked, "Whatcha got there?"

Kinsley held out her palm for Raven's inspection and was taken aback when she gasped. Raven covered her mouth with her hand and uttered, "*Oh nooo! It can't be!* Where did you find that?"

"*Raven?*"

"I mean," Raven sputtered. "It's nothing . . ."

The hairs started to stand up on the back of Kinsley's neck. She closed her palm and held the glass tightly in her hand, for fear of losing a crucial piece of evidence.

"*Raven?*"

"It's nothing," she repeated, walking away from her. "Just toss it."

Kinsley reached out and touched Raven's arm, causing the other woman to spin around and face her.

"It's *not* nothing, Rave. You know *exactly* what this is. It's a piece of a Grey Goose bottle," Kinsley said, carefully studying her. "I bet if I moved a few more things around in here, I'd find more of it. Wouldn't I?"

Raven shook her head adamantly. "No, I cleaned it all up . . . I mean . . . It wasn't me," she stammered. "I just . . ."

"Raven . . ." Kinsley softened, taking a step closer to study her further. "What's going on? Talk to me."

Raven gripped her head in her hands and then shook it in disbelief. "I thought I swept it all up . . . How did I miss that?" she cried. "Please, Kinsley! Just throw it away and pretend you never saw it!"

Things started to come together in Kinsley's mind. Things she didn't want to believe. Part of her wanted to flee, but the stronger part wanted answers.

"Oh, Rave. Talk to me. I'm your friend. *Please.*"

Raven dropped her hands limply to her sides and met Kinsley's gaze but continued to slowly shake her head.

"It's okay," Kinsley coaxed, reaching out a hand and touching Raven's arm again to prompt her to talk. "You can trust me."

"He followed me in here." Raven spoke the words so softly; they were barely audible to Kinsley's ears.

"Chris did? The night of the parade?" Kinsley pressed.

Raven nodded.

"Help me out here . . . followed you from *where* exactly?"

"I was returning from the dumpster, and he followed me in here. He said I needed to tell my boss that he'd be back." Raven threw her slender fingers up in air quotes and added, "And that Pete couldn't tell him where he *could or couldn't go* in this town. He said that *he* made the rules for Harborside. Chris reminded me that he could convince the common council to shut us down for going over our occupancy limit because there were too many people in the bar the night of the boat parade." Raven swallowed hard and then pursed her lips. "Funny how the occupancy limit was fine until he got himself kicked out!"

"I'm not sure that's accurate, I think he could only issue a fine at best, but go on," Kinsley encouraged.

"I told him to take it up with Pete and leave me out of it."

"Then what happened?"

"He took his stupid Santa hat off and put it on my head. I told him to stop messing around and to get out of here. I told him that he didn't belong in the storage room and Pete would be *really* mad if he caught him back here . . . especially after having kicked him out of the bar." Raven clenched her hands into fists and held them firmly at her sides. "He wouldn't listen to me!"

Kinsley didn't speak for fear she would break the spell and Raven would stop talking.

"I tried to physically lead him out the door, but Chris was drunk and it only made things worse. He was swaying into boxes of booze, and I thought he was going to break something." Raven looked to the stacked crates of bottles and cans that surrounded them, and then her gaze returned to Kinsley.

"And then what?" Kinsley coaxed.

The words were rolling off Raven's tongue freely now, as if she was finally relieved to let it all go. "When I tried to ignore him, he got all handsy and attempted to pull me in like he was going to kiss me or hug me or something like that. Which is totally gross! I don't even know where his *wife* was while this was all going on! He wouldn't let me go so I grabbed the first thing I could and hit him with it."

"And that was a bottle of Grey Goose?"

"Yeah, an empty one. It was a bottle that Scotty had brought back from the bar and left over by the door, but I had already taken the garbage out," she admitted sadly.

"And then what?"

"Chris was so stunned that I hit him, he cowered. Honestly, I was just as stunned as he was that I had done that, but he brought me to my breaking point, ya know? He wouldn't listen!"

"I get it. Then you followed him outside and pushed him off the pier, right? Is that what happened?"

"No! You got that part all wrong! It's not like that at all." Raven shook her head defiantly. "After I realized what I had done, I panicked. I put the Santa hat back on his head and shoved him out the door. I swear, that was all! I never saw him again after that." Fat tears began to freely roll down Raven's cheeks. "I swear I didn't mean it, Kinsley! I didn't mean to hit him! But I'm not a killer! And I did not push him off the pier!"

"And when you ran into the bar and said a paramedic was needed by the pier—was that your way of trying to make it right by attempting to have someone come to Chris's aid?"

"No!" Raven adamantly shook her head. "You don't understand. It wasn't too long after that when I heard screaming coming from outside the storage room. When I ran out to see what was going on, someone stopped me in the parking lot and told me that a person had fallen in the icy water and to go back to the bar and find a paramedic. I didn't know *who* had fallen in. I swear on my life, Kinsley, I didn't know it was *Chris*! I didn't learn that until later and then I really felt guilty because I thought maybe he got dizzy from what I had done and fell in. But then I overheard that the police thought he was pushed. I was afraid to come forward."

Pete entered the storage room and stopped short when he saw the two of them.

"What's going on in here?" he asked.

"Raven has something she needs to tell you."

Chapter 32

Pete, Kinsley, and Raven were seated on empty wooden crates in the back storage room of the Blue Lobstah while Raven repeated the entire story to Pete. After which, Kinsley asked pointedly, "Then how did your scarf end up in the ocean? Can you explain that?"

"It didn't," Raven said.

"The candy cane–striped scarf you won from Toby's Taffy a few years back. You were wearing it the night of the boat parade, weren't you?" Kinsley asked emphatically. "I know you own one, I saw the picture of you, along with the other winners, on social media. So please don't try and deny it at this point."

"I'm not denying anything," Raven said doggedly. "I'm telling you the truth!" she added, rising off the wooden crate in defense. "I knew it would be too crowded and warm in the bar that night for me to dress up. I left my scarf at home. Don't you remember? I was wearing my Blue Lobstah T-shirt!" She looked to Pete to come to her aid. "You can even verify it if you want because Scotty and I took a selfie that night." Her eyes ping-ponged between the two of them nervously, as if she was desperate for them to believe her. "Ask to see his phone. Just ask him!" she pleaded.

"Now I'm confused," Kinsley uttered. "Where did the scarf with the green smear come from, then? At some point Chris's green face paint touched that scarf."

"Was Chris wearing one that night?" Pete asked.

"No, just the Grinch costume and the Santa hat," Raven said quietly.

"Were you the one who called Pete and disguised your voice with the toy and told him to put the scarf in the lost and found the night Bec and I were doing a stakeout?" Kinsley asked cautiously.

"No." Raven vigorously shook her head in denial. "That wasn't me, either. I swear to you," she said, lifting both hands in defense. "Besides, you guys saw me leave work that night, remember? How could I make the call if I was with you?"

"That's right, you came over and talked with us mid-stakeout," Kinsley muttered under her breath. "So, it couldn't have been you who called. If it wasn't you . . . then who was it?"

"I have no idea except that it wasn't me," Raven said firmly, crossing her chest with the sign of the cross. As if that hand gesture solidified that she was innocent of all charges.

Kinsley leaned forward, resting her arms on her knees, and steepled her fingers. "You didn't take the scarf from the lost and found, then? And steal the camera? It makes perfect sense now, as you had easy access to it and Pete probably was the one who told you to keep your eyes peeled on the lost and found in the first place."

"I did tell her that, along with the rest of the staff," Pete agreed with a nod.

"I've been trying to figure out when and how someone could've gotten away with stealing all of that from right under your noses. And no one seems to have seen a thing," Kinsley said, examining each of them purposely for an acceptable explanation.

"I never said that I didn't take it. I *said* I didn't make the call," Raven confessed.

"Okay, wait, so you did take it?" Kinsley kneaded her forehead with her fingers before pressing Raven for clarity. "Why on earth would you take it? Why not leave it there?"

"I panicked! I was afraid someone was going to try and pin this whole thing on me, just like you're doing right now!" Raven shouted. "It was only a matter of time before someone found out I owned an identical scarf. When I knew you were all looking at that as a hot clue, I freaked and threw mine out. I wanted to distance myself from the entire thing! And then I realized someone in Harborside would figure it out eventually and, well, that was a really stupid thing to do. I should have kept it for proof because I've implicated myself even further!"

"Now you have nothing to substantiate your claim to prove your innocence," Pete said grimly. "No offense, Rave, but the authorities aren't going to believe you didn't follow Chris outside and finish the job."

Raven slumped back onto a crate and put her head in her hands. "I can't believe this," she uttered. "I can't believe that stupid freebie is going to bite me in the ass."

"Please tell me you were not the one who attacked Toby to destroy any evidence of you winning it," Kinsley said evenly. "Because that would be unforgivable."

Raven looked up and eyed Kinsley squarely. "What? No! I swear on my life, that wasn't me! I didn't even know Toby *was* attacked. When did that happen?"

"Are you sure?"

"Kinsley! Come on, you know me!" Raven's eyes grew wild. "I couldn't hurt him, he's like the nicest man in town! Everyone loves Toby! Including me!" she added, jutting a thumb to her chest.

"Where's the scarf now, the one from lost and found, the one with the green paint smeared on it?" Pete asked.

"I wrapped it."

Raven's comment left Kinsley speechless.

"You wrapped it? As in . . . like a Christmas present?" Pete asked.

"Yeah."

"*Why?*" Kinsley asked.

"So I could hide it in plain sight! I thought the police might find it at my house and think it was mine! But they never suspected me, they never even searched my house. Anyway, I wrapped it and it's under my Christmas tree at home. I was trying to figure out if I could get a DNA test on it or something like that. I was trying to figure out who it belonged to so I could get out of this mess!" Raven cried.

"Let's get back to the main goal here," Pete interjected with an uplifted finger. "What I'm gathering from all of this is that someone else was wearing the scarf that night. And after Chris left this storage room, someone else killed him. That's the most important thing to get outta this whole conversation. The rest of this is incidental."

"That's one hundred percent correct!" Raven said excitedly. "*Finally*, you understand!"

"Why didn't you come forward, Raven? When you knew the lengths we were going through to solve this thing?" Kinsley asked. "Why not tell Rachel all of this? It might've helped in the investigation."

"Because I didn't want to implicate myself in a murder charge! And spend the rest of my God-given life in prison over it! I was only defending myself from that creep. And now this is all gonna get pinned on me!" Raven wailed. Her eyes darted around the room nervously. "I mean, no one's going to believe this! Everyone is going to think I'm to blame! I'm having a hard enough time convincing you two, and you're my friends. What are a set of jurors going to think? *You* don't even believe me!"

"We believe you," Pete said, rising from the wooden crate and putting a comforting hand on Raven's shoulder. "Don't we?" Pete then looked to Kinsley to back up his unwavering statement.

Her reply was resolute. "Yeah. I believe you, Rave. But the only way you're going to get out of this mess is to find out *who* pushed that alderman into the sea."

Chapter 33

Kinsley could hardly wait for Rachel to arrive so she could share her findings. She wanted to know if the detective would be willing to disclose what she had learned in the past few days, too. Because she knew that more information had come to light, based solely on Rachel's being summoned by the chief of police back at the Salty Breeze Inn. Not to mention things her brother had alluded to, like the fact that Rachel had been following new evidence. Those things alone proved the police department must be onto *something*. She just hoped whatever evidence they had unearthed, it didn't point back to Raven. Pete would never forgive her if he lost his number one employee over this. If Kinsley's idea to call Rachel and explain everything backfired, or if Raven had indeed lied, they all could be facing a heap of trouble. Not to mention, Raven could be facing lifelong incarceration.

Kinsley watched from the door and waved the detective over

from across the parking lot as soon as Rachel had stepped away from her unmarked vehicle.

"What's going on?" Rachel asked when she was in earshot. "You mentioned you found pieces to the Grey Goose bottle? My team scoured the area out here and never found a shard of glass! We just assumed the bottle was in the bottom of the Atlantic or long lost at sea by now."

"Hurry in out of the cold! There's a lot more we need to share with you. Not just that. But yeah, if Raven wasn't moving crates back here, I never would've found it, either," Kinsley said, ushering the detective out of the winter breeze that was rolling off the ocean and seeping into the storage room as she held the door for her.

"Hiya, Rachel," Pete said with far less enthusiasm. "Hey, if you don't mind, let's move this conversation inside of the restaurant and get comfortable. I've got the main door locked and I won't open my place until this is all resolved. I don't want you to have to sit on one of those." Pete moved the empty crates that they had been occupying from the floor and stacked them off to the side of the storage room. He then walked in the direction of the bar, where they all followed like a train of cars until they entered the Blue Lobstah, eerily devoid of customers. Kinsley had never been inside the eatery when the restaurant wasn't fully open, and it felt oddly quiet.

When the four were comfortably gathered around a table, Kinsley removed the shard of glass from the Grey Goose bottle and set it in front of her. After Rachel had learned everything, Kinsley asked tentatively, "Please tell me you have a solid lead. Away from our friend over here?" She gestured a hand to Raven, who laid her head on the table and covered her ears as if scared for her life and desperately wanting an escape.

"Do you know who killed him?" Pete prodded. "And you're just solidifying your case? You have this wrapped up like a Christmas present, right?" He looked to the detective intently as if hoping it was true and this would all go away.

Rachel, on the other hand, slumped back in her chair and steepled her fingers and said thoughtfully, "Well, unfortunately, I don't think any of you are going to like what I'm about to say."

Raven looked up, her face riddled with fear as her gaze bounced among all of them expectantly. She looked as if with her sudden pent-up energy, she could leap across the room. Her anxiety was palpable. So much so that Kinsley could feel the vibration of the table from her leg bouncing beneath it.

Rachel pointed to the shard of Grey Goose, which was now reflecting the sunlight seeping in from the window. "This isn't something we can just brush under the table and pretend didn't happen. Can we? It's something we need to address."

"I was just trying to get him to leave me alone!" Raven squealed, pointing to the evidence. "I didn't mean to hurt him!"

"I have no other choice. I'm going to have to take you down to the station," Rachel said flatly.

"I didn't kill him, I swear!" Raven shrieked, leaning forward and gripping her hands on the edge of the table. "I promise you! He was alive when he stumbled out of the storage room. Please— I didn't do this!"

"Can anyone corroborate that?" Rachel asked pointedly.

Tears began to stream down Raven's cheeks and her lip quivered. With a shaky hand, she took a small sip of water from the glass Pete had gotten for her, and then tried to blink back the tears. She wiped her tears away with a napkin, but her eyes continued to fill instantly.

"I'm going to put a forty-eight-hour hold on you until we

can sift out some of this evidence and officially clear you," Rachel said, rising to her feet. "But for now, if you come willingly, I won't have to call another officer to bring you in. I'll save you that embarrassment."

"I can't believe this," Raven whispered as she looked to Kinsley with begging eyes to put a halt to what was progressing.

Rachel cleared her throat and said, "Raven, would you please stand?"

Kinsley couldn't believe what was happening, either. Her heart began to hammer in her chest. She glanced to Pete, who looked as if he'd been hit with a Mack truck—completely crestfallen, yet his eyes were alert and anxious. Pete's number one employee being led out of his establishment in handcuffs was not at all what he expected when showing up for a day's work. None of them did.

"You have the right to remain silent . . ."

Kinsley started to protest again but Rachel stopped her with a warning glare.

"Don't make this harder than it is," Rachel said, and then put the handcuffs on Raven. While continuing the rest of her "remaining silent" speech, she led Raven by the elbow out of the restaurant. Meanwhile, Raven's tears morphed into a full-on sob, which reverberated inside the empty restaurant.

Kinsley's and Pete's only response was to stand by helplessly and silently watch this all unfold.

"I'm so sorry, Pete," Kinsley said, finally breaking the silence.

Pete rubbed the back of his neck so hard that he left a mark on his skin. "Look, Kins. Don't take it upon yourself. This ain't your fault. We had no other choice than sharing with the authorities everything we know."

"No, I know. But . . . it doesn't make me feel any better," Kinsley stammered. She wished she could find the words to comfort him. Or words to fix everything. But nothing came to mind.

"Do you believe her?" Pete asked.

"Raven?"

"Yeah." He pressed, "Do you believe her?"

"Yeah," Kinsley said resolutely. "Don't you?"

"Yeah." Pete eyed her squarely.

Pete's penetrating gaze suddenly made Kinsley slightly uncomfortable. "*What?*" she asked.

"Hey, you love diggin' into this kinda stuff. And truth is, you might be the only one who can save her at this point," he answered, running his hands nervously through his hair again. "You said it yourself, you're already knee-deep into this thing. Now it's more important than ever that you figure out who did this."

"Me? How about *we*?" Kinsley held a hand to her chest. "How can I be the only one responsible to save her?"

"Do that thing you do!"

"The thing I do? What exactly are you saying? Prove that Raven's innocent and was only defending herself?"

"Yeah, that's exactly what I'm saying. I mean—prove it."

Chapter 34

Alate dinner tucked inside a private corner booth at the Blue Lobstah was called to order when Kinsley made emergency phone calls to round up the troops. They needed to come up with a game plan to clear Raven of all charges. Becca was seated directly across from her, and Kyle and Tilly were en route to the restaurant. Pete had mentioned he would pop into the conversation every now and then but being that he was now short an employee, he wouldn't be able to linger. However, he offered a free meal to anyone who would be willing to provide help.

At the very least, Raven might have to face assault and battery charges, but if it was up to Kinsley, she would work to get those charges dropped, too. After all, she had watched how Raven had handled herself on numerous occasions when things seemed out of hand at the bar, and never *once* did she witness Raven lose her cool around a patron. She knew Raven. And she believed her. More important, she knew Chris and how he often behaved. Therefore, Pete was right. It was up to Kinsley to solve this thing and put it to rest. And they had forty-eight hours to do it before Raven would officially be booked on murder charges.

Kinsley looked up to see her aunt and brother with worry-filled faces rushing toward the corner booth.

"Rachel arrested Raven today?" Tilly asked as soon as she slipped into the seat next to Kinsley. "And you mentioned on the phone that you don't think she gave him the final push?"

"I know she didn't," Kinsley said confidently. "Thanks for coming. We're going to need to put our heads together to get our friend out of this mess. She doesn't deserve to pay the price for someone else's actions."

Kyle slipped into the booth, next to Becca, and faced Kinsley directly. "I hope you're not taking this out on Rachel. You know, she's just doing her job."

"I understand that she's doing her job, but we need to do our part, too. Listen, Kyle . . . if you don't want any part of this . . . if you're uncomfortable with it in any way . . . you don't have to help." Kinsley looked her brother squarely in the eye and held her gaze there. "I don't want you to go against Rachel's wishes and jeopardize your relationship with her. You can totally just head back to the inn, and I'll give Aunt Tilly a ride back when we're through."

Kyle's brows furrowed and he studied her. "You're *sure* she's innocent?"

"I wouldn't have asked you here if I didn't believe it."

"Okay. That's all I needed to hear," Kyle said, folding his hands atop the table and looking to the rest of them. "Tell us what you want us to do."

Pete interrupted briefly, carrying a tray of steaming French fries and a round of lobster rolls for all. He handed them out and then offered a pitcher of soda, which they all agreed would wash the food down perfectly. When he returned with the pitcher of Pepsi he said sincerely, "You don't know what this means to me that you're all willing to help Kinsley clear Rave of this. I've known that girl a long time now and I know what she's capable of. And intentionally hurting someone is not even on her radar." He held up Scout-salute fingers to drive the point home. "I promise you; she was only defending herself. And between you and me, Raven's had to defend herself from this kind of thing on more than one occasion with that man. She'd never have taken it as far as she did that night if Chris didn't have it coming. That's all I'm going to say about that matter."

"No worries, we got this," Kinsley promised.

"Thanks for the food, Pete," Becca said, picking a French fry off the plate and blowing the steam off before popping it into her mouth.

"Yeah, thanks," the rest of the group chimed in.

"No problem. There's more food where that came from, so don't be shy." Pete jutted a thumb behind him. "If you guys need anything else or have any other questions for me, I'll be behind the bar. Just come get me." He tucked the empty tray beneath his arm and tapped his hand on the table twice before pivoting away from them.

While they shared dinner, Kinsley brought everyone up to speed on what she knew thus far. She then scrolled on her cell phone and held up the photo from Toby's social media account, where he had shared the winners of the candy cane–striped scarves. "We know that Mallory and Jackie both won a scarf that year—Raven wasn't the only one."

"So, you think one of them is the culprit?" Kyle asked.

"I know Jackie still has her scarf because I saw her wearing it that day in the parking lot, so in theory that takes her off the list," Kinsley said.

"Who else won a scarf that year?" Becca said.

Tilly leaned over Kinsley's shoulder to view the photo and pointed. "That older woman standing next to Jackie is her mother."

"Wait. That's Jackie's mom?" Kinsley asked.

"Sure is," Tilly said, wiping her mouth with a napkin.

"That means Jackie had access to another scarf. What are the chances that Jackie's mom let Tim borrow one that night? Maybe they were twinning?" Kinsley considered aloud.

"Who's the last person in the photo? Anyone you recognize?" Becca asked Tilly.

"I think that's Mildred. I believe she died of a heart attack last year. Rest her soul," Tilly replied sadly.

"Okay, so our suspect pool includes Mallory, Cole, Jackie, and Tim. Could be that one of the couples were in on it together. Cari is still not completely cleared, either. Which way are you leaning?" Kyle asked, and then took a bite of lobster roll.

"I dunno. Cole swore to me that night when I caught him in the kitchen that he didn't push his brother. But was he lying to me?" Kinsley said pensively. "That is the big question . . ."

"How are we going to solve this thing?" Becca asked. "What clues do we have left?"

"We can't forget about the toy," Kinsley said, pushing her plate aside. All this stress was ruining her appetite.

"The toy that disguised someone's voice to sound like Rudolph?" Tilly asked.

"Yeah. Whoever made that call was most likely the killer. If we know who has the toy, maybe Rachel can check the cell phone records to show that same person called the bar. It's slim, but it's just one more building block to add to the case," Kyle suggested.

"We need to find that voice-changing toy. How the heck are we going to do that?" Becca asked.

Kinsley twirled her straw in her Pepsi and pondered. "Well, if we're looking for a toy—we're looking for kids. Mallory doesn't have any."

"Jackie does," Becca interjected.

"Process of elimination?" Kyle asked.

Kinsley smiled. "I think I have an idea."

Chapter 35

Kinsley and Becca stood elbow to elbow on the front porch of Tim and Jackie Horn's residence while they waited for someone to answer the door. It was twilight, and the neighboring Christmas lights were lit in full glory as snow fell softly around them as if they were standing inside a recently shaken snow globe.

Becca leaned in and whispered, "You really think this is going to pay off?"

A porch light flicked on, and Kinsley replied, "All we can do is try. Just smile and act natural. It's go time!"

Jackie opened the door and a look of surprise washed across her face. "Hey, what are you two doing here?" She looked beyond them as if wondering if there were a group of others behind them and they were all about to break out in Christmas carols.

Kinsley held up a kissing ball. "After decorating the town of

Harborside, would you believe we have a few extra of these? We decided to deliver them to all our volunteers in gratitude. Can we come in? It's freezing out here." Kinsley chuckled.

"Oh, how nice of you. Of course, please come in!" Jackie opened the door wider for them to enter and had to kick an oversized rubber ball out of the way to do so. It seemed they just stepped into utter chaos. Kids were running circles around the house and toys were strewn everywhere beneath their feet. "Sorry," she explained. "Had I known you were coming I would have cleaned up this mess." She accepted the kissing ball from Kinsley's hands and set it carefully on the floor out of the way of any trip hazard. "Thanks for bringing that over. I'll have Tim hang it on the porch for me." She smiled kindly. "That will look so lovely! I'll be the envy of the neighborhood."

"You know, Kinsley and I were just saying on the ride over here that we'd be happy to babysit if you and Tim need a night out to finish your Christmas shopping," Becca proposed. "Would you like us to stay for a while? We'd be more than happy to help."

Jackie's expression reflected sincere gratitude. "That's so kind of you to offer, but believe it or not, I've already finished all of my holiday shopping." She wiped a hand dramatically across her forehead. "Phew! Dodged that bullet." She laughed. "I actually found everything on my list this year, if you can believe it!"

"Well, we can certainly stay for a little bit if you and Tim want to reconnect and go and grab a drink somewhere. A holiday cocktail at the Blue Lobstah, perhaps? I know Pete was playing around with some new concoctions. Maybe you'd like to try one?" Kinsley suggested. "I bet you could use a night out, away from the kids."

By the look of Jackie's perplexed expression, Kinsley wondered if she'd blown it, taking the niceties a bit too far. Jackie's eyes narrowed in on her further still. "Tim's not even home right now."

"Oh, bummer," Becca replied. Her eyes then darted to the floor of toys beneath their feet as if hoping to miraculously stumble onto the evidence they were in search of.

"Yeah," Kinsley agreed with a nod. "We were hoping to be of service. You see, Becca and I are not exchanging gifts this year, but instead we've decided to do something we're calling our own Twelve Days of Service. We have decided to volunteer for twelve days over the season in twelve different ways. And we're doing these acts of kindness together. So far, we rang the Salvation Army bells, but that's only one. And then we're delivering the extra kissing balls, that's two. In any event, if you decide you need a babysitter, we could qualify that as one of our volunteer efforts." Kinsley smiled sweetly.

Jackie mirrored her smile. "What a lovely idea. I'll talk to Tim about it and get back to you. Thank you for considering us as one of your twelve."

"You bet!" Kinsley said, rocking on her heels.

A long pause ensued but Kinsley was not at all ready to turn and head back out the door. "Are you baking? Or is that a scented candle? It smells delicious in here."

"Yeah, you can smell that? I just took an orange cranberry bread out of the oven. I make it every December, as it's a festive recipe my family really enjoys around the holidays. Would you like to try a slice before you go?" Jackie offered.

Kinsley inconspicuously elbowed her bestie. "We'd love a slice, wouldn't we, Bec?"

"Yeah, sounds great," Becca said, already removing her boots and coat and setting them by the door. Kinsley followed suit and then they traveled with Jackie into the kitchen, dodging toys along the way. Unfortunately, a microphone was not one of them.

"Coffee?" Jackie turned to them after both had taken a stool at an expansive center island that cut the room in half.

"Sure," Kinsley and Becca said in unison, and then smiled.

Kinsley looked down at the gloves she still held in her hands. She was so consumed about the plan, she hadn't thought to leave them with her coat. She tucked them under her leg and then folded her hands in front of her and rested them on the island.

As Jackie was making a pot of coffee, a girl about seven years old with bouncy strawberry blond pigtails ran through the kitchen squealing, with a little boy chasing after her. Jackie turned from the coffeepot to scold them, but they had already gone past them, into the next room.

"Can you excuse me for a minute?" Jackie asked.

"No problem," Becca replied, drumming her fingers atop the island.

As soon as Jackie had left them, Kinsley whispered, "I gotta go and look for the microphone. This might be our only chance!"

"Okay," Becca said nervously, biting at her thumbnail. "But please hurry."

"Just try and stall her, okay? Tell her I went in search of the bathroom. But whatever you do, do *not* let her come looking for me." Kinsley was on her feet and walking quickly toward a long hallway of the ranch-style house before Becca could even reply. She popped her head into the first doorway, which looked like the primary bedroom, as a queen bed was neatly covered with a burgundy duvet. It was probably the only room in the entire house that looked uncluttered of toys. Kinsley quickly moved on. A bedroom with dark blue–painted walls and glowing planetary stickers on the ceiling caught her attention. She stepped inside but, not wanting to alert anyone, kept the lights off. It took a moment for her eyes to adjust to the darkness before she moved toward a toy box in the corner of the room. She looked over both shoulders before opening the lid and sifting through the toys but came up empty. Kinsley dropped to her knees and looked under the twin bed, which was covered in a spaceship-themed comforter. A stuffed animal and a few Matchbox cars were coated in dust bunnies beneath the bed. Suddenly she heard heavy footsteps approach. Kinsley leapt to her feet, but it was too late to make it out of the bedroom. She held her hand to her heart and tried to even her breath for what was to come.

Tim Horn crossed the threshold and asked accusingly, "Who are you and what are you doing in my son's bedroom?"

Kinsley cleared her throat. "We're just visiting with Jackie . . . and I was looking for the bathroom . . . and I got turned around . . . I felt a little dizzy and sat for a moment on your son's bed to catch my bearings," Kinsley stuttered. "I'm so sorry." She rushed past him before he had a chance to respond and ducked into the safety of the nearest bathroom. She closed the door, held her back against it, and gripped her hand to her heart while she evened her breath. After taking a few moments to calm herself and flushing an unused toilet, she returned to the kitchen, where Becca caught her gaze and sent a questioning glance.

Kinsley inconspicuously shook her head *no*, and Becca

seemed to receive the message, as her smile faded and her eyes turned downcast to the island.

"Everything all right?" Jackie asked.

"Fine." Kinsley waved a hand of dismissal. "Honestly, I think my stomach might be acting up. I somehow got turned around looking for your bathroom and ended up in your son's room." Kinsley chuckled. "And, by the way, your husband is home. I met him back there."

"Oh, I thought I heard the garage door open," Becca chimed in, clearly not understanding that Kinsley had been caught red-handed in the wrong place at the wrong time.

Tim strolled into the kitchen then and looked to his wife. "Can someone please tell me what's going on here?"

"Oh, hey, honey! I'm glad you're home. Remember when I volunteered to make the kissing balls for the downtown? Kinsley and Becca stopped by to give us one of the leftovers. Isn't that nice?" Jackie said, smiling up at her husband.

"Oh," Tim uttered. He seemed to buy Jackie's explanation, which gave Kinsley her first full breath since she'd left the child's bedroom.

"I don't think we've been formally introduced," Becca said, lifting from the stool and shaking the man's hand. "I'm Becca."

Kinsley mirrored her friend's action but then stopped short and grabbed her stomach instead and grimaced. "I'm Kinsley. I'd shake your hand, too, but suddenly my stomach isn't feeling very well. I don't want to pass off any germs with the holidays coming up. In fact, we'd better get going." She nudged Becca, and her friend instantly got the message.

"Thanks for the cranberry bread, Jackie," Becca said, tucking the stool beneath the countertop. "It was delicious. I'd love the recipe when you get a chance if you want to text it to me."

She lifted a real estate business card from her back pocket and added, "My number is on the card."

"Sure, I can do that. Do you want to take yours to go, Kinsley? I can wrap it for you," Jackie said.

"Nah, that's okay," Kinsley replied, holding her stomach and leaning forward dramatically. "Suddenly food isn't sounding very good."

"Let me walk you to the door." Jackie moved to their side of the island and led the way, leaving her husband behind in the kitchen, which Kinsley was secretly relieved about.

As they were slipping into their boots and coats, the kids came marching back into the room as if lined up in a holiday parade, and one was holding a microphone. "Ready, Santa!" he bellowed.

Chapter 36

Kyle had insisted that he drive the getaway car from the Horn residence. Because, in his words, he *"needed to take part just in case something should go down."* Therefore, Kinsley's overprotective brother had been waiting nearby like a hawk, ready to pounce.

Kyle pulled alongside the curb in Aunt Tilly's vehicle just as soon as Kinsley and Becca exited the house. Kinsley felt like she was going to toss her cookies, but only because of the recent revelation. She held the bile in check with the back of her hand as she slipped into the back seat of the car.

When the three were safely seat belted and pulling away from the curb, Kyle asked expectantly, "Well? What's the good word? You get anything? Or was this shindig a complete waste of time?"

Kinsley scurried to reach for her cell phone, which she had left inside of her purse in the back seat of her aunt's car. "I'm calling Rachel. I'll put her on speakerphone so you can hear the lowdown, 'cause I don't want to have to explain everything twice. But yeah, I think our little visit might pay off, Ky."

As soon as the detective answered the call, Kinsley said, "Rachel, I think you need to issue a search warrant for the Horns' residence. You're never gonna believe this, but the Rudolph voice-changing toy was at Jackie and Tim's house! Becca and I were just over there and heard one of the boys playing with it. See if you can try and get in that house before it's too late. Or one of them disposes of it. A thorough search could potentially provide even more crucial evidence."

"Hey, thanks for the info," Rachel said curtly. "I'll catch up with you later." And hung up the phone before Kinsley could even wish the detective a proper good-bye. She held the silent cell phone in her hand, somewhat shocked at Rachel's quick exit. She hoped the detective wasn't upset with her.

"You found it, huh?" Kyle asked, interrupting Kinsley's reverie and meeting her eyes through the rearview mirror.

"Yeah, I really wasn't expecting to find it. Were you, Kins? We weren't having any luck with our search until we were half-way out the door!" Becca said excitedly.

"What do you think will happen now?" Kinsley asked, unbuckling her seat belt. She ducked her head through the center console between her brother and Becca to continue the conversation.

"I know Rach well. And I know how she works," Kyle said, gripping the steering wheel tight with both hands. "Since she didn't linger on the phone, I'm guessing our favorite Harborside detective has more up her sleeve and evidence that the Horns are somehow involved to back your theory, too. She just needs enough evidence to build her case. Finding the toy is probably exactly what she needs to bring this investigation to a close. I'm just glad you two got out of there safely. You don't think they caught on to why you were there?" Kyle looked in the rearview mirror nervously as if he was expecting something to occur.

Kinsley laid a comforting hand on her brother's arm. "Not to worry, I think we're good. Although, I do think we should deliver a few more kissing balls to our volunteers," she added, making a mental note, more for herself than the two seated in the front.

"Yeah, I agree. Jackie was excited about getting one so the rest of the volunteers should have one, too. We should've let them take a kissing ball home the day we made them, but we probably wouldn't have had enough for the downtown then," Becca said, and then adjusted in her seat to face Kinsley. "I think we did great, didn't we? We executed the plan perfectly," Becca continued proudly, sending Kinsley a fist bump.

Kinsley didn't share with her brother the near miss and being caught red-handed by Tim inside of his child's bedroom. Instead, she said, "I hope you're right, Kyle, for Rachel's sake, that she has everything she needs to bring this one to a close. I for one am ready to be done with this and get along with celebrating the birth of Jesus. How about you two? Don't you think it's just about time for the holidays to officially begin? I can almost taste the gingerbread," she added, licking her lips. Her appetite was returning now that the stress level had come down a few notches.

"I hate to say anything to crush your festive mood, sis, but I think we're being tailed," Kyle cautioned. "The car behind has been following us since we left Harbor Lights Road and seems to be gaining speed." He looked to the rearview mirror again nervously.

Kinsley laughed. "I think you're overreacting, bro," she said lightly.

Becca turned her head to regard the rear window. "I don't think he's overreacting. Someone is definitely following us. Look!"

Kyle took one hand off the steering wheel and pushed Kinsley to the back seat. "Put your seat belt back on!" he warned. "Either we have a case of road rage on our hands, or Tim Horn figured out what you two were up to back there and he's attempting to silence you."

Kinsley didn't get a chance to turn around and look for herself before bright headlights flooded the inside of Aunt Tilly's car and filled the space with a light so brilliant, it almost blinded them. Kinsley put her arm in front of her eyes to shield herself from the light and catch her bearings. She had no idea how her brother was managing to keep the car on the road under these conditions.

Suddenly, a jolt catapulted Kinsley from the seat to the floor, because she hadn't listened to her brother and hadn't yet reclicked her seat belt.

"Sorry! I hit the brakes trying to get them to stop!" Kyle exclaimed. "Sis, you all right back there?"

"I'm okay." Kinsley scrambled from the floor and settled herself into her seat and hurried to click on the seat belt.

"Hang on, I'm going to try to lose 'em!" Kyle said, hitting the gas pedal hard.

Kinsley dialed 911 and explained the situation to the dispatcher, who promised to send out a cruiser immediately. "Help is on the way!" she shared after she hung up from the call.

Despite Kyle gaining speed, the car behind them strobed

their headlights, causing her brother to grip the wheel tighter and let out an expletive. "Whoever this is, they mean business. I can only conclude that it's the Horns trying to silence you. But it's hard to see what color the vehicle is with them so close on our tail!"

Primal fear began to settle in Kinsley's chest, and she clutched her heart and uttered a silent prayer for safety.

"This is nuts!" Becca squealed.

"Kins, can you see the make and model of the car?" Kyle asked.

Kinsley turned to look but the brilliant light only blinded her further. "No, I can't. Sorry! Go faster!"

That's the last thing Kinsley remembered before the vehicle hit a patch of ice and rotated into a tailspin. The car continued to spin out of control before hitting a giant snowbank, which covered the car in a cloud of white, as if they'd been dumped in cake flour. This caused the frontal airbags to eject and the horn to blare nonstop.

A few moments passed before Kyle asked, "Is everyone okay?"

"I'm okay. You guys?" Becca choked out.

"I'm okay," Kinsley replied before thanking God that she had reclicked that seat belt just in the nick of time.

The three exited the car and a hysterical Jackie ran to meet with them. "Oh my goodness! Are you all okay?" she cried.

"*Jackie?*" Kinsley asked tentatively. "What are you doing here?"

Jackie handed Kinsley her fur-lined leather gloves. "I was just trying to get your attention to pull over. You left these at my house, and I know how harsh our winters can be. I only wanted to return them to you." She put her head in her hands and fat tears fell down her cheeks. "I'm so sorry, I didn't mean for you to land in the ditch!"

"It's okay," Kinsley replied to soothe her. Though she thought Jackie's reasoning was totally absurd. Was she the killer and trying to off the three of them in an automobile accident?

"No! It's not! I didn't mean to cause an accident. Tim told me to just let it go, but I couldn't. He never listens to me to dress for the Maine weather. You could get frostbite out here, for Pete's sake! You need your gloves!"

"So that's why you made him wear the matching scarf the night of the boat parade?" Kinsley asked evenly. "You wanted him to dress for the weather, so you could both enjoy an evening out. Is that it?"

"Yes! Exactly!" Jackie blurted. Then her eyes doubled in size from the unintended admission. As if suddenly panicked, she then held up both hands in defense. "Wait. No!" she said, backtracking as she took a physical step backward. "That's not what I meant . . ."

However, Kyle and Becca had stepped behind Jackie so she couldn't escape. The three surrounded her, which caused Jackie to crumble to her knees.

"It was an accident! Tim didn't mean it! He didn't mean to push him! It was a stupid accident!" Jackie cried, pounding her fists to the snowy ground.

"No. It wasn't an accident," Kinsley replied firmly. "It was murder."

Red and blue lights signified the arrival of the police. Rachel rushed on scene and exclaimed, "Anyone hurt? Paramedics are here if you need to get checked out."

"No, we're fine. Just a bit shaken up, is all. Right, girls?" Kyle looked to Kinsley and Becca to validate his answer and they both uttered a weary "yes" to the detective in unison.

Meanwhile Jackie was cornered in the center of them, slouched over with her head touching the snowbank. It was as if the cold completely evaded her now.

"The three of us heard her admit that she and her husband were wearing matching scarves the night of the event," Kinsley said, pointing to Jackie, whose eyes then lifted to the detective.

"They've got it all wrong!" Jackie pleaded, but even her words lacked energy and tone. "It didn't happen like that! My husband and I are innocent!"

"The police are at your house right now; a search warrant has been issued. You may as well just give it up, Ms. Horn," Rachel stated matter-of-factly.

"But it's Christmas!" she wailed.

"Exactly," Kinsley replied. "And this is the best present ever."

Chapter 37

Twas the night before Christmas, when rosy-cheeked visitors congregated around a glowing fireplace to get toasty while a local violinist played old-style Christmas carols. All had returned to the inn after an evening of singing carols door to door while carrying battery-operated candles throughout the streets of Harborside. Upon their return, Aunt Tilly provided appetizers and mouthwatering treats, along with music throughout the evening. As anticipated, guests would often bring along their favorite holiday dishes to share as well. There was never a shortage of food and yummy deserts, which lined the walls of the stately decorated living room and kept everyone happily fed until the clock struck midnight, when they'd officially call it a night. This was a lovely tradition to celebrate the season at the Salty Breeze Inn for close friends and return guests who had become like family.

"Hey. You look like you're zoning out," Kyle said, purposely hip-checking Kinsley to gain her attention.

"Hey, yourself." Kinsley smiled and shared a half hug with her brother. "I'm so glad you're home for the holidays this year. It's quite a treat, bro. I really hope you make it a habit," she cajoled with a playful elbow to his side. "All the Harborside ladies in your life—Aunt Tilly, Rachel, and I—have gone to great lengths to try and entice you to do so. Just wait until you see the next dessert tray."

"I have to admit, it's good to be home. And I appreciate all you've done for me, including the Christmas tree in my room with our parents' ornaments. It's pretty special, Kins. Maybe you and I can make a wish under it before I go." He grinned, swiping a cookie off the nearby table and taking a bite. "I think I've already gained ten pounds, but it's not stopping me from eating," he snorted with a chuckle. "Hope I fit into my uniform after this."

"Yeah, you gotta be careful with Aunt Tilly's cooking. No doubt, food is her love language! And she's incredibly lovable." Kinsley patted her stomach. "Hey, we're okay, right?"

"What do you mean?"

"I mean, we didn't exactly get off on the right foot when you arrived and I'm sorry for that. I don't want to argue when you're home on leave. It makes me sad."

Kyle turned to his sister and held her gaze. "You and me will always be tight. Remember that. It wouldn't be normal if we didn't disagree about things from time to time."

Kinsley leaned into her brother and gave him a squeeze. "I'm glad you feel the same."

"I do. Very much so," he added before releasing her.

"I saw you over there taking a phone call a minute ago. It looked serious. Everything, okay?"

"Just a greeting from Germany," he replied between chews. "A bit of a Christmas present coming my way, actually."

"Oh yeah? What kind of present? Do tell!"

"A friend of mine said he has more intel to share about Dad after the New Year. He said he wants to wait and tell me in person. But that I'd be very happy to hear it." Kyle finished his cookie and brushed the crumbs from his hands and then reached for a handful of sugary nuts and began popping them into his mouth one by one.

"Great. Sounds like this guy is going to keep us both waiting, then." Kinsley sighed. "You know how I *love* to wait," she added sarcastically, with a chuckle.

"Yep, I know you hate waiting, which is why Rachel is bringing your Christmas present and I'm giving it to you tonight." Kyle grinned devilishly. "I'm not waiting until Christmas morning this year. No sirree!"

"Seriously? You made Rachel wrap it for you?" Kinsley laughed.

"Something like that," he taunted.

Tilly then entered the room with her famous gingerbread cake roll, and Kyle turned to follow, clearly dying for a piece. Becca was behind Kinsley's aunt with a platter full of cookies and brownie bars and had set it down on a nearby table that was already covered with food and barely had space to contain it. Kinsley rushed over to help her make room.

"Thanks," Becca said after setting the tray down and simultaneously plucking a cocktail from Pete, who was walking by them with a tray full of drinks. Pete was handing out a new holiday beverage that he had concocted, which he had named Merry Bliss. A delicious cocktail sure to keep cheeks rosy throughout the evening.

"You bet, and a hap-hap-happy holiday to ya." Pete turned his attention to Kinsley. "And one for you, milady?"

"No thanks, not just yet. But I'll come looking for you in a bit," Kinsley promised with a wink.

"I look forward to it." Pete returned her wink before moving along with his tray.

Rachel entered the room and she was carrying what looked like a balled-up holiday blanket, causing Kinsley to frown in confusion. She thought her brother had said that Rachel was bringing a Christmas present, not laundry. When Rachel reached Kinsley's side, Kyle rushed over to join them, too.

Kyle and Rachel said in unison, "Hurry! Open it!" and then shared a laugh.

"I'm confused . . . Open what exactly?" It was then Kinsley noticed a light tuft of fur poke its head from beneath the edge of the blanket. "Oh, my heart!" she squealed. She opened the blanket further to reveal an English cream golden retriever puppy. "Ohhhh!" Kinsley cried with delight as she gathered the little pup into her arms. "Goodness, I'm shocked! But elated! Is it a girl or boy? I'm so excited." She giggled as she snuggled into the dog and it nuzzled beneath her neck. The dog's fur felt like Santa's velvet suit across her skin.

"It's a girl," Kyle said, grinning ear to ear, quite pleased with himself.

It was then Kinsley noticed the puppy's unusually long eyelashes, colored a slightly darker hue, and when she blinked, it looked as if the pup were wearing artificial lashes.

"Oh my! What a cutie!" Becca cooed, leaning in and giving the dog's head a scratch.

Tilly moved to greet the puppy, too, while Kinsley held the dog protectively in her arms. "Did you know about this?" she asked her aunt accusingly.

Tilly's eyes danced merrily. "Of course I did! Kyle asked if it would be okay with me if you had a puppy over at the caretaker's quarters. And quite frankly, I thought it was a splendid idea! You've been talking about taking a dog along on your gardening jobs for a long time now. I'm so happy for you, Kinsley. What are you going to name her?" she asked, stroking the puppy on the head.

"Well, I always thought if I ever got a dog, and it was a girl, I'd name her Willa." Kinsley nuzzled into the puppy's head and said, "Welcome to the family, Willa."

Willa responded with a giant kiss to her face, and the group shared a laugh.

"I'm so in love already." Kinsley fussed gleefully. "Kyle, you've officially won in the present contest!" Her smile grew wide. "I'm not sure the wool socks I got you are gonna cut it this year," she teased.

When Becca took a turn holding the puppy, Kinsley leapt into her brother's arms. "Thank you! Thank you! BEST Christmas present EVER!" she cried, hugging her brother tight. "I can't believe you did this for me. I'll never forget this night! I can promise you that!"

"You're very welcome, sis," Kyle said. When he released her, he ruffled her head as if she were ten years old again. Which this time, she was fine with.

Kinsley turned to Rachel while Becca continued to cuddle

with Willa and said, "I hate to change the conversation away from this bundle of joy, because she has quite literally stolen my heart, but I have to ask. How is Raven holding up? I haven't been able to get her off my mind."

"She's good, actually," Rachel said. "Holding charges were low enough that she was able to post bail, so she'll be able to spend the holidays with her family. Pending trial, her attorney thinks she'll have enough character witnesses in her corner to lessen the blow or completely drop the charges. She's confident that the assault and battery charges will be waved because she was defending herself, even though we'll never be privy to Chris's side of the story. Not to mention the medical examiner claimed there was water found in Chris's lungs. Which means his death was ruled a drowning—not due to the bottle over the head."

"That's a relief. And the Horns? Are they both going to jail? Did Tim admit to giving Chris the final push?" Kinsley asked.

"When we cornered Tim and he realized *both* could be charged with murder, he confessed to pushing Chris into the ocean. He didn't want to see the mother of his children be put in jail for something he himself had done. Though it was Jackie who attacked Toby in search of destroying that photo where her mother was wearing the winning scarf. So, she's facing charges as well, whether her husband likes it or not," Rachel said straightforwardly. "She won't come out of this with a slap to her wrist, I promise you that."

"Jackie attacked Toby, then," Becca confirmed as she handed back the puppy. Kinsley gladly took Willa into her arms and snuggled with her once again. "How did she remember about the photo? Did something tip her off to search for it?"

"Yeah, Jackie said that when Kinsley asked about the scarf

in the parking lot downtown, and she and Tim had already received that cryptic email to pick it up from the lobster tree, she knew it was a crucial piece of evidence. To compound the problem, Jackie realized that by sharing with Kinsley that she'd won it from Toby's, she accidently put herself on the chopping block. She figured the photo from Toby's Taffy would be the only remembrance of her winnings and she wanted the photo destroyed to protect her husband. Jackie had completely forgotten that her mom allowed Tim to borrow hers that night. She didn't want to implicate her mother, either, who wasn't present at the boat parade, instead she was down in Boston to see a live performance of *The Nutcracker.* Jackie felt that if she wore *her* scarf around town, no one would pin her family to the crime because she was wearing one, making her look less suspect. Her mother letting Tim borrow hers was the real problem here," Rachel confirmed.

"Wow," Becca murmured.

"Anyhow, I have you guys to thank because once we obtained the search warrant and connected the voice-changing toy to the timing of the call via cell phone records, we were able to trace the call back to the exact time Jackie phoned the Blue Lobstah. And then of course, the connection of the second scarf. We also located a few photos by a local photographer who was taking pics for Harborside's social media pages the night of the boat parade. These photos show Jackie and Tim talking with Chris alongside the pier in the background of a few shots, so we can place them at the scene of the crime. Not to mention, her confession to you three about Tim wearing the scarf. Anyhow, we had more than enough to approach the district attorney to file the charges. But just so you know; it'll be hard to prove Jackie was intentionally trying to run you off the road that night. She's sticking to her story that she was only trying to return Kinsley's gloves. We'll just have to let the other charges be the justice we've all been looking for. Thanks again for the assistance in this case."

Kinsley and Becca shared a smile. "You're welcome!" they said in unison, and then shared a laugh.

"We really do love solving crimes and officially bringing this one to a close. Don't we, Bec," Kinsley said, eyeing her bestie.

"That we do," Becca agreed with a smile.

"Uh-oh!" Rachel interrupted as she glanced at Willa. "I forgot your puppy's leash in the car, and she probably needs to pee. I was so excited, and I didn't want to get her paws wet before you met her. You mind if I take her back for just a moment to the car with me while you stay here with your guests?"

"I guess I can part with her for a second." Kinsley smiled as she handed Willa to Rachel. "And thanks for taking her out for me. I appreciate it."

"I'll go with you," Kyle said, turning to Rachel. "I have to get Willa's crate and the rest of her stuff out of your car." He turned to his sister then. "I wanted you to meet her before we put her in the crate for the night. I didn't want Rachel to have to house the dog at her place for a third night in a row. This hasn't exactly been an easy present to hide!" he said, chuckling.

"I bet! Thanks for helping my brother with the surprise, Rachel, and taking care of my new puppy," Kinsley said sincerely.

"No problem. It was my pleasure." Rachel's voice turned to baby talk as she addressed the dog. "We had fun, didn't we, Willa?"

Kyle, Rachel, and Willa left them while Becca simultaneously received a text message. "My parents just got here!" she said eagerly. "I'm going to greet them at the door. I'll be right back."

Suddenly Kinsley was standing alone at the party. She gazed around the room to witness her friends having a wonderful time. The room was filled with smiles and laughter. Toby and Jenna were dressed as Mr. and Mrs. Claus—and pulling the act off quite nicely. Jenna was singing carols alongside the piano while Toby handed Adam a handful of taffy. Adam took the candy willingly and was showing off his gleaming white teeth in a grin that was no longer filled with tinsel. And she heard a hearty "Ho! Ho! Ho!" come from Toby's lips, which made her smile.

As Kinsley looked around and noted all the people she loved so dearly, her heart was full. She silently gave a prayer of gratitude.

There was only one last Christmas wish that Kinsley longed to fulfill. Before thinking twice and talking herself out of it, she moved across the room and encouraged Pete to set down the tray of drinks. Kinsley boldly led him by the hand and didn't stop until they reached the doorway, beneath the kissing ball.

"Where are you taking me?" Pete asked.

"I couldn't let this holiday pass and let this Christmas be remembered as the one where only murder happened under the mistletoe, now, could I? I just need to fulfill one more Christmas wish," Kinsley said sweetly.

"Oh yeah? What's that?"

"*Merry Christmas, Pete O'Rourke*," Kinsley whispered.

And then planted a heartfelt kiss upon the bar owner's stunned lips.

RECIPES

AUNT TILLY'S FAMOUS GINGERBREAD
CAKE ROLL WITH EGGNOG FROSTING

Kitchen equipment required:
    10-inch-by-15-inch high-sided sheet pan
    Parchment paper
    Mixing bowls
    Stand mixer (helpful) or can use hand mixer
    Hand mixer
    Rubber scraper
    Flour sack cloth or dish towel
    Nonstick silicone mat

Ingredients for gingerbread cake:
    4 eggs, cracked and separated, at room temperature
    ⅓ cup packed light brown sugar
    ¼ cup molasses

1 cup cake flour

1 teaspoon baking powder

1 teaspoon ground ginger

1 teaspoon ground cinnamon

½ teaspoon ground cloves

⅛ teaspoon salt

⅓ cup granulated sugar

Powdered sugar (to dust)

Ingredients for eggnog filling:

1 8-ounce brick cream cheese, brought to room temperature

¼ cup unsalted butter, brought to room temperature

¼ cup prepared eggnog, brought to room temperature

¼ teaspoon pure vanilla extract

¼ teaspoon nutmeg

¾ cup powdered sugar

INSTRUCTIONS:

FOR GINGERBREAD CAKE:

1. Preheat oven to 350 degrees F and line 10-inch-by-15-inch baking sheet with parchment paper. Set aside.
2. In large stand mixer, using whisk attachment, beat egg yolks for 1 minute. Then add brown sugar and molasses and mix on medium speed until combined.
3. In separate medium bowl, whisk together cake flour, baking powder, ginger, cinnamon, cloves, and salt.
4. Add flour mixture to egg yolk mixture and beat until combined but don't overbeat!

5. In another large bowl, whip egg whites until soft foamy peaks form. With hand mixer running, slowly add granulated sugar, and once all the sugar is added, increase speed to high and whip until stiff peaks form.

6. Using rubber scraper, gently fold egg white mixture into bowl of batter. Note: Be gentle—don't eliminate the air you whipped into it.

7. Pour batter onto prepared pan, using a rubber scraper to evenly distribute batter.

8. Bake until cake is spongy and bounces back when touched (11 to 14 minutes, depending on your oven).

9. While cake is baking, lay out flour sack or kitchen towel on a silicone mat and sprinkle it with a layer of powdered sugar. Also, a helpful tip: You can use a flour sifter to sprinkle a snow layer of powdered sugar for an even coat.

10. Cool cake for a few minutes on baking sheet, then carefully turn it out onto flour sack and remove parchment paper from underside.

11. Before adding filling, starting from one of the shorter ends, roll up the cake (rolling towel with it as you go). Lay the wrapped cake seam side down to cool completely.

FOR EGGNOG CREAM CHEESE FILLING:

1. In large bowl, using either stand mixer or hand mixer, combine room-temperature cream cheese, butter, eggnog, vanilla, and nutmeg on medium speed until well combined.

2. Slowly add powdered sugar and turn up speed to medium-high to combine.

ASSEMBLE CAKE ROLL:

1. Once cake is completely cooled, carefully unroll it. Using rubber scraper, add even layer of eggnog cream cheese filling to top of cake, leaving about a ¼-inch space on each edge.
2. Gently reroll cake and move it seam side down to a serving platter.
3. Dust with powdered sugar, slice, and WOW your guests.

—*Merry Christmas with love, Tilly, Kinsley, and Kyle* ☺

CRAFTS

HOW TO CRAFT A ROUND
HOLIDAY KISSING BALL

(Mainely—Kinsley Clark's way)

Supplies for kissing ball:

Wilt-Pruf (comes in spray bottle, and used to mist your
greens for freshness)

Floral foam (Oasis)

Bucket of water to soak Oasis

Chicken wire

Wire cutters

Floral wire

6-inch cuttings of greens: use a mix of evergreens such as
cedar, fir, white pine boughs, and boxwood for different
texture and to add whimsy to your kissing ball. Winterberry and holly, too, for festive red pops of color.

Ruler

Ribbon for bows—about 7 yards long and 1½ inches wide,
   per kissing ball, will allow a top and a bottom ribbon for
   your ball, along with a hang ribbon.

Scissors

Glue gun

Christmas decor (pinecones or glittered spikes to use as
   stick-ins can add a real personal flair!)

TO MAKE THE EVERGREEN BALL:

1. To make the center: Use a piece of square Oasis soaked
   with water. (Yes, the square will be covered, to make a
   round ball.) And soaking is important, as when it freezes
   outside, the branches will freeze in place!

2. Cover the Oasis with chicken wire, wire close the ends, and
   snip with wire cutters. This will look like a suet-cage bird
   feeder, but again, it will make a round ball in the end!

3. Fold 18 to 20 inches of floral wire in half and then in half
   again. Attach to chicken wire basket. This is the hanging
   loop. So, make sure it's sturdy! These kissing balls look
   amazing hanging from a porch and blowing in the winter
   wind!

4. Make 6-inch greens using the ruler. You can use pine
   branches of your choosing (see above for ideas). Pinch and
   pull the ends off!

5. Now you're ready to assemble. Fill in the holes of the
   chicken wire with 6-inch cuttings. When each chicken wire
   hole is filled, go to the next one. Go all the way around and
   then you're ready for a bow.

TO DECORATE THE BALL WITH
TOP AND BOTTOM RIBBON:

For the bow: 7 yards of 1½-inch-wide ribbon loops are easier
to make when double-sided ribbon is used. Make 6 total loops.
These sit on top and rest on the kissing ball.

Choose how long the "hang ribbon" will be. The hang portion goes through the top loop of your bow. (The bow sits atop
the ball and rests there.)

Bottom loops that hang beneath the ball: Measure out
4 loops with bottom tails secured upside down for a bottom
bow using floral wire and attach to the bottom using a pick or
stick. Fan out loops for definition.

Now you're ready to hang your kissing ball in a prominent
location for all your neighbors to envy!

Acknowledgments

Sandy, thank you! Without you, this novel and the seven before it would have been but a wish and a dream. I can't believe how far we've come. I'm absolutely convinced that something divine had to happen for our paths to cross. I consider myself lucky to have you in my corner.

Leis, thank you for sharpening your pencil and tightening these pages. I appreciate the candid discussion on how to bring this manuscript to the next level. And the time you invest in the work (and me) does not go unnoticed! Thank you for taking a chance on me!

Cover artist Joanna Kerr and art designer Sarah Oberrender, I tip my hat! Great work, ladies! And for all at Berkley behind the scenes, the copy editors, audio voice actors, and publicity team, thank you! I share with you a fist bump. Your work is very much appreciated!

Mark, I'm losing ways to express my gratitude. Thank you

for loving my fictitious friends as much as I do. I count myself blessed to have you in my life. One of these days, I'm going to reward you with a Harley-Davidson with a Screamin' Eagle kit. (Wink! Wink!) Until then, we'll just keep riding our bicycles and making memories.

For you, dear reader, I hope you enjoyed this holiday tale and it brought you a pinch of seasonal joy. If so, drop me a line. I'd love to hear from you.

ABOUT THE AUTHOR

Sherry Lynn spent countless summers on the coast of Maine knowing she'd one day return to write about the magical location from her youth. Curious by nature, she found sleuthing to be the perfect fit for her, and she has written multiple cozy mystery series under several pseudonyms. Currently, Sherry lives in the Midwest with her husband, but she dreams about one day retiring oceanside with a good book in her hand.

VISIT SHERRY LYNN ONLINE

SherryLynnBooks.com

 SherryLynnBooks

Ready to find
your next great read?

Let us help.

Visit prh.com/nextread

Penguin
Random
House